PRAISE FOR
RISING FIRE

"Terri Brisbin weaves a richly imagined, spellbinding romantic fantasy in *Rising Fire*! Atmospheric, absorbing, infused with dark magic, gripping intrigue, and mesmerizing sensuality, the Stone Circle series is Terri Brisbin at the top of her game. I'm totally hooked and I can't wait for more!"

—*New York Times* bestselling author Lara Adrian

PRAISE FOR
THE NOVELS OF TERRI BRISBIN

"A carefully crafted plot spiced with a realistic measure of deadly intrigue and a richly detailed, fascinating medieval setting."　　　　　　　—*Chicago Tribune*

"A sharp-tongued and sharp-witted heroine clashes romantically with a dark and dangerously sexy hero in Brisbin's latest captivating medieval romance. Expertly laced with danger and sweetened with sensuality, *Taming the Highlander* is an absolute delight."　　　—*Booklist*

"Excellent. . . . The quick-moving story contains several twists readers may not see coming."

—*Romantic Times* (4 stars)

"Historical romance fans will fully enjoy *Once Forbidden* . . . a powerful relationship drama."

—The Best Reviews

continued . . .

D0595182

"As always, Terri writes compelling characters and a riveting story that totally draws you in to the world of medieval Scotland. . . . The kind of story that will stay with you long after you finish the last page."

—The Romance Readers Connection

"Beautifully written . . . [and] filled with surprises, passion, and danger, *Surrender to the Highlander* has something for all our reading pleasures. Terri Brisbin pens another excellent read." —CataRomance.com

"A seductive, vivid love story between a sexy hero and a strong heroine . . . a highly emotional tale that is vastly entertaining. It's rich in historical detail, laced with the perfect amount of passion, and enhanced with intrigue. . . . Ms. Brisbin continually delivers highly satisfying romances, and *Surrender to the Highlander* is another winning effort from her; don't miss it."

—Romance Reviews Today

"A great historical romance with rich characters that will delight and entice readers . . . [an] engaging story of a powerful Highland beast and the lovely lady who tames him. . . . Fans of Brisbin's novels will not be disappointed with her work, and newcomers will find in Brisbin a great new author to add to their historical romance list . . . a lively, frolicking tale of life in the Highlands; truly a must read."

—Historical Romance Writers

"Empathetic, well-defined protagonists, solid historical detail, and a well-crafted plot filled with spies, treachery, and intrigue keep things on track in this lively adventure." —*Library Journal*

RISING FIRE

A NOVEL OF THE STONE CIRCLES

Terri Brisbin

A SIGNET ECLIPSE BOOK

SIGNET ECLIPSE
Published by the Penguin Group
Penguin Group (USA) LLC, 375 Hudson Street,
New York, New York 10014

USA | Canada | UK | Ireland | Australia | New Zealand | India | South Africa | China
penguin.com
A Penguin Random House Company

First published by Signet Eclipse, an imprint of New American Library,
a division of Penguin Group (USA) LLC

First Printing, March 2015

Copyright © Theresa S. Brisbin, 2015
Penguin supports copyright. Copyright fuels creativity, encourages diverse
voices, promotes free speech, and creates a vibrant culture. Thank you for buy-
ing an authorized edition of this book and for complying with copyright laws
by not reproducing, scanning, or distributing any part of it in any form without
permission. You are supporting writers and allowing Penguin to continue to
publish books for every reader.

SIGNET ECLIPSE and logo are trademarks of Penguin Group (USA) LLC.

ISBN 978-0-451-46907-6

Printed in the United States of America
10 9 8 7 6 5 4 3 2 1

PUBLISHER'S NOTE
This is a work of fiction. Names, characters, places, and incidents either are the
product of the author's imagination or are used fictitiously, and any resemblance to actual persons, living or dead, business establishments, events, or
locales is entirely coincidental.

If you purchased this book without a cover you should be aware that this book
is stolen property. It was reported as "unsold and destroyed" to the publisher
and neither the author nor the publisher has received any payment for this
"stripped book."

To Val Luna—librarian, writer, friend: You loved this idea when I first told you about it and urged me to write it. I hope it turned out as you thought it would. Yours was a life well lived. It ended too soon with stories yet to be written, and I will miss you always.

Acknowledgments

This series has ruled my thoughts and writing for more than three years—from the first idea to finally bringing it to readers now. During that time, many, many friends and readers pushed me on to write it, and I'd like to thank several:

To Jen and Lyn Wagner, my unofficial brainstorming-critique group—thanks for talking me off the ledge too many times and for always being supportive of my crazy creative process—you keep me grounded, or, at least, away from the whisky.

And to Carolyn Sullivan, a writing colleague from New England—thanks for believing in this series and for giving me a message about the future for it.

THE LEGEND

Centuries ago

The earth buckled beneath her feet, its roar fearsome and deafening, and the sky tore itself open to hurl torrents of rain and lightning at her. Chaela soared through the air and laughed as the others used their powers against hers.

The goddess of fire and chaos, she inhaled the acrid smoke of the destruction she wrought as her enemies and their minions scattered before her might. Chaela savored the taste of ashes in her mouth that foretold of the victory that would soon be hers. Raising her voice, she formed the words and sounds that would bring forth the fire from within her. That fire would bring an end to this battle and to her enemies gathered there.

A moment away from sending brimstone and flames at the last of them, a freezing burst and a terrifying silence flooded through her mind. Like a woolen blanket swaddling a newborn, the silence strengthened, surrounding her until she could hear nothing, feel nothing, and think no words of incantation or spell-making.

She gazed across the desolate plain and discovered the other six gathered among the only stones left standing. Her weakling son stood with them—*against her!*—but she would make sure he'd pay for his betrayal. Soon . . .

Another sound began, invading her thoughts, pushing her down to the ground and forcing even the breath from her body. Their voices rose, chanting words she did not know, until the eerie melody was everywhere.

"No!" she screamed against the overwhelming power of it. They could not defeat her! She could not let them.

She sought the words of a protective spell, but they scattered, as those who had chosen to follow the six traitors had. Chaela drew upon the fire inside her, searching for the power that was hers to burn and destroy, but it, too, was gone.

Cernunnos forced the ground beneath Chaela to thrust up, tossing her into the air. The winds, guided by Taranis's powers, carried Chaela to the stone circle and held her motionless above it as the enchantment grew louder around her. And still she could not release herself from the bonds the six created.

"Chaela," Belenus, the god of life and order, called out to her. "Cease this and you will be allowed to live."

"Fools!" she roared back when her voice would serve her mind. "I cannot be destroyed!" Struggling against the bonds that held her, she could not do more than scream out in frustration. Elemental powers such as hers were created by the universe and could not be extinguished.

"You can be defeated, Chaela. You will be imprisoned in the endless pit and never return. Your name will be forbidden and forgotten," Sucellus, the god of war and change, told her.

She would never be forgotten—she had seen to that. Her name and her legend—and her blood—would go on no matter what these betrayers were able to do here today. Her very being held an elemental power of the universe and could never be extinguished. Chaela laughed then, the sound echoing across the decimated landscape. The people who had served and gained powers from their gods should be afraid, very afraid, of her wrath and the extent of her powers. Gathering every bit of the power that lived in her blood, she pushed out one final time, trying to force herself loose from the binding spell.

Spiking tendrils of pain and terror seeped through her as she watched a huge black hole open beneath her in the center of the standing stones. The seven continued chanting, and each word pierced her like a sword, her powers leaching out of her as they forced her closer and closer to the yawning pit. Her body levitated over the chasm, and then she fell. Though free of the binding spell, she could not break through the barrier they placed over the opening.

"Free me!" she screamed, beating at the invisible wall between them.

Lashing out with her remaining powers, Chaela pounded against the wall that kept her from the world she would rule. She could feel a weakness in it, and she thrust all she had against it. She watched as the seven standing above her startled, and she threw her head back, laughing at their stupidity.

To bind a power such as hers to this place, there must be a sacrifice to strengthen the spell. A sacrifice of blood, of her blood.

"You do not deserve the powers we have!" she yelled

through the barrier. "You do not—" She could not speak the rest because her words were cut off by the sight before her.

Her son, the only one of her human-kind children who'd inherited some of her power, threw himself over the pit. Sucellus sent a spear of iron through his heart, and his blood spilled across the barrier. Instead of freeing her, his sacrifice sealed the portal over her.

Chaela pounded fruitlessly against the now-impenetrable divide and then fell back into the blackness, unable to see or to feel an end to it. The opening of light disappeared above her as she fell farther and deeper into the void, but Chaela stopped fighting it and allowed herself to drift downward.

Let those traitors above believe her conquered. Let them believe themselves and the other puny humans safe. They may have won this battle and thrown her from the human world into this void, but they would not win in the end.

They would eventually die off in the human world while she lived on forever in this prison, searching for a way back.

And she would find a way back—to take her rightful place as ruler, to avenge this wrong, to destroy those who could band together against her.

She would find a way to return, and every one of them and their descendants would curse this day when they turned against her.

PROLOGUE

Late winter, AD 1286
An island off the Scottish coast

Marcus woke from a deep sleep with a scream tightening his throat. He caught himself before the sound escaped and sat up on his pallet. Sweat poured from him, and he pushed his hair back from his face as he climbed to his feet. Staggering in the dark of his hut, he found the jug of ale and downed a good portion, trying to ease the terror inside him. His heart raced in his chest, and his thoughts filled with danger and turmoil . . . and fire.

He pushed open the door and walked out into the cooler, misty air of night, hoping to regain his calm and clarity. Taking deep breaths did not help, and he found himself shaking as sheer and absolute terror filled his mind, heart, and soul.

This could mean only one thing, and he dreaded even thinking of such a possibility. Marcus shook his head, denying the thought before it could form completely. The crunching of leaves underfoot startled him, and he turned toward the sound.

And her.

Aislinn stood before him, her eyes glazed over and her body not her own. She was a seer of immense power, sent by her mother to him when still a child to train in the old ways. Her skills and power grew as she matured, and now she began to speak in the language from ages ago. The language of the time when priests like the two of them had served the old gods. The words floated into his mind, and he memorized them as she spoke them in the singsong voice of prophecy.

"When the threat is revealed, the sleepers awaken. A Warrior seeks the truth while Fire burns away the deception. Begin in the East, then North, then South, then West. . . . Find the true gate among the rest."

Marcus's rising blood told him that this was the moment they'd trained and prayed for throughout their lives and the lives of the generations of priests before them. Now he waited for the rest of the words that would give them guidance in their task to save humanity from the darkest evil they would face, but none followed. Instead Aislinn opened her eyes as if she were waking and stared at him in fear. She rarely remembered the prophecies or knowledge she gained, but she understood the import of what had come to her this night.

"Marcus? Is it begun?" she asked, walking to his side.

He wrapped his arms around her and drew her close, both giving and receiving comfort in the physical gesture. "Aye, I fear it is."

"And she is . . ." Marcus put his fingers to her mouth

to prevent her from speaking about her prophecy anymore. They could not afford to discuss it openly.

"Aye," he repeated.

In the silence, he felt the heat of his powers rising in his blood. It replaced the fear and gave him the clarity to know what they must do, or at least whom they must seek. He knew that Aislinn would lead them throughout their quest, and as he watched the emotions flash across her face, he realized she must be feeling the same thing.

They had valuable weapons for their battle against the ancient evil one. For thousands of years, they'd prayed and worshipped the gods who had been forgotten or transmuted by other, newer religions. They'd studied the old legends. Marcus doubted that anyone in the outside world was as prepared for the bloody battles and tremendous displays of power that were about to unfold.

Suddenly, the skin of his forearm burned, and he raised his arm to look upon it. Aislinn did the same. A mark appeared in the same place on both of them.

They watched by the light of the moon as the ancient image of a small man burned a patch into his skin. Hissing against the searing pain, he nodded as others left their dwellings to join them in the center of their village. Each held out their arm as they were marked with the symbol of their power. Only Aislinn's was different— the silver crescent moon marked her skin. Would she be for some higher purpose than the rest?

"It has begun," he said, meeting their gazes and then closing his eyes in silent prayer. "Ready yourselves for the journey."

As he watched his followers obey his instructions,

he knew that some would fall, some would stand, and some would die in this war against true evil. Marcus offered up new prayers to the old gods, hoping they could still hear the pleas of those who remained faithful to the old ways.

By daybreak they were ready to leave their island for the first time in generations. Standing on the shore, staring into the thick mist that protected them from discovery and kept outsiders forever away, he uttered the words to disperse that fog. Four boats—twenty men and women—would leave on this perilous journey while the rest remained hidden here, protecting their knowledge from the outside world.

Marcus watched the island disappear from view as they crossed the miles to the mainland, where they would face dangers unlike any they had faced before. As he turned away from the island, he realized one cause for his fear—the seer had never finished her prophecy.

Gods help them all.

RISING FIRE

When the threat is revealed, the sleepers awaken,
A Warrior seeks the truth
while Fire burns away the deception.
Begin in the East, then North, then South, then West . . .
Find the true gate among the rest.

CHAPTER 1

Late winter, AD 1286
Yester, Scotland

With the morning's cool mist long burned away by the strong rays of the midday sun, Brienne waited until the villagers were all seeing to their daily chores and tasks before deciding that this was the day.

And it was—she could feel it in her bones and in her blood. Something called to her, and some growing urge within her pushed her feet toward the place where she would find out the truth about what lived inside her. There had been tiny glimpses at what it might be, times when fire seemed to answer to her, but she would attempt something this day that she had not dared before.

Taking a deep breath, she lifted the latch and tugged the heavy door open a crack. It creaked on its hinges as she eased it open only wide enough for her to slip inside. Then, after stepping inside the smithy's dark cottage, Brienne closed the door behind her, wanting no interruptions. Since her father was off on an errand, she expected none. Entering into the small building that served as his workshop, she circled the fire pit and tossed in more wood, watching as the existing fire licked at the new pieces and then consumed them. She leaned over and pressed down on the bellows that fed air to the fire, encouraging it to spread and grow hotter and hotter with each breath of air that blew from the pump.

The flames flared higher before her and she could not resist the urge to look deeper into them. Brienne tried to fight their call, tried to fight the strength of it, but lost the battle. She inhaled slowly, trying now to control the fear that simmered in her belly while she moved closer to the fire's heat. As it called to her, icy tendrils slid along her skin in spite of the heat in the smithy. Shivering and sweating at the same time, she lifted trembling hands from her side and held them out.

Not knowing how to do what she planned, Brienne stretched her fingers, wiggling them, and watched as the flames did the same. Then she flexed each finger separately, and single bursts of flame followed each movement. When she twisted her hands, the reaction of the fire was overwhelming.

Each flame danced before her, swirling and dipping this way and that before joining the others in the growing swarm of heat and light. Even when she dropped her hands and closed her eyes, they remained vivid and shifting in her mind.

They danced for her—*they danced for me!*—moving in every direction when she simply thought it, and the sound of their movements surrounded her. Holding her arms out over the fire, she wiggled her fingers over the hearth and laughed as the flames writhed and swirled in answer to her gesture. This was not new to her. She'd done this many times before.

What she planned to do next was different and daring.

Moving her hands in a gathering motion, Brienne pulled the flames together and then spread them out until they filled the space before her, no longer limited to the fire pit and no longer dependent on wood or peat to fuel them. Staring into them, she searched for the center of the brightness and heat and waited.

"Mine."

She strained to keep her eyes on the fire and listened as the whispers came from the heart of it again.

"Come to me."

A shudder coursed through her body, and the fear overwhelmed her as the whispered words surrounded her, enticing her, entreating and tempting her. The back of her neck tingled, and her skin burned as the heat of the flames—nay, the flames themselves—encircled her. Keeping her body still, she waited to hear more, waited to recognize the voice or to learn who called to her through the fire. From deep within her soul, she drew the strength she needed to regain control over the flames and, standing within their embrace, she listened and waited to hear more.

"Daughter of my blood."

Brienne laughed aloud, feeling the power course through her, stronger and stronger each moment. The voice, the words, the flames at her command all confirmed her suspicion that she could control the fire. After hours or minutes—she knew not which—of her standing untouched within the flames, they began to sway and spark around her. As she gathered them once more under her control, they parted for her to move away.

When the voice disappeared completely, when she knew that presence was gone, her fear heightened. The heat began to burn her skin, so she tamped down the flames, guiding them back to the hearth of the smithy, easing them back into the coals of burning wood there so that they would be ready for her father's use. A smile teased the corners of her mouth as inappropriate pride flooded her.

She had done it!

Each time she dared, her power over the fire seemed to grow. And grow stronger. But this day, this time, she had stepped within them without dire consequences. Next time she would—

"Brienne."

She jumped at the interruption and spun around to face the door to the small building. Her father stood there, staring at her. Had he seen her move the fire? From the blank expression on her father's face, she could not tell. Pressing her now-sweating palms on her gown and adjusting her veil back into place, she waited for his reaction.

He closed the door quickly behind himself and checked the shutters, just as she had before attempting to call forth the ability to command the flames. But she'd not barred the door, so he could have seen everything she'd done. Would the flames follow her commands if another were present, or was this something she could do only in secret?

Brienne watched as concern and wariness entered his gaze. Leaving some tools near the doorway, he walked slowly toward his hearth, glancing between it and her several times.

"Are you injured? Are you burned?" he asked as he

took one hand of hers and then the other in his larger ones, searching for signs of damage. Then he met her gaze. "How is this possible? What have you done?"

His suspicious, accusatory tone hurt her, but Brienne understood that he was worried about her. She stepped away from him and away from the constant draw of the flames before answering.

"I . . . ," she stammered, not truly knowing how to explain it all to him. Brienne glanced at him, imploring him to understand.

"Come here, lass," he said softly, opening his strong arms to her as he always did.

Embraced by him, she felt safe . . . for the moment. These feelings, these powers, these changes that grew stronger and stronger with each passing day frightened her. There was no one she could speak with about them. No one who could understand or accept that she was more like her true father than anyone had guessed. Even though Gavin the blacksmith had raised her and loved her as his own, she was not.

She shuddered at the thought of her true father, and Gavin responded by hugging her even tighter. The tears gathered in her eyes as she kept silent.

"I will keep ye safe, Brienne," he promised. His words and warm breath tickled her ear, and she nodded, accepting his pledge even if it were not the truth.

"I know you will, Father," she said, nodding her head and granting herself another moment of comfort before moving out of his embrace. "I have so many questions."

As always, her words stopped him. Gavin hated her questions. He hated the reminder that she was not his, that there was another who could step in at any time and take her. And though years had passed since any interest had been shown, all it would take was the untoward word and unguarded action to draw the wrong attention.

"I fear there is little I can add to what you've heard from your mother or ken already, lass. The lord had you brought here to us when you were but days old, giving you into our care. He gave no explanation, no instructions other than to care for you, and he has not interfered since that day," he said. Staring off into the corner, Brienne knew he was thinking on that long-ago day. Turning back to her, he shrugged. "We never had the courage to ask his reasons or why he gave you to us for fear he would take you away."

Brienne smiled at his admission. She knew of no one in Yester Village or in the area who would question Lord Hugh—or anyone who had survived questioning him. A shiver traced a path of icy sparks along her spine. She'd never even had the courage to approach him before, but now, now that she was discovering these powers and understanding he was the only person who could answer her questions, she might.

"Do not!" her father warned, taking hold of her arm and drawing her close. "Do not even think about speaking to him on such"—he glanced at the fires now banked low in his hearth—"such matters as these."

The fear gazing back at her from his eyes should have been enough to steer her from such a path. The whispered warning should have been sufficient to caution anyone not a bairn or a fool. The need that grew ever deeper and stronger within her pushed her in that dangerous direction. The desire to know her origins and the extent of these strange powers that inhabited her never diminished.

Words drifted to her in that silent moment, and she shivered. The power in them tempted her and called to her deepest longings.

Mine. Come to me.

Daughter of my blood.

Brienne, who had belonged to no one, who could call none family or kin, longed to be part of something. And this whispered invitation called to that deep need within her. She tried to shake off the fear and the temptation, but it all settled within her, keeping her blood heated and that unspoken need stoked. Gavin's sad expression called her back to this cottage and this moment.

"Nay, you are right, Father. 'Twould be foolish to speak to him," Brienne assured him, nodding her head.

Gavin kissed her on the top of her head, just as he always had when reassuring her, and released her from his arms.

"You should be thinking about that offer from Dougal's son James rather than . . ." He nodded his head, lifting his chin in the direction of the hearth. "Marriage and bairns should be your concern now, lass. Surely your mother has spoken of such matters to you?"

Brienne smiled, trying to convince him that such matters did interest her, while her heart broke over her deception.

"Aye. She has spoken of little other than Jamie's offer." That much was true. "I have taken her counsel on it seriously." A truth, but getting closer to the lying. "It is appealing to me." There was the lie. Would he believe it?

"Any man would be proud to have you to wife," he said. "Your weaving skills do you much credit."

No matter that the skills she wanted to practice and develop did not involve a loom and threads. Brienne let this lie stand between them as well.

Noises began to leach into the cocoon of silence that surrounded them, warning them of the approach of others and the return of their everyday tasks and chores. Gavin walked to the window, unlatched and opened the shutters, throwing them wide to allow the cooler breezes in. Though the cold air of winter had barely warmed these last weeks, Gavin could not work the smithy without a flow to feed the flames.

Strange. The flames needed no such flow when she called them forth. Even with the shutters and door closely firmly against intrusion, they grew stronger and higher at her command. Her fingers tingled, reminding her of the power that had directed the heat from within her. Shaking them for a moment, more to erase the memory than to ease any tightness, Brienne reached for the two buckets by the door.

"I will get water," she said, tugging open the door. She found comfort in the ritual of helping her father work.

Brienne stepped into the path leading from the smithy to the well at the center of the small village, which was not as large as Gifford itself. Those who lived here worked the lands owned by Lord Hugh or provided some necessary service to those in the keep. Now, as she made her way through the village for the noon meal, she nodded to everyone who passed her by. Reaching the well, she chatted with the women there as she tossed the dipping bucket down and then tugged the rope up until it peeked over the stone wall's edge.

An eerie feeling invaded her body and soul at that moment, just when everything around her seemed so much the norm as it was each day. Instead her blood raced through her veins, and Brienne could feel it as it moved through her. Her heart pumped so strongly that she was certain others must hear it. Glancing around at the gathered women, she saw that they took no untoward notice of her. Then her skin began to heat, and she was tempted to pour the cool contents of the recently filled bucket over her to ease the growing warmth that seemed to control her.

Only when the pounding grew too loud to ignore did she realize it was not her heart making the ground shake beneath her. A group of mounted knights broke through the bushes and headed along the pathway to the keep. Twenty armored men, none taking notice of the villagers as they passed—save one.

Her.

The one who led the group slowed his horse before passing the well and met her gaze. Brienne quickly lowered her eyes, whether out of respect or out of fear she knew not, but when Lord Hugh rode through the village, no one dared look directly upon him.

Now he directed his horse toward her. She watched as the other women began to edge away from the well and from her. No one wanted the lord's attention, for it usually ended badly for anyone involved. Over the years she'd heard the warnings from her parents about the rumors of the lord's powers and his attitude toward the women under his control, so Brienne tried to blend in with the others, lowering the buckets to her sides and shuffling back away from his approach. This time it did not work. Glancing up, she saw Gavin walking toward her from the direction of the smithy, but when the lord moved closer to her, Gavin stopped.

She put the buckets down and waited for Lord Hugh to say or do something. Silence filled the area, and she knew that many watched this encounter from safer distances and from behind cover that would keep them from their lord's sight. No one wanted his molten-silver gaze to fall on them.

"You there," he called out. "You, girl!"

She startled and began to shake, so she clasped her hands together as she nodded. How could she have wished for just this very thing a short time ago? It was as she raised her eyes that the skin on the inside of her forearm began to itch and sting. Trying to ignore it, she nodded and met his gaze.

And wished with all her heart and soul she had not.

Lord Hugh lifted his helm off and pushed back the chain-mail coif that covered his head. Tossing the helm to one of his men, he examined her from her head to her feet and then focused his fearsome gaze on her face. The patch on her arm stung now even more, and she covered it with one of her hands while waiting on Lord Hugh's next words.

"Your name, girl," he demanded as his horse fought his control and pranced in the dirt, throwing up dust and stones in his wake.

"Brienne," she said. Though her voice shook as she spoke it, she surprised herself with being able to speak at all.

"Daughter of?" he asked, pulling the reins hard and forcing his mount to his will. The huge warhorse relented and stood still under the lord's iron grip.

Brienne tried to force down her fears. Her bold idea to seek him out and ask him about the powers became one of such folly that she could not speak at all. Whose name did she give him? Should she declare her his get or claim the one who raised her?

"Gavin, my lord."

Both she and Lord Hugh turned at the same moment as the blacksmith strode across the clearing and placed himself between the two of them. She stepped closer to him, but to his side so that she could yet watch the lord. Some look passed between the two men that she did not understand.

"Yours, then?" the lord asked.

Gavin reached out for her hand, which she gave him. 'Twas an expression of possession and belonging. She wondered if the lord would let it stand.

"Aye, my lord. Mine," Gavin proclaimed in a low but somehow bold tone. Before any other words could be exchanged, the lord grabbed at his forearm and hissed. When a new flash of pain seared through hers, she fought to keep from doing the same thing.

Lord Hugh seemed to want to say something, but he pulled the reins tightly, causing his mount to sidestep and whinny its displeasure at the tight control. This time the lord released the reins, giving the horse its head. Spinning back toward the keep, he rode off without saying another word. Just when she believed them safe from additional scrutiny, the warhorse rose on its hind legs and spun to face her once more.

"Brienne, you are mine!"

Though no words were spoken aloud, they echoed in her mind. The same words as the one who called from within the flames, but these were in Lord Hugh's voice. As the dust flew up, the horse and rider turned again and disappeared up the path out of the village.

The rumors about his otherworldly powers must be

true—for he had sent those words into her thoughts without saying them. He had touched the same place on his arm as the stinging had affected on her own. Sliding her sleeve up, Brienne watched as the skin there burned away, leaving some kind of mark in its place. Shivering, she wondered at its origin. Gavin turned just then to face her and noticed her arm.

"You burned yourself on the flames, Brienne?" he asked, reaching out to touch the now-raised burn.

"Nay, not on the flames," she replied.

It was hard to deny it, as the singed area now resembled any other burn gained from not tending the fires with care. The intricate pattern disappeared within the patch of reddened skin. Brienne met his eyes and read the doubt in them. He would have lifted her arm had she not pulled away from him.

" 'Tis well, Father," she said. If she'd not been looking in his direction, she would have missed the grimace that flashed across his face as she called him "father."

Without another word, he bent over and picked up both buckets. Gavin did not wait for her or ask her to follow, but she did. But not before looking back at the road to the keep and wondering what other rumors about Lord Hugh were true.

If he had other powers, had she inherited them as well?

CHAPTER 2

Early spring, AD 1286
Dunfermline Palace, Dunfermline, Kingdom of Fife, Scotland

William de Brus awaited the king's pleasure, now for the fourth day in a row and with little patience or good cheer about these infernal delays. Still, as his friend Roger reminded him once again, this time for the twentieth time, beggars such as he could not afford to be demanding when it came to the king's attentions. Called to Scotland by Alexander for a resolution to his problem—the other branch of the de Brus family's intrusion onto the lands he would inherit at the king's command—he tried to convince himself that it would be better if he did not anger the king or his ministers.

Standing in the crowded Presence Chamber of the palace, William gazed around at the others who also held out their hands to the king and wondered what their causes were. Would they, or he, be successful in their pleas to Alexander for help? He held one advantage over many of the others, one he hoped would soften the king's heart toward his request to rid his lands of the other de Bruses.

Roger made his way through the crowds and held out a small, wrapped bundle to him. Peeling it open, William found a steaming pasty. Nodding to his friend, he bit into it. Since he dared not leave and risk being absent when finally called to the king's chamber, Roger ran errands and brought food for him.

"Any news?" Roger asked.

Biting into the meat pie once more and chewing, he shook his head. After swallowing, he added, "The king is at his noon meal and will hold an audience after for . . . some."

"The men wait for us at the inn," Roger said. "Though they grow restless." A company of twelve men had accompanied him on this journey, all hoping for a place at his board. Twelve knights would be critical in controlling his new lands and in convincing the king to award the title to him.

"Tell them—" William began. The herald's call interrupted his orders.

"William de Brus! The king will speak with you now. Come forward!"

Heads turned to see who the lucky one was and then began to mutter as their names were not also called. William thrust the rest of the pasty back at Roger as he pushed his way to the other side of the chamber, where the herald waited. He'd forgotten his manners for a moment, and he turned back to Roger and handed him his helm, short dagger, and gloves. It would not do to appear in the king's presence armed.

It took a few minutes to reach the herald and then a few more to walk down the long hallway to the king's private chambers. The guards opened the door to him, and the herald announced him to the king.

"Come, William. Eat with me," Alexander called out as William paused to bow before him. "My lord bishop, this is the son of my cousin, late of Brix in France."

"I am familiar with the de Brus family, Your Grace," the bishop of Dunfermline replied, inspecting William from his place at the king's right hand. William approached the bishop and kissed his ring. He could read nothing from the churchman's expression, though he surely knew William's true parentage.

"Ah, but William is from a different branch of that family," the king explained. Though the words sounded benign, the tone and the wink that accompanied them explained all the bishop needed to know.

William was a bastard. The king's own.

"Come. Share this meal and tell me of your mother."

A servant pulled out a chair at the table, and William sat there. Another presented platters of food until his expensive, silver plate was filled. A matching cup held what was certain to be a similarly expensive wine, for the king ate and drank only the best.

Whether strange or not, considering that the king had recently lost his own mother, William spoke about his mother as requested. 'Twas no secret at the royal court that William's mother was the king's cousin and something more. Madelyn of Coucy had caught the royal heir's eye before he was crowned king and then she herself had been caught. She was married to a compliant de Brus before her condition was known, and William was given her husband's name, but the truth of his parentage was widely known in France and Scotland. All because of the royal wink and nod.

William spoke of the time his mother had spent with the dowager queen in Picardy instead of their largely ignored personal relationship. Alexander did not suffer an empty bed, whether now or in his younger years, so William was but one of many royal seeds sown in willing woman. 'Twas simply the way of things for kings.

Soon the meal came to an end, and William waited on the king's pleasure. With a wave of his hand, Alexander cleared the chamber. All of his servants and ministers, even the bishop, left with silent bows. The doors closed, and William waited to discover the true cost of his request of the king.

It was not long in coming.

"I know you wish me to rule in your favor in your dispute with the other de Bruses," Alexander said in a quiet voice. "And I am willing to do that. . . ."

William heard the pause that signified the conditions of that ruling and waited, holding his breath on the coming words.

"But I have a small task for you to carry out first," the king said.

"Anything, Your Grace," William answered quickly. Truth be told, he would agree to do anything to have his claim settled and the lands his for the taking.

Alexander reached over and lifted the pitcher of wine before him, filling both of their cups and drinking half of his before continuing. And that worried William, as did the glances toward the doors and the king's increased nervousness.

"Is there aught wrong, Your Grace?" he finally asked.

"Come," the king directed. He rose and walked closer to the huge stone fireplace and as far, William noticed, away from the doors, windows, and tapestry-covered walls as one could get. William followed and waited, a shiver of warning tickling the back of his neck as he watched the ever-confident, ever-in-control king change into someone very different.

Mayhap the king's grief had caught up with him? Mayhap the lack of suitable heirs and his yet-unfruitful new marriage and the possible end of the Canmore dynasty had changed him from the decisive strong king he had been?

"I have a matter that requires the utmost of discretion and cannot trust it to someone else," he explained as he sat on a stone bench before the fire. "You . . . you I trust, William."

"I am honored, Sire," William began, but a furious wave of Alexander's hand stopped further words.

"I am not so sure you will feel honored once you hear the matter. Sit close by and listen to my plight. I must have your word that you will speak of this to no one."

William hesitated, both intrigued and wary of such secrecy as this seemed to be. Still, the king held the power to grant or deny him his lands, so he would be wise to carry out regardless of his feelings on it. "You have it."

"Good. I'd hoped I could count on my kin in this, but none are so trustworthy as I know you to be," he said, glancing toward the door once more. "For some time, I have begun to doubt the sincerity and loyalty of one of my councilors. Rumors persist, and his behavior answers not my questions about him. Strange stories abound. . . . " He paused and glanced over his shoulder.

William wondered about this suspicious demeanor,

but the man was his king and was to be obeyed without question. "Which of your councilors, Sire?"

"His advice has recently become less dependable and there are stories. . . ." The king shuddered as he spoke now. "Demons, William. 'Tis rumored that he calls forth demons from the other world."

The silence in the chamber surrounded and pressed down on him at the accusations. The old beliefs were long gone from the lands of the Celts and Gaels, but there were always rumors of those who had ungodly and otherworldly powers. William never believed in such things. They were for the fearful and the weak. He believed in the one true God.

A sudden burning in his arm took him by surprise. Had he been sitting too closely to the fire? Tugging on his sleeve, he watched a patch of redness spread on his forearm.

"William?"

He pulled the sleeve down to cover the strange spot and turned his attention back to the king. Meeting his gaze, William asked again, "Which of your councilors, Sire?"

"De Gifford."

William leaned back, shocked to hear this name. From another part of Brittany, the de Gifford family was old and powerful. The current lord, Hugh, was one of the most important men in the kingdom, having been one of Alexander's regents. Lord de Gifford had continued in the king's closest circle in the years since the king came of age and proceeded to succeed where his father had failed.

"Hugh de Gifford? The rumors are about him?"

"You must understand how important this is. My

kingdom is at stake. My life and the life of my queen and"—the king paused to whisper—"and the possible heir she carries is at stake. I must know if I can trust his advice or if he has ulterior motives for his words and wisdom."

William felt the irrational fear behind the words spoken as he considered them and did not answer immediately. So the queen was enceinte, then? Dredging up the logic that usually suited his purposes, he glanced at his king.

"Sire, what accusations have been made? What makes you suspicious about Lord Hugh?" He ran his hand through his hair and stood, staying close to the king so he did not have to raise his voice. "Demons, Sire? Who says such nonsense?"

Alexander's gaze sharpened and darkened. "Many. And I am beginning to suspect there is more to this. I scoffed at the first reports brought to me." The king brought his head up as though listening for something and then shook it. "I would not have believed it either had I not witnessed . . . something."

It took only a glance at Alexander's face for William's urge to laugh to be quelled. The king took in a deep breath and let it out slowly and, for just a moment, the confidence of someone born to royalty slipped and Alexander appeared a tired, old man filled with fear.

"Tell me, Sire. What makes you think that Lord Hugh is something other than your man?" The king held out his cup, and William retrieved the pitcher from the table and filled it. Thinking on this situation, he filled his own and waited on the king once more.

"I was journeying south to visit Melrose Abbey, and we stopped to see the progress Hugh was making on his new keep. He invited us to stop to see the high tower he had designed himself. It was . . . ungodly," the king ended on a whisper, as though afraid to say the words aloud. "He wore the strangest garb when he greeted us. A long robe unlike any I have seen before. It seemed to glow as he moved, and his hands shimmered," he said, staring at his own hands as though living the moment again and again.

The king reached out and gripped William's wrist. "And the sounds coming from the lowest vault made my skin crawl and caused me to want to rush forth from the place and never return. I prayed two novenas at the abbey and still the feeling of being near evil remained." The shivers that shook the king's body reinforced his words. "He controls demons, William. He casts spells. He"—he paused and swallowed several time before finishing the words—"he speaks to the otherworld."

William stood then and walked away. How could this be happening? It did not surprise him that the king would not speak of such things before other witnesses, for the words would damn him as a madman. Demons? Spells? What folly was this that plagued the king's mind? He turned back to urge the king away from such . . . fears when his arm began to burn once more. Clapping his hand over the intense pain, he tugged the sleeve of his tunic up to look at the area.

Where there had been nothing before, a raised and burning red patch took form on his arm. It changed before his eyes into something . . . something he could not yet discern. Covering it from the king's view, he realized that this situation was quickly growing out of control. Worse, there was something now wrong with him.

William reached up to touch his head and felt the sweat pouring down his forehead. His lungs could not draw in a full breath, and his skin burned everywhere. His thoughts jumbled, and the chamber before him grew hazy and smeared as though rain had run over it all and washed away the colors and textures. He lifted his hand to find support and instead grasped the king's hand.

With a jolt, his head cleared. Then plans for attack appeared before his eyes, as drawings would look. A stone castle surrounded by acres of farmland. The hills in the distance. As he watched the scene unfold, William knew the weaknesses in the castle's defenses, the best path to approach and the strength and numbers of the guards. His blood heated and surged through him as his vision strengthened and his mind raced with options for deploying his men for the attack, how to control and even destroy Lord Hugh's unholy demesne.

He stumbled back at the realization of the vision before him. The king watched without a word, slowly nodding as though he could see what William did.

"Something is awry in my kingdom, William. You are part of it." At the solemn declaration, William shook his head, denying the truth of it.

"Sire, I know not of what you speak," he argued, but the visions flooding his mind and the need to fight, defeat, destroy, and conquer filled him, body and soul. His fists clenched against the strength of the need now flowing through him. He shook his head again, but it convinced neither him nor the king.

"I was led to you, William. I cannot explain that part

of it, but I knew you would be the one to help me in this task," the king assured him.

Whether the king's words were madness or part of some bigger plan, William knew not. He was publicly a minor member of a very large and powerful family, and the king had had no way of knowing that William would arrive to request his sanction against another branch of the family.

"I am your man, Sire, but this . . . this is not something I have experience in. Why not speak to Bishop—" Before he could continue with a list of possible people who could help him in this endeavor, the king leapt to his feet and grabbed William's shoulders, forcing him close.

"You must do this for me, William. For my kingdom. For all of Scotland and more," he demanded.

Regardless of the unexplainable things going on, no matter the strangeness of the request, this was his king. Obedience was a foregone conclusion, even if the methods of executing such a task were questionable.

"Aye, Sire," he said, with a bow of his head. "I am at your service."

The mad expression in the king's eyes seeped away, leaving the one he recognized. With a nod of his head, Alexander released him. Stepping back, the king called out to his ministers.

"Speak to no one about this, William. No one. The royal Exchequer will provide what you need. Mention the name of your holdings and he will understand."

The king's councilors and servants returned quickly at his call, and soon they were surrounded with many other courtiers and concerns. William met the king's gaze and bowed his head, acknowledging his orders.

He backed from the chamber and turned down the hallway to return to Roger . . . and sanity.

But as he strode toward the larger waiting area, the intense burning on his arm increased as some shape was drawn—burned—into him. Between that and the plans rushing through his thoughts, he was convinced that he, too, might be part of the king's madness.

With only hours left before darkness fell over the city of Edinburgh, William led his two closest and most able friends to a table in an alcove at a noisy inn. Doubting this whole endeavor, he had followed the king's instructions and visited the Exchequer. The bag of gold coins now lay beneath his hauberk, tied firmly to his belt where none could see. They'd eaten their fill and consumed a fair share of the inn's finest ale before he allowed himself to think on what to say to them.

Their lack of questions to this point in time spoke of their longtime friendship and their shared past of covering one another's backs in battles large and small. Their patience was wearing thin now—he could tell from their exchanged glances and nods—but he doubted that either one of them would believe the tale if he told it.

Which he could not, for so many reasons.

"You were with the king a long time, Will." Roger's keen blue eyes watched William's face for any sign and signal that he could not speak openly. Lifting the mug to his mouth, Roger asked, "Did he relent and promise his support?"

"He has," William began.

"What is his price?" Gautier interrupted. When William and Roger looked at him, he shrugged. "There is always a price for the king's consent."

Nothing came free in this world, and even kings commanded a fee of some kind—whether men to fight, gold to pay, or in this case, his soul. William needed to examine whether the cost of his claims to his lands was worth the odd price the king placed on it. To reveal it to his friends, however, the ones he would rely on to carry out the task, was against the king's orders. So for now he would keep Alexander's strange behavior and request to himself and give only the most general of explanations.

"The king"—he lowered his head and his voice to keep his words from going too far—"would like me to investigate one of his councilors. A question of . . . loyalty." That was plain enough with sufficient substance to leave the bewildering details to him alone.

"Do you take up this task?" Gautier asked after downing the rest of his ale. "Do we take up this task?"

William met their gazes and nodded. "I have no choice, but you do. I cannot give you more than I just have, and I do not expect you to agree blindly." Blindly, without knowledge of the king's possible madness. His friends deserved more than that. More that he could not—would not—give them now.

"Will there be fighting?" Roger asked, drinking down the last swallow in his cup.

"Aye, there will be fighting," he replied without hesitation. He knew—he could feel it in his blood—that there would be fighting and death. He nodded to Roger.

"And women?" Gautier asked. The randiest of the bunch, Gautier could be depended on to find the willing woman, or women, in any village or town where they journeyed.

"I suspect so," he said, laughing. Growing serious, he looked at each of his friends. "This will not be an easy task. But it is the one I must carry out to get clear title to my lands . . . and our future home."

"The others?" Gautier asked. They'd left the other ten of their group outside the city, camping in a clearing near the ferry road.

"Too many," William said, shaking his head. He leaned back on his stool and rested against the wall. "The three of us and one more. I will send for the others if they are needed."

"Just do not bring Herve. He is too pretty and will steal the good ones," Gautier offered. The two were often in competition over women.

"You will just have to hone your skills, Gautier. Herve is one of my best warriors." Gautier slammed down his hands on the rough wooden table in mock anger.

"When do we depart?" Roger asked, sliding his empty cup closer to the pitcher for him to fill.

"Two days hence. It will not be a long journey, but I have arrangements to make first." William emptied his cup and stood to leave. "Finish it. I will meet you back at the camp." There were people he needed to speak with in Edinburgh and then in Dunfermline before leaving on this mission for the king.

"Do you wish us to accompany you now?" Gautier asked.

"Nay. I will meet you at the camp and we will make preparations for our journey. I hope to have more news to tell once I complete my tasks."

He was not able to tell them anything else, and they would keep asking questions. They had done so in the past and most likely would do so this time as well.

By the time he rode out of Edinburgh toward his men, William had more questions than answers and little more to go on than what the king had said.

And the mark on his arm continued to burn and form a shape that he did not recognize.

The bad feeling that he'd had all day, the one that resembled the warnings his warrior nature received before a battle, increased, until he wondered if he would survive long enough to lay claim to his lands at all.

CHAPTER 3

Spring, AD 1286
Yester Castle

He was angry.

And when Hugh de Gifford was angry, everyone around him scattered, daring not to do something that would focus his anger on them. Unfortunately for the man who lay crumpled on the floor before him, the daft man had indeed drawn his attention.

The moans emanating from deep within the mass of burned flesh, twisted limbs, and soiled, torn garments warned the few who stood witness that Hugh would not accept failure. He kicked him once more, but it did not ease his fury.

"A simple task, John. Never allow the king to be alone with anyone. And what did you do when he chased his other sycophants out of the chamber to speak alone with someone?" he asked, kicking the now-silent pile at his feet several more times before meeting every gaze in the chamber. "You left."

He held out his hand and smiled as the others began

to tremble. His power, he knew, was awesome to watch, which was why he exercised it before his subjects. This lesson would be useful and would ensure that the others did not fail in their tasks as this worthless piece of dung had.

The fire spread in his blood, and he felt it grow and gather within him. Hugh smiled and aimed his hand at the downed man, and he watched as the flames arced out from his fingers and incinerated every bit of flesh and cloth before him until only a pile of ashes remained. Then he gave those ashes a final kick of his boot, spreading them across the floor.

"You have your assignments," he said quietly since there was not a sound in the room. "Do not fail me."

Hugh smiled again as they nearly knocked one another over, trying to escape his presence as quickly as possible. The extent of his power invigorated him. Once they were done, Hugh walked to the corner and pressed on a series of stones there until the secret door swung open, allowing him access to his private chamber. After he removed his garments and boots, he walked down the steps through the windowless tower and soon reached the oldest part of his keep. The power that had placed each stone surged through the entire vault and he breathed it in. Somehow, his goddess had found a way to contact him, and this chamber was the result.

Chaela, goddess of chaos and fire, had directed him to build this underground chamber and had been instructing him on how to help her open a path back into the human world. Exiled hundreds of centuries ago by fools, she now sought out her descendants, and he was only too glad to help her. Hugh, his father, and his grandfather before him had prepared and waited for such things. His ancestors were her descendants, and through the centuries they had kept the knowledge about the old ones and their betrayal alive.

They'd also practiced the power that they inherited from the goddess until they'd honed it and controlled it. Perfected it.

Now only Hugh and his knowledge and powers could open the doorway to the other realm and allow Chaela back in. Since the bloodlines of those who worshipped the other old gods had dissipated so much, now was the perfect time to attempt it. There was barely enough of it left in any of the other six families. Hugh's father had known the time was coming, so he'd sought out others descended from Chaela to ensure that his son would be powerful enough to guide the goddess back into the world and serve her.

Hugh nodded as his blood heated and he heard the goddess calling to him. Closing his eyes, he inhaled several slow, deep breaths and let them out, trying to calm the excitement coursing through him. He was close, so very close now, and nothing could stop him in his quest.

Chaos would reenter the world, throwing kingdoms and their rulers into confusion and disarray. Chaela would rule as she should have eons ago. Hugh would be her right hand, as one of her blood and her rightful consort. Together they would control everything in the human world. No one, nothing, would be able to stop them.

He opened his eyes, and the flames appeared before him. He spread them across the width of the chamber, like a wall. Heat built, and his skin grew hot, but he forced the fire out of his body and into the flames. Everything in the chamber disappeared as another place opened before him.

And out of that dark emptiness, she floated. Sometimes she appeared in the shape of the ancient flying beast; other times she took human form. Though he was tempted to fall to his knees before her, he remained standing, his power holding the portal open. She came close, but she could not enter here or leave the realm where she was still imprisoned.

"My faithful servant," she whispered. "Hugh."

"Always yours," he answered, feeling her nearness and the surge of heat and power in his blood whenever he was in her presence. He walked closer to the wall of flames and held out his hand, penetrating the barrier as he could. Knowing what would happen, he prepared himself for it.

So much power! So much strength! So much pain!

He clenched his jaws together to keep from screaming at Chaela's contact. The touch of her fire seared him to the soul, and the intensity began to burn his skin away, but he forced himself to remain still under the pain and anguish of it.

The rewards would be so great and worth every second of agony he suffered at her touch. The pleasure that came from such agony coursed through his body.

Images filled his mind, and words raced through his ears, circling in his thoughts and overwhelming him. His cock stood and hardened and throbbed as though his body readied itself to join with a woman.

She did this to him. The pain and fire did this. His heart beat so fast and strongly that he thought it might burst. His lungs burned with every breath. His muscles pulsed and strengthened with each second. Then he fell to his knees, crying out loudly, but he never removed his hand from inside Chaela's wall of fire. Completely in her power, controlled by the pain and the promise of ecstasy and release, he waited as she told him all she wanted him to know.

Seconds or minutes or hours passed. Hugh was not certain how long he remained kneeling before her, burned and burning within and without and overwhelmed by all she shared with him through their link. Then, in an instant, she released his hand, and he fell to the floor, spent in every way and yet invigorated by this exchange. The flames surged around him, singeing his skin until he climbed to his feet and called them under control. Peering through them, he realized that the portal was closed and the goddess gone.

"Chaela, my goddess," he said, bowing deeply in homage.

"My faithful one." Her whisper filled the chamber once more, sending waves of shivers through his heated and burned flesh. "It is time to claim all that is mine."

He could not contain his joy. For years he'd waited and watched and learned and prepared for this moment, the time when he could unleash his powers and gather his minions to seek out those of the other bloodlines and use them to open the doorways to the goddess's prison world. Use them and then destroy them for their ancestors' betrayal those eons ago.

Hugh spread out his arms, leaned back his head, and roared out his joy. Finally, he'd be able to serve the goddess and gain all he deserved. His battle cry echoed through the chamber and then out into the night.

His moment of celebration over, Hugh strode back up the tower stairs into his own chambers and readied orders to his followers of this wondrous news. It was time to free Chaela and fulfill their ultimate mission.

Closing the doorway, he sent out riders to begin the search for the others. Now that Chaela issued the call, the other bloodlines would rise to it as well, just as her followers would. Time would be crucial to find the gatekeepers who would open the doorways closed by the blood of Chaela's son. He needed to find the priests who would even now be making their way to the first of the circles.

Only a passing glimpse of himself in the looking glass as he gathered his garments to dress slowed him.

Touching his chest, Hugh watched in the reflection as his hand moved over skin that was now more youthful and unmarked by the ravages of time and age. His face had changed, appearing twenty or so years younger, the wrinkles gone and his cheeks no longer sallow or drawn. He laughed and noticed his voice was different as well, stronger and deeper, as it had been when he was in the flower of manhood.

But the most shocking change was his hair. No longer did gray and white mix with the black of his youth. Nay, instead it was black once more, as it had not been for more than a score of years.

He smiled, realizing that the touch of his goddess had done this. Imagining all that could be done when she crossed to the human world, he laughed again. Only then did he notice the other change to his body.

The patch of skin that had risen on his forearm now bore the mark of his goddess. As though burned and marked with ink, two flames intertwined there. His mouth lifted into a grin when the flames moved, twisting and dancing as he caused real ones to do. They burned as they moved but did not destroy the skin there. 'Twas a constant reminder of his link to Chaela, and he found it pleasurable to feel the burn. It made his blood and the flesh of his body simmer with arousal that did not diminish as he dressed or as he ate his evening meal.

And when he took a wench to his bed that night and plowed her with the relentless vigor and force of youth, the flames leapt and pulsed on his skin, increasing the strength of his release. The constant pain there magnified his pleasure and his desire for satisfaction.

It burned its mark on his bedmate when he touched it to her skin. As he took the woman repeatedly through that night, marking her again and again with his new, burning insignia, he found even more pleasure in her terror and anguish. He wondered at what other changes would come with the goddess's return.

This particular one he liked.

CHAPTER 4

S even days.
   Seven days after speaking to the king and hearing his disturbing words and suspicions, William traveled along the road that approached the village of Yester. Two days of preparation had turned to five as he sought out and discovered more bits of hearsay and gossip and, he hoped, some truths about Lord Hugh de Gifford. Some of it, if shared, would make him sound like a raving madman. Not unlike the king had sounded during their shocking conversation.

He knew better than to share those suspicions or thoughts with anyone, or he'd find himself hanged for treason. Glancing over at the men riding at his side, William thought on how to parse out the needed details without revealing what the king had prohibited him from sharing. Roger and Gautier had guarded his back more times than he could remember. Herve, though new to his men, had proven himself valiant and strong in battle. All of them were worthy of the truth, but did he dare?

Shielding his eyes from the midday sun, he studied

the road ahead of them. Upon leaving Dunfermline, their journey proceeded without interruption or delay, first to the south and then to the east, where Lord Hugh's lands and keep lay.

"Have you been this way before, Will?" Gautier asked as he brought his mount to William's left.

"Nay. I have visited but a few places in these lands and not this one."

Even as he spoke those words, images filled his thoughts. Three other approaches to de Gifford's village and at least one secret way into his castle. Secret no more. Searching farther away from the castle, William saw three guard posts along the road from Gifford to Yester, too. They need not worry about those for now.

"You seem familiar with these lands." Gautier said, almost in accusation. The words hung in the air between them.

William shrugged and shook his head, letting the gesture hang out there in the space between them. Whether good fortune or the fates, a small traveling party appeared on the road behind them, coming through the thick line of forest and onto the more open, exposed fields.

"These people may know of the route we should take."

In a few minutes, the group of peasants caught up with them. A man who was tall, broad-chested, broad-shouldered, and older than the rest led them. William's gaze fell on a young woman standing behind the man, to the side of the horse-drawn cart.

"Good day, my lord," the man said as he stepped, William noticed, between him and the girl. The small group made as to pass them by, but William eased his mount farther onto the path, stopping them.

"Good day," William said, nodding only at the one who would meet his gaze. "Do you travel to Yester Village?" With a touch of his heel to his horse's side, he made the animal sidestep enough for him to see the girl.

"Aye, we are from the village," the man replied. With a nod of his head, he added, " 'Tis just over the next hill and about a mile on."

"And Lord Hugh?" William asked.

What William could only describe as a shudder passed quickly through the six villagers at the mention of the lord's name. Only the girl remained unaffected. Damn her, who would not raise her eyes to his! The older man moved as their gazes met once more, preventing William from getting a better look at her.

"Is Lord Hugh in residence?"

With neither of them willing to reveal their intentions or knowledge to the other, William might never get an answer. He also could not explain the compulsion burning through him to see the young woman and to speak to her. Was this man her husband then, protecting her from other men? The age difference was no indicator to him. His daughter?

"Sir," a soft voice began in faltering French. "I fear we know not."

She stepped from the shadow of the large, older man and glanced up at him. Although braced for something, he was not ready for the reaction of his body or mind as their gazes met. A roar filled his ears, and the ground seemed to shake beneath him.

Older than he'd first thought, she had amber eyes that resembled molten metal, a color that also seemed to surround and outline her form. But he must just be imagining it, for no one else appeared to notice how truly different she was from the rest of them. Everyone else faded, as though they'd lost all the color in their skin and hair and garments. Then, as if in answer to her heated gaze, the patch of skin on his arm burned more, a searing pain that threatened to take his breath away.

His blood rushed, and the beating of his heart pounded in his ears, both making any words impossible to hear. Without thought, his hand moved to the hilt of his sword as though some danger approached. And, as happened before any battle, his muscles tensed and prepared to give and take blows.

"William." It took him a few moments to realize that Roger spoke and shook his shoulder because his gaze and his senses were filled with her. "William."

He felt unable to pull his gaze from hers, but he finally tore himself free of the power of it and nodded, once he was able to hear his friend's words.

"They are returning to Yester. We will have to ride on to see if Lord Hugh is there."

"Brienne?" the man said, touching the woman on her shoulder. "Are you well, lass?"

He watched as the young woman, as *Brienne*, came back to herself and nodded to the man. "Aye, Father," she whispered, but William heard the words. *Father!*

Whatever had happened, they'd both felt it. The man tugged the girl back closer to his side and then nodded at William and the others.

"Good day and safe travels to you."

Without waiting for his approval or permission, the man guided the group back along the road. No one spoke until they were far enough away not to hear their words.

"*Merde!* I thought you would bed her in the road before all of us," Herve said with a laugh. "Though I've never known you to pay heed to a woman of that kind." William did not seek out virgins, and he did not seek those in service to their lords who could not gainsay him.

"Her father saw your intention with one look, and now he will lock her away until we are gone from this business with Lord Hugh," Gautier said. "A bit homely for my tastes, but to each"—he nodded at each of them—"his own."

"Homely? You think her plain of face?" he asked. She was radiant and stunning to him, her eyes glowing like a fiery ingot, her womanly curves outlined by the same glow. How could they think her otherwise? The three laughed aloud at his words and nodded. "Truly?"

"Aye," Herve said. "Though a woman's beauty or lack of it ne'er stopped me from bedding her if she were willing."

"Nay, it does not," Roger agreed. "I have seen you take all manner of women to your bed. Be they young or old, infirmed or in fine mettle, plain-faced or a beauty. You have no refinement in your choices of a bedmate, my friend."

William let them continue in their boasting and stared off down the road at the travelers, who'd reached the hill and soon disappeared over it. He motioned to Roger, who rode to his side.

"There is another road that leads to the village and the keep," he explained. Raising his hand, he pointed to the east. "Through this field and the other side of this wood. We will go that way."

"They said this is the road," his friend replied, nodding in the direction they had been heading. Then Gautier stared at him. "You think there is danger in following them?"

"I think—I know—there is danger in Yester for us. Following them or not, it will find us."

And know it, he did. To the marrow of his bones, he was certain with every step along this path, they were in grievous danger. When the cover thrown over the back of the wagon had shifted, he'd seen the swords and axes there. A cache of weapons for Lord Hugh's purposes, whatever they may be. His men, his friends, deserved to know the truth of it.

"We will camp in the woods there and bide our time before we venture into Yester. I would not enter a battle unarmed and will not enter this fray unprepared. Come," William said to all of them. "We should not remain here in the open."

They rode through the farmland in silence as William led them along a path only he could see. The road would curve up along the stream and then come to a small clearing. He shook his head, still not believing that he could visualize almost as though he flew above it all. They set up a small camp inside the woods near that clearing. Once night had fallen, William shared the fantastical tale of what the king had told him. He would not put their lives at risk without them knowing why. Asking them to think on his words, he gave them the night to decide their willingness to join in his mission.

As dawn's light crept into the thickly clouded sky, William's three companions remained with him.

By the time the morning's fog burned away, he was making his way, alone, into the small village to discover the whereabouts of the lord of Yester.

And mayhap a chance to observe the intriguing and puzzling young woman whose face and voice and eyes now filled his thoughts. With only that thought, he could see exactly where she stood now, sweeping in the small cottage in which she lived.

William shuddered as he realized the impossibility of such knowledge even while it flowed into his mind with a certainty difficult to ignore.

Brienne tugged the woolen shawl tighter around herself to ward off the chill of the morning as she walked through the village. Another errand for her father kept her busy for now. Though this was the kind of day when the cold and fog would have made her wish to remain under her blankets for a while longer, the excitement of meeting the four strangers on the road had kept her awake all night long. The anticipation of them arriving in the village and seeing their leader pulsed through her veins.

She met very few strangers here in the village. She traveled outside Lord Hugh's lands and control infrequently. But even living such a sheltered life, Brienne understood to her core that this man, this *William* as she had heard him called, was someone very important.

And important to her in some yet unknown way. The way his gaze caught hers and made her blood heat had shocked her. But it was more than a man lusting for a woman. Oh, that she'd seen before in men's eyes enough to recognize it. Though most men here would never dare anything, even young James's eyes had flashed with wanting when he'd wooed her gently.

No, this William's gaze felt like a thousand suns, and something within her answered with a heat unlike any of the fires in her father's smithy. The area on her arm yet burned, the pattern rising once more and becoming clearer to her—two flames moving on her skin, swirling and dancing and burning as they did. Brienne lifted her arm, allowing the woolen shawl and the sleeve of her shift and gown to slide up, revealing the strange patch.

She heard some villagers nearby, so she dropped her arm and let the clothing fall back in place. Continuing on her path, she considered her reactions to this stranger. For a moment, everything else had faded away but him. And he'd seemed to grow in size and fierceness as he stared at her. Yet, instead of the fear she should have felt and should be feeling now, she felt protected and safe.

The fog thinned and the sun's light tried to pierce the dullness of the misty morning as she brought water from the well, carried bread to the baker's ovens, and made her way from task to task as she did on a usual day. But this day was different from all that had passed before. Brienne knew that but would never have been able to explain her certainty. As she spoke to the miller's wife, her body changed.

As though a strong storm's wind had blown over her, something moved over her body, awakening the heat within her. The fire within her pushed at its bounds, strengthening and filling her in a way she'd never known before. For a moment she wanted to hold out her hand and let it escape. Turning to see if the change within her was noticeable by anyone, she saw that she'd walked away from the miller's cottage and down the path without even noticing where her steps had been taking her.

She'd controlled the flames with her power, but she'd never created it. Yet from the strong urge within her, she thought she could. Shivering against such a thing, Brienne glanced around to see if anyone was near.

And that was when she spied him.

William.

Brienne stepped back into the shadows of the cottages and watched him, for from his demeanor and gait, it was clear he did not wish to be recognized or seen. He'd taken only a few strides toward the village when he lifted his head and met her gaze.

The fire pulsed in her now, not just heat or something indefinite as before. The flames urged their release from her. She closed her hands into tight fists to keep them within.

"Brienne." His whispered voice spoke her name. He took one step toward her and then another and again until he stood before her.

Power flowed from him, much as hers had in the presence of her fath— of Lord Hugh. But his was different and didn't seem to come from fire. Strength. Loyalty. A man of war. A defender.

Brienne shook her head and realized where she was. She stood barely a pace away from a complete stranger, a man, a noble perhaps, but at least a knight, capable of all manner of things. Her parents had warned her of the danger in such situations as this, and yet she did not feel threatened.

Intrigued. Curious. Drawn. But not threatened.

When his gaze moved to her mouth and then down her body, a shiver passed through her. Those eyes, like the icy surface of the loch when it froze, seemed to look right through her.

What would his touch be like?

"Aye, how would it feel, lass?" he asked, lifting his

hand toward her face. As he turned it so that he could skim down her cheek, she closed her eyes and waited for . . . for . . . The moment before his hand touched her, she shook her head and stepped back.

"Can you hear my thoughts?" she asked, putting a short distance between them. "Who are you?" In truth, she should be showing him respect and not nay-saying him, but she wanted to know. He was unlike any man she'd ever met.

"I am William, the king's man." He bowed slightly to her as though she was worthy of such regard. "I come to meet with your lord."

"He is not yet returned," she blurted out.

In spite of her father's warnings not to speak of Lord Hugh to outsiders, she just had. Did he hear her thoughts *and* control her speech? His mouth curved into a smile then, easing the masculine sharpness of his features.

"I suspected as much," he said. "Where is your father?"

Brienne glanced over her shoulder and in the direction of their cottage and the smithy. "He is working in the smithy now."

"Ah, so he made the weapons you brought in your wagon?"

Finally gathering her scattered wits about her, she did not let the words leave her mouth. It would be unwise to be caught speaking to a stranger, let alone giving him information about anything that involved Lord Hugh. He was not tolerant of those who spilled his secrets or spoke unwisely about him.

"My father is there, if you wish to speak to him."

The warrior, for that was what he was, turned and

looked back toward the woods and then at the village as though deciding which path to take. When his foot took a step away from the village, her heart ached.

She needed to ask him . . . She wanted to speak to him. . . . She wanted to know . . . everything. If he left now, Brienne knew she would never discover why his presence seemed to strengthen her powers when no one else's ever had.

Except for Lord Hugh, her true father.

"Will you return?" she asked.

"I have business with your lord," he said, nodding. Then, with a quick glance over her shoulder, he disappeared into the thick copse of trees faster than she thought a man could move.

The crunching and crackling of leaves behind her told her of another's approach. Now she understood William's hasty leave-taking—he did not wish to be seen here. Puzzling over it, Brienne turned and watched as James made his way to her.

"Are you well, Brienne?" he asked. "My mother said you left hastily when she spoke to you."

"I am well. I will apologize for my rudeness," she said.

He took a step closer and towered over her. Taller but thinner and not as muscular as the warrior who'd stood with her, James did not upset her feelings or cause the heat to blossom within her.

"She did not speak of rudeness, she but worried over you." He lifted his hand and lightly placed it on her arm. "As I do, Brienne."

A fortnight ago, even earlier this day, she would have welcomed his touch and his company. Now, though, everything in her world had tilted and changed. She had changed. Now . . .

"I spoke to your father, Brienne. He said I may court you." The hope she heard in his voice, full of promise and a shared future, made her stomach tighten. "If you consent, we could be married in the spring."

James tilted his head down and touched his mouth to hers. It was a warm and gentle kiss. He canted his head, and his lips pressed against hers until she opened to him. A slow, tentative slide of his tongue into her mouth startled her. He drew back in response.

"So, will you, Brienne? Will you take me as your husband?"

As his brown eyes searched hers for an answer, she considered that only a fortnight ago, he would have been the perfect husband for her—the son of the miller marrying the daughter of the blacksmith. They would live in the village with their families, as generations had before them.

A perfect match.

Except that she was not the blacksmith's daughter. She was the get of one of the most powerful and terrifying lords in Scotland, who'd recently taken notice of her. She held some power within her that allowed—nay, pressed—her to control fire. The burning place on her arm flared then, reminding her of the unknown and that this possible future as the wife of James, Dougal's son, was simply not possible. As she tried to choose the right words that would kindly dash his hopes, he shook his head.

"I am not pressing for your answer now. I know you would speak to your mother and father now that the offer is made to you. Take some time to consider how good a marriage we would make." James took a full pace back and smiled at her.

All she could do was return it in silence.

"I must return to my father now that I know you are safe," he said, leaning in for a quick kiss. "I will seek you out later."

With those brief words of farewell, he was gone, striding back along the path toward his family's cottage.

Brienne stood in the dappled shadows, watching the wind move the branches above and around her. So much had happened this morning, and she was no closer to answers than she had been when she'd opened her eyes on this new day. All she had now were more questions and more doubts . . . and a marriage proposal. She shook her head at that, for her answer to James was the only thing of which she was certain.

Glancing around the clearing, she shook off the confusion and decided she must return to her errands. Mayhap by doing those tasks and daily chores that were part of her everyday life, she would begin to find her path in all the uncertainty. Taking a deep breath and letting it out, she put one foot in front of the other and forced herself back to the path.

The skin on her arm, two flames dancing and burning without destroying, reminded her that, regardless of her wishes on the matter, nothing would ever be the same again.

CHAPTER 5

He stood in the shadows, planning the death that would visit the man who'd touched her. Who'd kissed her. Who'd whispered to her. His sword drawn and ready, William blew hard against the urge to walk into the clearing and kill the one who dared so much.

She was his.

His to touch.

His to kiss.

His . . . to claim.

His vision narrowed, and red ringed the edges of it. His body strengthened and broadened, his muscles elongating and tightening until his garments felt too small. He breathed hard and deep, preparing for battle, and the hand that clutched the sword appeared larger, as though it were not his own. Then the sword became as one with him and his focus sharpened onto only one thing— making certain that no man left his scent or mark on the woman destined for him.

His.

He'd taken one step back out of the thick copse that hid him before his control overruled the possessive compulsion that nearly forced his hand. Shaking off the stranglehold of pure fury that raced in his veins and pumped his heart hard and fast, he watched as the young man escaped the death he did not know was coming for him.

Then she left, walking back along the path that led to the center of the village.

Though the skin on his arm ached and burned, his gaze and his head began to clear. Then a wave of shudders racked him as whatever had fueled his rage dissipated and left him. His own body returned and the red tinge left his vision, allowing him to notice the cool breeze rustling through the trees around him. Now, when he lifted his arm, the sword appeared to be a separate thing, the weapon he'd always known it to be.

Not an appendage to his body.

His knees buckled and he landed hard, shaking and trembling, as though he'd not eaten in days. Sweat poured down from his brow, trickling over his face and neck and under his garments, as it did after a battle or a strenuous training session with his men.

But he'd done none of that. Had he?

Rubbing the back of his hand across his forehead, William wondered if he was getting ill. A fever? Some contagion that caused the strange changes in his body and mind? He must return to his men. There must be an explanation. One that made sense. One that did not seem too close to the king's peculiar claims.

Oh God! Was the same madness that claimed his father's reason now taking his?

Pushing to his feet, William retraced his path back through the darkest part of the forest to their camp.

When he broke through the trees, his men stared at him in silence.

"What happened?" Roger asked as he approached. Glancing behind William, he stared into the forest. "Were you attacked? Are you being followed?"

As William expected, the three formed a line and drew their swords, expecting an attack at any moment. They'd fought many times before, and he welcomed their presence in any battle. But this was not one.

"Nay." He waved them off, walked directly to the stream just at the edge of their camp, and drank the cold, fresh water. He even splashed some of it on his face and neck. He hoped it would cool whatever fever controlled him, but the shaking would not desist. "No one comes. I was not attacked," he said, standing before them. "If I did not call out to you, why would you think that?"

The three looked at one another and then back at him, disbelief etched on their faces.

"Did you see the girl?" Gautier's gaze narrowed. He stood more at ease now. "Or did her father see you?"

"The girl," he replied, choosing not to lie about it. Pushing his hair out of his face, he shrugged.

Gautier nodded to Herve then; for them this was a simple thing—if they lusted for a woman, they sought her and eased the itch. Roger motioned the two of them off and walked up to William.

"You look like bloody hell, Will. What happened?" he asked in a low voice. "You look as though you've seen the devil himself."

"I am beginning to understand the king's strange behavior and suspicions." That admission eased something within him. "Something is going on here, something I have never encountered, Roger. I am part of it, as the king said, but now you and the others are as well."

"I do not understand," Roger said. He walked a few paces back to the camp and brought back a skin of wine. After taking a long drink from it, he offered it to William. "Something like treason? Or"—he paused and glanced around before whispering—"some madness? Surely not witchcraft or deviltry?" Roger made the sign of the cross over himself after saying the words. "And the girl is part of it?"

"I am part of it. And, aye, the girl. I could see something was different about her when I first looked upon her. Just now, while speaking to her . . ." He shrugged, not knowing what to say or how to explain the change that had happened. "When someone approached, I left. Then I watched, and I . . . lost control of myself somehow," he admitted.

That's how it had felt to him—as though someone else had taken over his body, changing it, changing him. Only at that last moment had he regained control and stopped the young man's death. He shivered against the heat that yet filled him.

"Sweet Jesu, man! Did you take her? Did you kill her or someone?"

"Nay," he answered. Shaking his head, he knew that whatever had happened had occurred so he could protect her, not threaten her.

Roger asked nothing else, which suited William, for he had little or nothing else he could say in reply to queries. In battle, William was skilled, strong, and ruthless, but he always controlled his actions and the path he took when fighting. Just a few minutes ago, he'd felt like a madman, ready to kill for no reason.

Though his control had returned, William could not rid himself of the suspicion that this was but the first strange incident and that many more dangerous incidents would follow in his quest for the king. Peering over the rolling lands just beyond the forest's edge, he knew he and his men were not safe.

"Send Herve to Gifford to find out what he can about Lord Hugh's whereabouts," he said, handing the skin back to Roger. "And send Gautier for the rest of the men. They should travel in small groups so they do not draw attention." When Roger nodded, he continued, first pointing to a place higher on a nearby hill. "We will move our camp up there. Better to see the whole of this valley and easier to defend ourselves."

"Defend?" Roger stared at him. "You think we will be attacked?"

"Aye."

William *knew* they would be. He could see it in his thoughts, the waves of men pouring from the keep and out into the forest and running up the hill at them. No, not men . . . Though they resembled men, there was something almost inhuman about them.

He could also not determine the time or the day of his vision; he knew only that they would come. "Aye, we will be attacked."

He spent the next few hours making a list of supplies and discussing the weapons they would need. Two of the men waiting outside Dunfermline were experts at the long bow and would be sorely needed in the coming battle. Battles.

William had gold from the king and could buy the weapons they needed—and that might be the course of action he would take. First he needed his men in place. Then he must determine Lord Hugh's plans.

And he must discover the reason why the young woman Brienne was so important to him.

Later, when the sun was high in the late-February sky, he and Roger moved their camp higher on the hillside.

Suddenly it made sense to William: This was more than just the king's quest. There were other players in the game that was unfolding around him. He just could not see his place on the board yet.

The fire hummed inside of her, whispering its call, its invitation, quietly and testing its bounds. She could not ignore or resist it now that it had awakened. Though Brienne carried out her daily tasks over the next days, her thoughts drifted to the extraordinary exchanges she'd had with both James and the warrior William.

James had never kissed her in spite of his obvious affection for her. His proposal and her father's permission had emboldened him to take such an action now. A pang of sadness pierced her, as she knew that she would never marry him. The words she would use to tell him eluded her, but that did not change the result or the disappointment she would see in his eyes when she did.

William had not returned to the village. Gavin had warned her with stern words to avoid the strangers. He'd reminded her of what could happen to women caught outside the village by strangers. He begged her to stay within the well-worn paths and among those she knew. And for all his concern and warnings, Brienne watched along the shadows and at the edges of the village for any sign that the outsider had returned.

After she'd finished her chores, Brienne walked along the stream, feeling the fire push at her control. What would happen if she let go? Would she truly be able to create fire? Could she control it as she had in her father's smithy? Would it do her bidding?

Searching for a secluded spot where she would not be seen, she decided to test out this new power. As she crept along the water's edge, she saw him. He knelt there, scooping water in his hands and drinking it. His brown hair hung down, hiding his face from her, but she remembered his fierce gaze and his pale blue eyes. After her father's words of warning and her mother's plea to remain close, Brienne knew she should be wary and probably afraid, but all she noticed was a shameful amount of curiosity—about the man, his purpose, and the world from which he came.

"Good day," he said when he'd turned and noticed her. Standing, he shook off the water from his hands, wiped them on his cloak, and nodded to her. She noticed how he towered over her, though not as much as James did.

"Good day," she replied. Glancing around the area, she saw no one else. He was alone.

"You are looking for the others? My men?" he asked. She nodded. "They are not here."

His gaze did not waver, and a small shiver of excitement and nervousness pooled deep within her. No man ever stared at her in this manner or took more than a sidelong glance at her. Oh, her father could meet her eyes when they talked, and her mother as well, but few others in the village dared. Brienne's molten gaze was something she had inherited from her true sire, and everyone who'd seen him knew it.

Could he sense it?

"I must get back," she began, lifting her hand in the direction of the village behind her.

"So soon, demoiselle?" The word spoken in such a soft tone seemed strange coming from such a large and dangerous warrior. Then he continued. "I did not mean to frighten you away from whatever task brought you to the stream. I will go."

"Nay. Stay," she said, shaking her head. What she wanted more than anything was to talk with him. Talk to someone whose life was from outside Lord Hugh's demesne and control. Yet she could not say such a thing to him, knowing he had business with Lord Hugh. "I was but walking before helping my mother with our supper."

"Very well," he said, turning back to the water and dipping his hands once again.

Her feet would not move. In spite of the warnings, she wanted nothing so much as to remain here and speak with him. Part of her wanted to speak with him about Lord Hugh, while another part knew the dire consequences that could happen to her or, worse, to her family, if she did. Brienne doubted that being his natural daughter would stop Lord Hugh's hand if raised in retribution. She shivered at the thought.

"Are you chilled? Here now. Come into the sun and out of the shadows," he said. Reaching out, he took her hand and tugged until she took the few paces out from the cover of the trees to where he'd crouched at the water's edge. Then he tugged the edges of her cloak together. "Better now?"

She nodded, knowing it was a lie. She never suffered the cold and wore a cloak only to avoid questions and inquisitive glances. She never had felt chilled, now that she thought on it. Closer to him, the fire inside her grew even more, swelling and pushing against her limits. Every step toward him made it intensify and strengthen.

Brienne gritted her teeth and clenched her fists, hoping to keep it within. If she had doubted she could bring forth fire without a hearth or pit, she did not do so any longer. It was there, barely contained, barely restrained, waiting for a slip in her grasp. She dared not.

She dared not.

"Why are you not at the keep?" she asked, trying to distract the heat within her from its purpose. "If you have business with Lord Hugh, surely you would be welcome there."

He wiped his hands against his trews and tunic and met her gaze. "Lord Hugh knows not of my visit or my business yet. I did not wish to ask for the hospitality of his house until he arrived."

She sensed that those few words, that short admission, cost him much. *Does he think me a risk?*

"Aye, it is not my custom to speak of my matters with others."

"How did you know? Can you hear my thoughts?" she asked. Then, gasping at her words, she covered her mouth with her hands. *Why did I say that to him?*

"Not hear them so much as sense the questions you have," he said, shaking his head. "I cannot fathom how it happens either." He glanced at her, and his eyes narrowed. "Nor why I need to tell you things I should not as well. Why do you draw me as surely as if you call my name?"

He touched her hands first, lifting them away from her face, and then he outlined her cheek and jaw with only a finger. She lost her breath, for it was the lightest of touches, but it held the power of a blow. His eyes never left hers as he turned his hand and let the back of it caress her cheek.

Now the heat pulsing through her body had nothing to do with the fire she controlled. This heat came from a growing ache in her core, her breasts and skin. It was a different kind of heat, and he leaned in closer and touched his lips to hers.

In that moment, Brienne knew that this was what she should fear. This power, this heat. It wasn't the one she'd been born with that should terrify her. His mouth tasted hers in the gentlest of ways, not forcing or pressing her for more. Not yet. But she could feel his control, hear the shallow, panting breaths that spoke of his arousal, and she shook in response.

"Brienne," he whispered as he moved his mouth from hers to kiss along her jaw. "Brienne." He touched her ear with the tip of his tongue and she shuddered from it, her body not her own.

The loud whistling of a bird pierced the quiet of their secluded spot, and William stilled. A second one roused her from this stupor of passion he'd created. He lifted his head and canted it, listening, and then released her when a third one followed.

"I . . . I must go. Forgive me if I trespassed."

Within a few seconds, he'd disappeared from the spot where they'd stood, sharing an intimacy she'd never shared with any man before. The rustling of leaves as he walked away quieted, leaving her alone, confused, and filled with a feeling she'd never felt before.

Was this desire? Her body ached and throbbed in places she'd hardly noticed before. Her skin tingled and her lips burned. And this kiss, this touching, by a stranger made her body answer his caress in a way that James's had never done.

There was more, too. Sharing this personal, private moment with him aroused the deeper need within her to be with another, to speak about important matters. She wanted to speak of her dreams and fears with another person.

The cool water of the stream tempted her, and she walked to its edge. Pulling on the laces that held her cloak around her, she dropped it before kneeling beside the water. As she dipped her hands into the water, steam rose from the surface. Releasing her power, she watched as her hands turned red and then orange and then like gold when the metal was heated over the fire. With an unpracticed motion, she extended her arms, lifting her hands out of the water and cupping her palms together. And then she created fire in them.

Fire!

She had created fire.

Laughing, she stood and forced the fire higher and wider, spreading her hands apart and spreading the flames into the air and around her. Urging it on, Brienne strengthened it with whispered words she did not understand. Glancing around, she closed her eyes as the flames caressed her, never burning her as they became one.

She could do it!

She could bring fire into being and be one with it.

She swirled around inside the cocoon it formed, the flames moving around her as ribbons on a pole, outlining her body, moving her hair on its currents, making her feel their power and hers. Touching and caressing her almost as a lover would. And yet never did she feel in danger of being burned.

All it took to end it was the sound of a branch breaking behind her. Brienne stopped the flames with a thought and they were gone. She spun around and watched as William entered the clearing.

Had he seen her? Had he witnessed what she could do? From his level gaze, she could tell nothing. But she could feel that the fire wanted him, too. She could feel its need to surround and engulf him as it had her.

"I would speak with you, Brienne. About what happened," he said, striding toward her. He stopped only a pace from where she stood. "Meet me here on the morrow."

'Twas a bad thing, to be torn between wanting to meet him and knowing that there was such danger in doing so. The woman within her ached to explore the world he'd just opened to her. The passion and intimacy of the kiss they'd shared still echoed through her even while the daughter of the villager knew that it would lead to heartbreak and ruin. Yet the firemaker within also wondered how he was involved in her power, for she knew it for the certainty it was.

"I should not."

"Nay, you most likely should not. But," he said, glancing at the water that she'd turned to steam, "I think you will." His face gave away nothing to tell her what he'd seen. Or if he had. Since she did not want

Gavin to know of their encounters nor of her expanding power, she would concede.

"On the morrow?" He nodded. "I will come after my father breaks his fast, but I cannot remain long." The corner of his lip curled as though attempting a smile. She remembered the feel of his mouth on hers. That other heat filled her, and she felt a blush creep up into her cheeks.

"Until then," he said.

Brienne nodded and he left, not as quickly as the last time. She listened as his footsteps moved farther and farther through the trees and brush until only the silence surrounded her.

With questions filling her thoughts about what he could have seen and what had been between them, she made her way back to the village and to her parents' cottage. 'Twas times like this when she wanted—nay, craved—someone with whom she could talk about these things. None of the village girls would friend her because they feared her true father's attentions. Even the mother who'd raised her seemed to fear her at times as Brienne had approached womanhood. And Gavin knew about her power and yet he did not welcome talking.

So in the dark of the night as she sought sleep that would not come, Brienne wondered if the warrior had seen her bring fire into existence.

On the morrow, he'd said.

On the morrow, he'd tempted.

On the morrow, he'd promised.

On the morrow . . . she feared.

CHAPTER 6

Loanhead of Daviot, Northeast Scotland

Hugh strode across the rolling countryside . . . again. Each time he did, each time he circled the standing stones, his men drew farther and farther away. Each failure to locate and read the signs told those he controlled that someone would pay for his failure.

The stones had been fashioned centuries ago to mark the positions of the sun and the moon, the passing of the seasons, and to aid in the worship of the old gods here on this plain. Though the forests encroached, the view of the sky to the south was unimpeded. This must be the place for which he'd searched.

His first quandary was that there were two circles of stones, one lower on the hill and this one, farther up. But examination had revealed no symbols or signs or enchantments of any kind on the lower circle. And no altar stone. Which led him back here to this one.

"Well?" he called out to the man who dared to stand closest to him.

With the power to sense spells, Paulin was a druid's son whom Hugh's father had raised to this purpose. The man's own father had left some godsforsaken island where the priests and scryers yet studied and had somehow found his way to Brittany, another Celtic region. When the truth of his origins was discovered and the man would not reveal the island's location, Hugh's father executed him in front of his family, teaching young Paulin that obedience and service were the only correct answers.

"Still nothing, my lord," he replied, bowing.

"You said the changes in the moon would reveal the markings."

"I hoped it would, my lord," Paulin said. "I do not sense any trace of power here in the stones. Even the altar stone bears no sign of . . ."

"Sacrifice? Worship?" Hugh finished. Human blood left its own memory on sacred altar stones, and there were those like Paulin who could see and smell it decades and centuries later. Paulin nodded and watched him with the same wariness that everyone did.

Hugh's patience snapped like a worn thread, for they had been here for more than a sennight, watching the phases of the moon and waiting for the signs. He knew that those of the blood were waking, their powers stretching and opening. Soon they would be drawn to the stone circles. Hugh could not allow them to find the symbols and close the gateways, trapping his goddess for eons to come.

Hugh grabbed Paulin by the throat and held him off his feet. Shaking him, he watched as the man's face changed from red to purple.

"I cannot fail in this endeavor," he warned, shaking him once more. "So you cannot fail me," he repeated. "Where are the symbols? Where are they?"

"My lord."

Paulin's eyes bulged, and he gurgled as his throat closed under Hugh's grip. "You do not have much time. Where are they?"

"My lord!" The man who led his human troops called to Hugh, so he turned his gaze away from the seer clawing at his fist. "He is the last one, my lord."

Eudes's words gave him pause. As much as he wanted to kill the seer who could not see, he did need him. Hugh screamed his displeasure as he threw Paulin to the ground. Gasping and trying to suck in the air he'd been denied, Paulin struggled on the ground.

"See to him, Eudes. Two more days and we return to Yester."

"Aye, my lord." Hugh's half brother bowed and then helped Paulin to his feet and away.

How had the symbols—that must be here—been hidden from his sight and that of this druid? Walking to the nearest stone, Hugh placed his hands on it, feeling the heat that radiated from within. That was not magical, for some stones simply absorbed the warmth of the sun and held it, releasing it slowly over hours. They must be here. They must be—

The pain struck him quickly and took his breath. His fire raged within him, answering the call of another. Another?

Another fireblood?

Bending over and gasping at the pain that was neither exquisite nor arousing, Hugh knew it was not his wife or daughter Adelaide. His daughter had demonstrated no ability to control fire in spite of his sire's careful plan to find and breed the trait in the children of his son and daughter-in-law. So many years of planning and finding the right bloodline to breed with his own and it had ended in failure. It had seemed that Hugh was their bloodline's last chance.

Until now. Until this.

The excruciating waves pierced him, burned him, tried to tear his power out of him. He fought, grasping within to keep the fire there at his core.

Someone was calling it forth. Someone could call it. Someone . . .

By the goddess! Could it be his bastard after all?

He laughed now, loud and rough as the pain tore into his soul and his flesh. The girl was calling the fire!

And then it was gone. The pulling and tearing, the fire burning him, all of it. She must have ceased in her efforts. Or mayhap she did not yet know how to control it.

Gods! When she did, he could tell from the feel of this that she would be formidable. His dark mood evaporated, and he laughed into the terrified faces of those who served him.

He tried to remember on which slattern he'd bred this daughter, whether one of his villeins or some other woman taken as he wanted. Ever aware of the bloodlines of his goddess's enemies, he did not remember finding or swiving a woman of power. And yet this bastard girl of his had inherited his and clearly her dam's, if she could use it this way.

Having two firebloods in this quest meant everything. That the other was of his flesh and blood meant his power would be irresistible when combined with hers. Hugh roared out in pleasure at this, for he would now claim her and train her and she would belong to him and his goddess. She'd be used in their quest and discarded when her powers were depleted, leaving his untouched, undiminished.

None of the other bloodlines—not the warrior nor the healer nor the stormblood nor the waterblood nor the beastblood nor the earthblood—could hope to stand against him—against them now.

"Chaela, my goddess," he whispered into the air. "We are close. We are so very close."

He strode over to the altar stone, a large, flat stone that reclined between two taller, upright stones, and laid his hands on it. Blood had been spilled here, but it had happened too long ago to wake the seer's abilities. He would fix that and then return to Yester to begin the process of claiming his daughter's powers.

"Eudes!" His half brother came at his call, knowing better than to hesitate. "Summon Brisbois from the camp and find a suitable gift for the gods here." Eudes bowed and turned to leave. "And tell Paulin we leave one day after he reads the altar stone."

In a short time, for he would brook no delays or impediments, his executioner had arrived with their sacrifice. Handing Brisbois the dagger Hugh had forged and used for his own initiation, he instructed him in how to perform the ritual.

As Brisbois set to work, making the death last as long as possible, Hugh walked around the altar stone and chanted the prayers that would gain favor for their search. By the time the man's last scream echoed through the circle, the altar lay covered in the rich, dark blood that would replenish the force within it. Chaela had been properly worshipped. Now his seer should have no excuse.

When Hugh rode south the following day, back to his lands in Gifford, he knew that the circle was the first gate he must open. Paulin had been able to point out where the symbols were carved into the stones, but he could not make them visible to Hugh yet. Regardless, the potential of combining his power with another fire-blood made him smile with joy for the first time in a very, very long while.

It would take him another sennight to reach Yester and then the first steps in the quest would begin.

William divided his men into smaller groups so that they could hide on the hillside. In farmland like this, a large camp of armed men would be easily seen and reported. No one could find any word of Lord Hugh's whereabouts nor his intention of returning to Yester. He held lands here and in the west, though this was his seat and the place the king had sent him. Standing on the edge of his camp, he could see the towers of Yester Castle rise in the distance beyond the forest and the curls of smoke rising above the small village that sprang up at its entrance and served the needs of those who lived in the keep.

Without gaining entrance to the castle, William knew not if the lord's wife and daughter were in residence. He knew not how many guards were on duty nor how many soldiers lived within it. Nor how much food or supplies were on hand. Nor if the water supply was contained within the castle walls or if it came from outside. All crucial bits of knowledge needed before planning any attack on a fortified castle.

The sun struggled to rise this morn, the clouds thick and dark and threatening a late-winter storm. William nodded as the first of his men woke and rolled their blankets. He had said little to them when they'd arrived just after sunset, leading their horses on foot along a hillside path to avoid being seen. Uncertain of what Gautier had told them, he would wait and speak to them later, when all twelve of his men were present.

Roger walked to his side and held out a battered cup of ale and a hunk of cheese. He took them and nodded his thanks. It had been Roger's signal the day before that had stopped him before he could go further with the blacksmith's daughter—and regret it. There was no recrimination in his actions, simply a reminder of the task at hand and the dangers of seducing an innocent villager.

"Do you still plan to see her?" he asked, knowing of William's arranged meeting.

"Aye. I think she can tell me much about Lord Hugh," he answered, looking off in the distance. Roger's choking cough and then laugh spoke of his clear disbelief in William's plan.

"I saw you with her, Will," his friend explained. "I have seen the way you watch her. I have heard the way you speak of her. You want her and I would not naysay you on that. . . . " Roger turned and faced him, not allowing him to ignore the coming words. "But you know that there is something strange and powerful going on here, in these lands, with this lord. The king has sent you to look into the matter. Do not, my friend, allow her to distract you from the importance of or the danger of your mission."

Will could not argue with a single word Roger spoke. He knew all that and more, and yet he also understood that he could not avoid this young woman. For now he knew she stood at the heart of this quest.

The sight of her opening her hands and causing fire to burst forth from nothing was something he would never forget. He could not explain it, but if this were true, if she held this great power and magic within her, he could not dare to ignore her part in the king's mission.

How he'd managed to keep his shock from showing on his face afterward, he knew not. He'd fought to keep it from his gaze and his manner when he'd walked back into the clearing and saw her surrounded by those flames. And she did not burn. Nay, from the sound of her laughter and the broad grin on her face, she reveled in her talent.

Yet how could he admit this to Roger, when no God-fearing man would dare to admit seeing such things? He drank down the rest of the ale and handed the cup back to his friend.

"I hear your advice," he said, looking in the distance to where the stream meandered across the valley. To where she would be.

"But you will not heed my warning?"

Will smacked his friend on the shoulder. "I am too far into this, whatever this endeavor is, Roger, to turn back now. Control of my lands—*my lands*—lies within the king's hands, and to possess them I must do his bidding. The king said he was led to me. Well, I am led to her."

Those lands had been promised to him since his birth by the king in consideration of his friendship with William's mother, but always there were conditions and delays. Without his father's permission, he could not stand against the other branch of his family—the legitimate ones. Only the king could give him the standing, even if not the legitimacy, to claim them . . . and hold them.

And now, remembering the changes that had overtaken him a few days before—changes that were just as unbelievable as those he'd glimpsed the girl making— he realized that everything he thought he knew and thought possible were shifting, like the sands of a beach.

"I will heed your warning, Roger, though I know not if I could walk away at this moment."

William needed to find out what was happening here. Raised in the faith of the Holy Church, he understood good and evil. He understood that some people sought evil and did evil things. And that things that could not be explained were usually the devil's work. But he was not of the devil and he doubted that Brienne was either.

"I will have your back, Will," Roger swore quietly. "Fear not that you are in this alone. No matter what manner of danger comes at us, we will stand together in this."

Will felt that the coming times would task that promise, but he could not explain it to Roger. And he would not fault his friend or any of his men for choosing to leave when they discovered that all was not as it seemed to be. Indeed, from the look of things, very little in this part of Scotland was.

Nodding to Roger, he put on his sword belt and placed the dagger in his boot. He did not wear his battle armor, wanting to be able to move more easily among any villagers he would encounter. Wearing only a jack of leather over his tunic and trews, he covered it with his long cloak so he could pass for a merchant.

"I will return shortly. Herve is expected back this morn, and we will discuss what he has discovered and what I discover when I return. Keep everyone close."

William did not wait for Roger to acknowledge his orders, for his friend would follow them. Walking down the hill, into the forest, and along the stream, he made his way to the place where he'd seen Brienne the day before. If she arrived first, would she wait or would she leave? Should he reveal that he'd seen her?

Crossing the distance to the stream, he looked back to the hill to see if the camp was concealed. Satisfied, William turned back and found her standing there, watching him with an even gaze. When he nodded, those burning amber eyes filled with questions. Against his will, against all good plans and advice, he needed to answer them.

Brienne watched him approach with the cautious steps of a wary predator wanting not to be seen or heard. He turned and stared back at the hills that surrounded the roads leading to Yester Castle. At first she thought that he appeared different from other men to her because he was a stranger and because he was a warrior. Now, watching as he faced her and realized she stood before him, she saw that it was something more than that; there was something more about him. But she could not decide what that something was.

A subtle shift in the light that outlined his form caused him to appear brighter, as though the blue of the sky lit him from within. That was strange. When she looked at him, the rest of the world around faded to a paler version of itself. How had she not noticed it before?

He nodded to acknowledge her and walked closer, using that same stride that seemed to be what his lethal grace would look like in battle.

He reached her in only a few paces, his long legs covering the space between them quickly. Would he kiss her again? Would he touch her? Brienne found it difficult to draw in an even breath at just the thought of that. Clasping her fingers together to keep them from shaking, she forced herself to meet his gaze.

"Good morning to you, Brienne," he said. "How do you fare this day?" He spoke her language with an accent that made his tongue curl over certain words. Chills raced along her spine at the sound. He had not smiled yet; his face remained serious and intent.

"I am well, Sir William," she replied. "And I am here as you requested." As he'd ordered, she'd wanted to say, but she would not anger him by reminding him. If she did, he might reveal the things he might have seen. If he spoke of it to the wrong person, it would not go well for anyone, especially not her. Just as she thought to explain her words, the sunlight pierced through the dreariness of the morning and shone on them.

Brienne could not help but stare at him then, for the light reflected off him and once more she could see him glimmer. She began to shake, unable to control it or hide it from him, for she remembered seeing only one other person who appeared as this warrior did before her.

Whatever connected them, whatever business brought him to Yester, whatever pulled them together, it terrified her.

For the only other person who glimmered as this man did was Lord Hugh. And she knew what Hugh of Gifford was.

But what was this man?

CHAPTER 7

B rienne could feel the terror filling her veins.

Rumors and stories, shared in hushed voices in the shadows, spoke of her sire's abilities and dark passions. The villagers who entered the castle and never returned to their homes. The girls and women dragged screaming to his bed, most of them never the same again. The sounds of the inhuman cries deep inside the castle walls, which seeped into the night. And with her new knowledge of her abilities to create and tame the fire, she could only imagine the power he had within him.

This man standing before her was unknown. Other than his name, she knew nothing of him, his family, his origins, his . . . power. Having seen her father's body shimmer with it, she recognized it within this knight.

And it terrified her.

When her head began to spin, she tried to force a breath into her body. If she fainted, if she could not run, what would happen to her?

"Brienne," he said with that accent to his words that made her smile.

Her name echoed to her as though called from a distance away. Blinking, she tried to see him, but everything before her grew dark. Then even the shimmering blue light that outlined him faded, and she fell into the darkness.

The warmth surrounded her, urging her to remain. Brienne wondered if she had called the fire forth in Gavin's smithy once more, for all she could feel was the overwhelming comfort of it. Then noises trespassed into what she now thought must be a dream. Birds chirped, the wind rustled by, and the sound of someone breathing close to her ear became louder.

She realized it was not the fire but arms that held her. Forcing her eyes to open, she gazed into the icy blue ones of the man she wanted to escape. She tried to push free and found herself imprisoned in an embrace that would not yield no matter how she struggled.

"Hush now, Brienne," he whispered. The warm breath he expelled as he spoke tickled her ear and her neck and did not soothe her sense of impending danger. "You fainted."

"Let me go, I pray you," she pleaded softly. "I will tell no one." The fear that took hold of her would not recede even now that she was awake.

"Tell no one? Tell them what?" he asked, easing his grip and helping her to sit.

Gathering her wits, she thought about what to say. Did she tell him she knew he was . . . ? What did she know—that he was like the man he sought? Was he? She felt suddenly confused and lost, and the tears gathering in her eyes burned as they threatened to expose how naïve and unworldly she was.

"Brienne, fear me not," he urged, standing now and, grasping her hands in his, helping her to. "I wished only to speak to you this morn. Nothing more nor less than that."

The glint in his gaze belied the words. He wanted her. She'd seen desire in a man's eyes before; this was no different. And she was alone with him, deep in the forest, away from anyone who might help her. She'd been warned by her mother, by her father, never to let this happen, and here she was, alone with a man who was neither friend nor relative.

The fact that he intrigued her as no other man had should have been warning enough. The knowledge that she wished to talk to him frightened her. But she did wish it. He was the first man from outside the villages of Yester or Gifford to visit in a very long time. And she wanted to know about his life, his vineyards, him.

That longing, with the way he gazed at her intently, told her what she must do.

"I should go," she said, brushing her hands down her gown.

"I will walk you back."

"Nay!" she said, shaking her head and taking a step away from him. "You must not."

To be seen with this man would bring all sorts of attention and questions, from her parents, from the others who lived in the village, and especially from those who spied for Lord Hugh. Not only would word get to him that strangers had arrived, but he would also learn that she was seen talking with their leader. Alone.

And since that morning when Lord Hugh had wordlessly acknowledged their bond, she could not risk that. She could not risk the retribution that would follow for the people who had raised her as their own. No matter how much she wanted to see him.

"Very well." He reached over and took her by the shoulders. His hands gentled as he steadied her on her feet. "But do not rush away. Let your head clear before you try to return to your home." He reached one hand inside his cloak and brought out a small skin. "Drink."

As he held out the skin to her, she caught a glimpse of the sword he wore beneath the cloak. It was a warrior's sword. One she was certain he could wield with power and precision. How many battles had he fought?

Accepting his offer, she took the skin and drank a small amount from it. Not the water or watered ale she'd expected, the liquid was a lush wine, coming as a complete surprise to her.

"I brought it from my home," he explained, taking it back and drinking some himself. "I am partial to this one for it's made from grapes grown on my family's lands."

"France? Normandy?" she asked, knowing his accent must be from that region. Lord Hugh's family was from that area and still spoke French most of the time, regarding their Lowlanders' language as an abomination.

"Aye, Normandy. Though many other parts of the de Brus family hold lands here, in England, Ireland, and Wales."

Robert the Brus had held the position of tanist to the king, the next to take the throne if the king died childless. He and Lord Hugh had served as regents when the king was a child. They both stood high in the king's respect. That much her parents had told her, knowing her true origins. And this man was part of that other family.

"William de Brus? Is that your name?" she asked.

"Aye, though a distant cousin to the one who served with Lord Hugh as regents and as guardians to the king in his minority."

She could not speak. He was not simply a knight; he was a nobleman and a warrior, with as many connections to the king as Lord Hugh. What was he doing here, and why did he pursue her?

"I see the fear is back in your eyes, and I like it not," he said, shaking his head. "I am a simple knight in service to my king," he explained. Something in his words did not ring true to her. He held a secret or secrets back, from her and from the world, she suspected. But then, so did she.

"Here in Yester? What brings you here?" She watched for signs of a lie in his answer or his voice.

"Aye, I must meet with your lord on a private matter."

The truth. Every fiber within her said he spoke truly.

"He has been gone for a fortnight." She offered him that bit of truth in return, sensing that he did not wish to reveal a single detail to her.

"Do you know when he will return?" he asked. The softness of his tone did not fool her for a moment, but it did surprise her.

A man such as this was used to getting what he wanted and did not have to be nice to get it. Still, he needed to know, for whatever this matter was. The one that had him staring up at the hillside when she'd arrived. From the intensity of his expression at the time, it had appeared as though he was making a plan or worrying about an attack from above.

Even knowing all that and suspecting more, Brienne

felt as though she wanted to tell him. She wanted to help him. This man who was so far above her and could have no place in her life, who would do his duty and leave her life forever, made her want to tell him whatever he needed or wanted to know.

She nearly laughed aloud as she realized it. For it went against everything her parents and experience had taught her about the consequences of speaking about Lord Hugh to outsiders. And yet . . .

"Soon, I think. It is not his custom to leave the castle for much longer than that." The words tumbled out, in spite of her doubts about sharing them. He smiled at her, and it eased her fears a bit. She let out the breath she did not know she held inside and nodded.

"Are the lady and her daughter within?"

A terrible thought struck her at this question. Was he to marry her half sister, Adelaide? Had the king sent him to propose the match with their father? No! She wanted to scream out and stop him, if that was his intent. But the sight of Gavin standing a few paces away stopped her from uttering another word.

"Father," she said, nodding to him. Sir William faced him as well.

"Brienne, come with me. Your mother needs you," he said. He crossed his massive arms over his chest and waited for her to move.

Sir William did not seem surprised or bothered by the order given her. He stepped aside without a word and without looking away from her father and allowed her to walk from his side. When she reached him, she turned back and met the knight's gaze. Once more, he smiled at her, and Brienne knew her fear of him was gone. She nodded her reply to the question he last asked and waited for him to indicate he'd understood before looking at Gavin.

"Go, child," her father said softly, nodding in the direction of their cottage. "I will follow you."

What was he going to do? Try to protect her from this knight? This man of power? This knight sent here on the king's orders? Such a man could take anything or anyone he wanted and answer to almost no one—certainly not the blacksmith. A few coins paid to the lord would address any loss of honor, if it came to that, and it had before to other women here. Her lord, her true sire, used his people ruthlessly and cared little if others did as well.

Gavin moved so that he once again stood between her and Sir William, and she was forced to begin walking away. She would have to have faith that Gavin would not insult this warrior over any threat he thought the man held for her. Sir William had, other than one kiss, done nothing untoward, and Gavin should have no argument with him.

Only as she walked away did she realize how far from the truth that thought was.

This man had already changed her life, and he would change it more. She knew it in her bones. The fire in her blood knew it and teased her with it. Brienne simply had no sense of how it would happen or when, but it would be soon.

Very soon, the fire whispered.

William watched as Brienne left, and that strange feeling in his blood began anew. This man was her father and offered no threat to her, and yet something inside him knew that the man stood in William's path to claiming her. He fought against releasing whatever pushed from within, repeating to himself that this man protected her as well. And he would protect her until she belonged to him. The heat racing in his veins eased and the redness in his gaze faded then.

"I would ask ye to keep away from my daughter, my lord."

Though there was no disrespect in this man's tone, there was a hint of guilt there. Or another emotion that William could not identify.

"What is your name?"

"Gavin, my lord. Gavin the blacksmith."

"Gavin, I have done nothing to harm her. I would not dishonor or hurt her." The man's brow rose on one side, challenging him without a word. Others had tried; he knew that now. This man had kept her from harm. "I will not seek her out," he offered, knowing the words to be a lie as soon as he uttered them.

"Thank ye, my lord," the man said, bowing to him, at what William could tell was great cost. "She is our only child, and I would not see her abused or hurt."

This man would do what he needed to in order to protect his daughter, whether that meant challenging a nobleman or humbling himself. He loved his daughter.

A tightness fisted around his heart, squeezing it and reminding him that no one had done that for him. As a bastard raised by a man who knew him to be the son of the king, no soft words were spared for him. A nuisance and an inconvenience to his mother, he'd interfered with her time with the king, shortened more so then by the king's need for a legitimate heir. He'd learned early to depend only on himself and to expect nothing from even those he called parents. With only a small gesture, this man showed him all that was lacking in his life.

William could not force words past the tightness in his throat, so he nodded to Gavin and watched the man leave the clearing, following his daughter as he said he would. He wondered if she would be punished for being caught alone with a man, but then he remembered the glimmer in Gavin's eyes as he spoke of her. She was safe in her father's care.

As he made his way to return to his camp, waiting until he was certain no one could follow him, the pit of his stomach began to churn. William reached the camp and found that more of his men had arrived, so he spent the rest of the day organizing their weapons and supplies. Throughout the day, he thought about the cause of the pain he felt. Lying on his blankets that night, awaiting the rest of the troop, the truth of it struck him.

Brienne was not safe. Neither Gavin nor he himself would be able to protect her from whatever they would be facing. And chances were, William would be the one to hurt her worst of all. For if she were part of those endangering the king or his kingdom, William must stop her as well.

But the next morn, against his own better judgment, against the advice of his closest friends and his word to the blacksmith, William positioned himself along the path he knew she would walk.

And she did.

This time, she approached heading toward the valley, carrying a basket on her arm. He'd been waiting a short time when she passed the place where he sat, next to the stream and not far from where he'd met her the day before. When she noticed him, her step faltered a bit before she stopped and bent her head down in a respectful gesture.

"My lord."

"Good morrow, Brienne," he said, remaining where he was. She'd become frightened of him the last time, and he did not want that to happen again. "How do you fare this morn?"

"I am well, my lord," she said, watching him without moving toward or away from him.

"More chores?" he asked, nodding at the basket on her arm.

"Aye. They never do seem to end," she said, smiling. Then she spoke to him. "You seem at your ease, my lord. Have you no tasks to fill your hours?"

He laughed at her words and shrugged. "My task is waiting on your lord to return," he explained. "So here I sit, enjoying the cool breezes and the warm sun."

Now it was her turn to laugh as she looked above and around them at the customary Scottish weather—cloudy with an ever-present mist. Not the sunshine and breezes he'd said.

"Mayhap you are thinking yourself elsewhere than here? Mayhap your home in the south?" She walked closer and put the basket down on the ground. "Is it always warm there? In Normandy?" she asked.

"Nay, not always. But our land is tempered by the warm seas. It is sunnier there more often than here, though I know that some areas of the kingdom are more blessed than others," he said as he rose and walked toward her. "I have heard of places that have golden sands and turquoise waters."

"As your homeland does?" William picked up the

basket and looked at her before answering. "I take that to the men working the fields."

"Come. I will carry it," he offered. "And tell you of my homeland as we walk."

Though she hesitated for a moment, she did not refuse. Brienne walked at his side away from the village, clearly not apprehensive nor obedient to her father's wishes.

William began with a description of his favorite places in the lands held by his mother's family and those of her husband, his father-in-name. The rows of grapevines and other fruits. Verdant fields producing all manner of crops. The beaches and sea that he could see from the highest places on their lands.

"Tell me of the sea," she said softly. There was such a wistful wanting in her voice, it made him smile. "I would like to see it."

"You have never seen the sea, Brienne?" he asked.

As a nobleman and a warrior, serving a king who traveled his kingdom and owning lands here and across on the Continent, William found it difficult to conceive of not traveling. Whether on land or sea, his travels had taken him wide and far. He forgot for a moment that those who lived tied to the lands and the lords who held them rarely left them. She shook her head.

"Do you like the sea, my lord?" she asked.

"Aye, though it can be as fickle as the weather here in Scotland. And 'tis no place to be when it turns dark," he said. "Though on a sunny, warm day, I like to swim in it."

"Swim? In the sea?" Her tone was curious and horrified at once.

"Have you never swum in the rivers here?"

"Nay. Some of the children do, when the river is high, or in some of the deeper pools that gather at the turns, but I cannot swim," she said, with a forlorn expression on her face.

In that moment, he wanted nothing more than to take her to the sea. To let her feel the waves coming in and washing up against her feet and legs. To be there when she first viewed its expansiveness and might. William did not know why he reacted this way to her— to this village girl who belonged here and who had no place in his life.

But, then, watching her face come alive and her eyes sparkle as he spoke of his recent voyages, he wanted it to be so. They walked and he answered her never-ending questions about how it felt and how it appeared and sounded. By the time they reached the edge of the forest, she'd impressed him with the questions she'd asked and her interest and curiosity and enthusiasm about a number of topics.

Though he found himself staring at her mouth and remembering the innocence in her kiss and the taste of her lips, he held himself in check, for he had said he would not pursue her, and that would cross that line. From her blush, she remembered it as well. Instead he handed her the basket and nodded at the fields before them.

"One day, you will visit the sea," he said, somehow knowing it was true.

"I hope so, my lord," she said. "My thanks for carrying this for me."

The silence surrounded them then. He wanted to kiss her with every fiber of his being. He stepped back, breaking the spell, and bowed slightly to her.

"See safely to your chores this day, Brienne," he said, turning to leave before he acted on his desires. At this point, he would have given anything just to be able to continue to talk with her.

"And you as well, my lord . . . when you remember what your tasks are."

With a soft laugh, she walked off, leaving the shade of the forest and entering the open fields where men and women worked, preparing the fields for planting.

His heart pounded as he realized that, if he carried out the king's duty, he would oversee his own lands soon. By next spring, he would have fields to plant and a manor of his own. William headed back to the camp on the hill, not wishing to think on the rest of it. For now he would think only about the wonder in her vibrant amber eyes as he spoke of the sea.

Two mornings later, as he tracked a large group of mounted men riding along the road to Yester, he knew that the time when she would be in danger had just arrived. And when the leader of the riders stopped in front of where he stood hidden by the dense trees and brush and stared in his direction, William knew that Lord Hugh was back at Yester Castle.

Although he was careful about being out of sight of anyone down in the valley, the helmed man nodded at him, acknowledging his presence. Then heat filled him, and the warrior within pushed against its bounds, forcing William to fight to keep it controlled. He blew hard, like a winded horse, and clenched fists that even now grew larger, barely containing the growing power. The sound that echoed up the hills shocked him.

Laughter.

Deep, full laughter traveled through the air, mocking

and challenging him at the same time. Struggling against the need to release whatever this power was that now lived inside of him, William practiced his meager control, knowing that the time was coming when he would not be successful in holding it back.

The time was coming . . . soon.

Hugh felt one of them with each passing mile. Opening up his senses as they crossed the last few miles between Gifford town and Yester Castle, he attempted to discern who his opponent was. To determine from which bloodline this enemy had come to face him and test his resolve to free his goddess. Though close, he was yet too far to tell.

Hugh smiled first, relishing the thought that his plans and those of his creator were under way and there would be no more delays. If one had arrived, others would come. Others who knew not the location of the circles. Others who knew of the prophecy. More of the bloodlines who had no idea of their powers or his.

But they would learn quickly that he would not be refused. He had perfected the ways to find a man's weakness and use it to gain their compliance before he destroyed them. All he needed was to open one gateway, and then the goddess would be freed and could destroy the others.

One.

Surely two of these ignorant fools, untrained in the ways of the ancients, would bend to his will . . . and to hers. Once the gateway opened and the sacrifice made, they would be useless and he would see to their deaths. They, and anyone who stood in his way, would die, be they serf or king.

Pulling his horse to a stop, he stared up at the hills that surrounded his lands and castle. *He* was there, up there, watching and waiting. The first of those who would challenge his faith and resolve. And most likely the first to fall and be crushed for resisting the will of the goddess.

He leaned his head back and laughed, loud, hard, and long.

The game had begun and he was its master.

CHAPTER 8

They landed on the east coast of Scotland, having journeyed by water from their island to the west. Once there, Marcus led them as he was led in his dreams, toward the lands of Lothian. Not a one in their group remained unaffected by the power of evil that drew them closer and closer.

But Aislinn suffered the most.

Terrible dreams filled her nights and even crossed into her days. She revealed only small bits of them to him and said nothing to the others. Struggling to find the rest of the prophecy, she made him promise not to wake her when the dreams made her cry out or struggle in her sleep.

It was not fair that such a young, fragile woman should bear the cost of her gift in this way, but believing and being faithful to the old gods' ways had nothing to do with fairness. The old gods could be cruel, and this showed that eons had not changed that part of them.

The only thing Marcus could do was hold her when she screamed in the night and guide her faltering steps during the days that followed. Which he did and would continue doing until he was physically and mentally unable. In the years since she'd come to him, he thought of her as the daughter he never had and, like any father who loved his child, he wished he could take her burden on his shoulders.

The gods would have none of that, so he eased the pace of their journey so she would not be too weak when the time came for her to carry out her part of the prophecy and ceremony.

As the seer, she would understand the words of the prophecy and direct them to the right place and the right descendants needed to safeguard the gateways. Aislinn would chant the words and prayers necessary to seal the barriers. She would recognize the signs and the right stones and would heighten the powers of the warriors of destiny so that they could carry out their task.

As they crossed the miles, every person in their group began to suffer, so Marcus knew they were approaching evil. He ordered them to set up an encampment in a covered, secluded place in the woods before they entered the valley that would lead to the beginning of their challenge.

Choosing two of his men, he set them to the task of searching ahead for signs of the two descendants they needed to find. If they could convince the first two warriors of their history and their quest, Marcus believed they could stop the evil one here.

"Marcus?"

He turned to find Aislinn behind him, looking even more haunted in the light of day than she had during the last long, sleepless night.

"You should be resting, Aislinn. You get so little sleep and our journey is long."

"I would," she said with a wan smile, "but it is my duty to hear the warnings and the signs."

"And you have heard more?" he asked.

Guiding her to sit on a log, he found the skin of ale and held it out to her. She drank little and ate less, and he watched her losing part of herself as the cost of her gift. His duty was to see she accomplished her task. One of the men passed him some cheese and bread and he gave them to her. "Eat and drink first."

When she did not argue, Marcus knew she understood the risk of becoming weak, especially now. Once they found the circle of stones and deciphered the symbols, she would be called on to perform the ritual—and that ritual would have great physical cost. Her survival was as important as that of the descendants—without her, they could all be present and ready to use their powers, but would never succeed.

Once she ate a small amount, more than yester morn's, she gazed at him with an intensity he'd not seen since their departure from their island home. Her green eyes seemed so bright against her pale skin.

"There are two firebloods, Marcus. Two."

He shook his head. All the prophecies pointed to one of each bloodline being the only one left with enough power to close the gateways. "That is not—"

"Possible? I thought not, too, but the dreams show me two of them. And the warblood is here, as well," she said.

"Each one needs the other. What does this mean, Aislinn? Will we find two of each line now?"

"One fireblood is the goddess' minion; the other one is the one we need for our task." Confidence entered her weak voice, as it did when she spoke of the dreams or signs. "She is the path to the warblood's cooperation."

They knew that the two needed to close each gateway would be linked in some way, but Aislinn's visions could not see all of those details yet. Marcus suspected each pair would be a man and a woman, each with a power that either complemented the other's or controlled it, but he could not be certain. Until she could see it clearly, they were relying on their limited experience and other intuitions.

"Are the firebloods known to each other? To the warblood?" he asked. The men he'd sent would find out some of this, but Aislinn might know now.

"Connected closely," she said, nodding. "Though the warblood has not met both yet." She smiled then, a slight curve of her mouth, and then looked at him. "He will be a strong warrior against evil."

"If we can convince him to carry out his part."

"Aye." She stood then and brushed the few crumbs from her gown. "She is already his weakness. Their connection is only beginning, and yet it is nearly unbreakable. I had no idea it could happen so quickly."

"Nor I," he said. None of the priests understood it; nor would they, until all the pieces stood together in plain sight like a puzzle needing to be solved. "Rest now and gain your strength if you can. Donal and Colin will not return for at least a day."

Aislinn turned to leave him, but paused and looked at him over her shoulder. Her green eyes faded to the color of the shadows of the forest leaves now. "Will I be able to do my part, Marcus? Do you think I can?"

He smiled then, at her lack of confidence, which was not unusual for a young woman who'd never been tested. A seer himself, but with only a small portion of the power she possessed, he was certain of the answer. To his soul, to his blood and bones, he knew there was truth in the words he was about to speak to her.

"Aye, Aislinn. You will fulfill your duties in this. That much I know."

There were dark corners in his visions where the possibilities hid from exposure, and he shivered then as she walked away. Aislinn would succeed and guide those who needed her. He would aid her however he could, as would all those who'd journeyed with them from the island.

The problem was that he had no idea if any of them would survive once they'd carried out their parts. No matter how hard he tried to see that part of the future, no amount of praying or chanting or scrying revealed it. Marcus walked to a place where he could be alone and knelt on the ground.

So many strands and threads were coming together to be woven into the future. Of many colors and textures, the warp and weft would be put in place by those who carried the blood of the gods. He could see the parts, waiting to be worked into the cloth of the future, but he could not touch them or guide them himself. Only the others could bring this weaving to fruition; he could only show them the pattern to follow.

Marcus prayed now for the wisdom he needed in the coming days, and in a moment of weakness, he prayed for the life of the young woman he considered his daughter. May the gods be merciful in this.

Though he'd told the blacksmith he would not pursue the man's daughter, William found it impossible not to watch her. Over the next days, while he pondered his plan and decided when to approach Lord Hugh, he found himself standing in the shadows, just far enough away from her that he could not feel her influence, observing her as she went through her days. Roger's scowl remained in place, a constant reminder of the folly of such actions, but William knew he must learn about her to understand his quest and her part in it.

He also knew he was not alone in watching. There were others in the forest, just beyond the valley and on the opposite hillside, others who did the same thing he did—watch and prepare. From the number of weapons he saw stored throughout the village and the troops that had arrived that sennight, Lord Hugh was planning a large endeavor. Whether a treasonous rebellion against the king or something else, William knew not . . . yet.

So he watched.

And this morn he needed to be close to Brienne, so he followed her. She walked in a different direction from her usual one, heading along the stream and around the castle. She paused often, listening for signs that she was being pursued or watched, but his tracking skills had risen to a new level since he had arrived here. He could scent her, hear her steps, and feel her ahead of him. He stopped when she did and stepped as she did. Her destination this day was a cave, hidden away behind thick brush and plants.

William waited until she'd entered, clever enough to pull branches and leaves over its low entrance, and he listened. When the cave filled with a flash of fire, he pulled the branches out of his way and called out her name.

"Brienne? Brienne, are you well?" But no one answered. He knelt down and peered inside, seeing only the fire burning in the corner and no one there.

Had he somehow lost her trail in the forest? He looked around the cave, but still saw only that fire, and so he crawled back out. Racing the way he'd come, William looked for crushed leaves and inhaled to detect her scent along the path.

Nothing. And no Brienne in sight.

Trotting back toward the cave, he saw the flames flare again, and then the cave grew dark. Then her smaller form crawled out of the cave and stood. The branches were not where she'd left them, and she glanced around before climbing to her feet and brushing the dirt from her hands.

How had she . . . ? There had been nothing in that cave except the fire burning in the corner. Had he missed another entrance or hiding place within? Nothing there but a fire. William shook his head at the notion that took hold of him.

A fire burning with no wood or peat to fuel it.

A fire made out of nothing?

Had she created it as she had the fireball in her hands?

It was too nonsensical to accept. He must have missed the signs of another way in or out of that cave.

He shook his head again before realizing the absolute and sheer insanity of his thoughts. Thoughts that a month ago would have seen him imprisoned as a madman or a heretic now did not shock him at all.

Was his father so afflicted or had his strange words of warning caused this in him? How had things changed so quickly in his otherwise clear and orderly life? How had he changed so much?

The woman at the center of his speculations had yet to see him, so he stepped into the path and watched as her eyes widened in surprise.

"Sir . . . William," she stuttered out the words. "I . . ." He watched as she tried to come up with some excuse or words of explanation. William shook his head at her and shrugged his shoulders. "I did not see you there," she finally said.

"Nay, you did not."

Waiting for her to reach him, he noticed the way her cheeks flushed as she met his gaze. Innocent. He must remind himself that she was an innocent. Or, he had no doubt, the well-muscled fists of the blacksmith would remind him so. It mattered not, for nothing in this world could stop the desire for her that grew within him. And the need to protect her.

Who was this young woman?

When he was rational and thought on it, she could have no place in his life. That much he knew and understood. And as an honorable man, he would not dally with an innocent when he could not offer the protection of his name. As he could not. Once his lands were secured, once the king confirmed the grant and title, then he would seek a wife and establish his household. And it could never be this woman.

No matter that the need to claim her filled his body and soul every time he encountered her.

"Your expression is quite formidable, Sir William," she said softly, now right before him. "Have I done something to displease you?"

For a moment, he was diverted by her words.

"You need to have a care, Brienne. I thought you'd

gone into that cave and burned when I saw the fire burst forth."

"I thank you for your concern, Sir William, but these lands are known to me. I was searching for something left behind by one of the village boys in that cave. And I saw no fire there."

For a scant moment, he doubted his own sight, but that was before he remembered the other strange things he'd witnessed only a few days ago. Such things raised questions and could have been witnessed by any number of people, putting her in grave peril. Over the last several days, too many strangers had entered this valley—from the last of his men to the additional armed men who rode into Yester Castle's yard to the newest arrivals whose identities he knew not.

"There are strangers in the valley, Brienne. You should have a care not to be caught alone," he warned. The irony of his warning was not lost on him.

"Lord Hugh is in residence now," she said with a slight lift of her chin. "No one would—" She stopped as though revealing too much to him.

"Do you think that is enough to protect you? And if a man did not know you were under his protection? How long do you think it would take a man to . . . to . . . do this?"

He gave up trying to warn her and instead just took her in his arms and showed her what could happen to her. At least that was what he told himself in that moment. Then he kissed her as he'd wanted to for days.

The last time, the first kiss, he'd held back, exploring Brienne's mouth gently. This time he was not gentle. He did not explore. He claimed.

He possessed her.

What began as a way to show her the vulnerability of a woman alone became an exploration of the growing passion and attraction between the two of them.

Sliding his hands into her hair, he held her face close to his and kissed her long and hard. Then, easing back, he kissed along her forehead and along her chin, the same one she'd recently raised in challenge to him. Unable to resist the taste of her, he teased her lips with the tip of his tongue until she opened for him. His tongue plunged into her, finding hers and drawing it into his mouth.

She made soft sounds against him as he suckled on her tongue, driving him mad and making him ache to take all of her. Her hands crept up along his and yet he did not stop. Then she leaned in to him, the heat of her body igniting his desire even more. He slid his hands along her neck and shoulders and then down to her waist. He eased them around her and cupped the globes of her bottom, pulling her up hard and tight against his raging flesh.

And never for a moment did he release her mouth from his. When she wrapped her arms around him, holding him close, he kissed her until she was breathless and then moved his mouth over the gentle skin of her neck, kissing and nipping down to the place where her gown lay low on the swell of her breasts.

He should stop. He knew he should. He planned to. But her hands slid into his hair just then, her fingers tangling in the curls and pulling his head down. He let his desire flow, loosening the ties of her gown and chemise with one hand while his mouth played its way along her skin. Tugging the edges lower, he licked the stiff peak of her breast and drew it in his mouth.

Her legs gave way then, and he guided them down, first to a kneel and then onto the ground. Holding her gown away, he kissed the soft mounds and caught a tip once more, this time worrying it with his teeth and licking the pink bud of it as she gasped. Her body lay next to his, writhing and rubbing against him in the way of an innocent who did not know the pleasure before her. William caressed her body and placed his hand over her belly and then lower, grazing his fingers over that place where he knew she ached, even if she did not understand it.

An innocent.

The word and its meaning finally sank into his passion-riddled mind, as did the lesson he'd wanted to teach her about being caught alone. Instead she'd taught him about his own weakness when it came to her. A weakness that could be deadly in the danger that was coming.

He stilled then and lifted his head, releasing her lovely breast. She panted, breathing shallow and fast, under him. Her eyes were closed and her head tossed back in pleasure. A sight he would never forget. William waited a moment to catch his own breath before speaking the words that would drive her away from him and hopefully keep her safe. When she opened her eyes and looked at him, he nodded.

"And that is how fast a man could have you beneath him, taking your favors and your honor, if you get caught alone."

He knelt and then stood, grasping her hands and pulling her with him. She swayed on her feet, the rosiness of her breasts now hidden by the garments she tugged back into place. The blush on her cheeks faded, replaced by the paleness of shock. Brienne turned her back on him to finish tying her laces and then ran her fingers through the length of her now-loosened and tangled hair.

Facing him, she began to speak several times and ended up saying nothing. Then, damn him, those amber eyes filled with tears. His heart tore apart at the sight of her distress and humiliation. All he wanted to do was hold her. Tell her that he reacted this way because she was driving him mad with worry and the need to protect her and keep her safe . . . and that he knew he could not.

"Brienne, I . . . " He paused, for what could he say now that he'd turned his honest desire for her and her naïve, new desire for him into something tawdry? She shook her head and began to leave. "Wait, I pray you," he said. She hesitated, and he took the chance it gave him.

"Something strange and dangerous is going on. The king has asked me to seek the reasons. Everything points to your lord. Now more strangers are arriving each day, and I . . . worry that you will not be safe as you make your way through your errands and chores. Not as safe as you might think you are. Have a care and stay close to your father." Her eyes widened the tiniest amount, but he still noticed it. "He can protect you best." She crossed her arms over her body and rubbed her arms as she nodded. He stepped back to allow her to pass and added the final warning: "Even from me."

Without another word and whether she heard his last warning or not, Brienne ran off, back toward the village and—he hoped—safety.

Now she might think before wandering off and putting herself in danger. And mayhap his rude behavior would keep her from him and break the hold, the draw, the connection they had with each other. She must go back to her life and he to his. Pacing himself to stay far enough behind her not to be seen, he wondered if he would wake up on the morrow and discover that this strange journey on behalf of the king had just been some kind of nightmarish dream.

Ignoring the painful protest of how much his body disagreed with his honor's actions, William strode back to his men, intent on finishing their plan and on riding into Yester Village and castle and meeting with Lord Hugh. Those good intentions, like so many that lined another path, evaporated when he was about fifty yards from the camp.

For Brienne screamed out his name in terror.

CHAPTER 9

Turning around and around, he could neither see nor hear her. But . . . he *had* heard her. Roger must have been watching, for he and Gautier came running to his side.

"Did you hear that?" he asked, holding his hand to his brow to shade his eyes. "Did you hear her?"

"I heard nothing but you," Roger answered.

"You speak of the girl?" Gautier asked. "Is she nearby?"

Drawing his sword, he closed his eyes and saw her being half dragged and half carried through the forest by three men. A gag in her mouth, her hands bound now, she seemed unaware of herself and her surroundings. Worse, the image in his thoughts went completely and utterly black then, as though she'd lost consciousness.

"Aye, she is," he said. "Or was. I can sense nothing of her now."

William saw them staring at him as though he had three heads instead of the one and realized he needed to tell them more about . . . more about . . .

"I warned her not to be alone outside the village," he tried to explain, but the dark feeling of her loss tore at him.

"You warned her, Will?" Gautier asked. "You saw her again."

"She is in danger now." It was becoming hard to speak. The muscles in his neck and shoulders and back tightened, and his vision began to glow red like the coals left in a fire. "Come."

His body trembled and shook with each step, and then his legs lengthened, and his trews, tunic, and gown felt tight, too small for his body. Tremors moved along his arms until his grip around the hilt of his sword changed, his flesh becoming one with the metal and leather.

She was in danger.

He ran, faster and farther than the others, down into the valley, across the stream, and up into the hillside. He paused only to gain her scent in the air, noticing the signs of a struggle in the broken plants and furrows in the moist earth, and then he followed.

She was in danger.

The red washed over everything in his sight and colored the world in a different way; the sky, the trees, everything bore a scarlet tint to him. Glancing over his shoulder, he saw the others trailing behind.

His . . . friends . . . no danger there.

He gained the top of the hill and saw the small gathering of tents and people and smelled her there. Rushing toward her scent, he watched as they scattered out of his way. He did not find her among the tents, but knew she was beyond them.

He broke through the trees and saw her. The gag was off and her hands had been freed of their bounds. She faced him, staring at his face and shaking her head.

He would tear them apart for touching her, for scaring her. No one did that and lived. He reached for the one closest to her, the one holding her arm, and grabbed for him, but she stepped in front of him, placing herself between him and the one he would kill . . . first.

"Sir William?" Her voice shook, and she spoke as though she did not know him. Was that his name? Is that what she called him?

"William," she said again softly, leaning closer as she spoke. He sniffed her face and hair and knew she was his.

He wanted to push her aside to get to the ones who needed to be destroyed, but she reached out and put her hand on him. Looking down at it, so soft, so small, so hot on his skin, he did not recognize the body it was touching. Blue as the sky with markings swirling over the skin she touched as though moved by the wind. Muscular and strong enough to fight off all these puny men at once, with shreds of clothing hanging over his shoulders and around his waist. And with an arm that held—no, an arm that *was* his sword.

This close to her, he could smell that the terror had eased and the danger was gone. Still he waited on her word.

"There is no need to fight them," she said, stroking his chest. "I am well. I am safe."

He looked around. No one was near her now. A few men stood scattered around them watching, and one man, an older man, nodded at him. Had he given the orders to touch her? Did he need killing?

"William, it is over now," she said in a whispering singsong tone that made him want to let go of the fight. "Come back to me." Her smile eased the terrible need to kill that bubbled within him. "That is good. It is over."

He could feel his body changing, shivering and convulsing as it had before, until he could drop the sword from his hand and fit within his skin once more. He felt himself sliding back into control. The red in his vision melted away until he could see her in all her colors, even though the others paled next to her.

William turned as Roger and Gautier reached his side and read the confusion in their gazes and on their faces. Roger grabbed the sword from the ground and held it. Glancing around the group, he noticed that the others wore expressions of horror and terror. He looked back at the only one who did not turn away from his gaze.

"What happened? Brienne, are you well? I heard you screaming."

"I am not hurt," she said. Before she could say more, another man spoke.

"Sir William de Brus? I think we should speak." The older man watching him spoke in a calm voice.

"You did this? You took her? Why?"

When the older man did not deny it, William looked at her for his reply. She held the key. She was the key.

"Let Brienne sit over with the women while we do," the man offered. "She will come to no harm here, sir."

When Brienne nodded her agreement, a young woman escorted her away. Though she still glanced from him to the others, he allowed it. Seeing the same shock filling Roger's and Gautier's expressions, he nodded at her.

"Stay near her," he ordered quietly. Although they did as he said, he could tell it was more from rote than from agreement. Then he walked after the other man until they stood away from the rest.

"Has that happened before, Sir William?" the man asked.

"Who are you and what are you doing on Lord Hugh's lands?" he asked back. Studying the man, he noticed several things. He was older, he wore no weapons and, from his accent, he was a foreigner.

"We seem to be at a stalemate," the man said with a slight laugh. "I am Marcus of Far Island, and these are my kin."

"Far Island? I have never heard of it. Where is it?"

" 'Tis a small island, holding a small community, off the west of Scotland."

"A small community" made it sound like they were priests, but none wore the tonsured hair of monks or the vestments of priests. That women traveled with them did not say aye or nay, for many holy priests were known to enjoy the company . . . and beds of women.

"A religious community? You do not have the look of priests," he said. "So why are you here?"

"Sir William, we are priests of the old gods, not the Christian one."

Part of him wanted to call out "Blasphemy!" at such a claim, but the part of him seeking answers about what was happening to and around him pressed on.

"I see your disbelief," Marcus said with a nod. "The old gods are not gone, only forgotten. We keep to the old ways and worship and remember them still."

It was not unusual for fanatics and heretics to spring up out of the wild and secluded places, and William guessed that this was some cult. Even the old Celtic Church and their outdated practices existed out in the Highlands and islands, regardless of the Roman Church's and several kings' efforts to stamp them out. But why were these people here now and what did they know?

"We were led to you, Sir William. And to the girl." He gestured over to where Brienne sat talking with a young woman. "We are traveling on the same journey now."

"I know not who you are, but I travel on the king's business."

"But you know not why he sent you to Lord Hugh, do you?" William crossed his arms over his chest and considered this man. "And the changes that are happening to you make no sense to you, do they?"

"And you know these things? Who are you?" His fingers itched for his sword, but this man offered no threat that William could see. The rest of these people gave no indication of danger. He could also see Brienne speaking with that young woman across the clearing, and she seemed at ease.

"I am the chief priest for the old gods. I have trained most of these"—he gestured to the small group standing around the tents and in the clearing—"in the ways of prophecy and scrying. We are here to help you to carry out the task set for us."

"And what task would that be?" he asked.

He wanted to leave. He fought the urge to turn his back on this man and the lunacy he spouted, but something in the man's face and voice made him listen. He wanted to return to the time and place where he knew himself and before he had embarked on this task for the king.

"To claim your blood rights and keep the evil one away." With that, William shook his head, refusing to accept this.

"I carry out the orders of my king. I answer to none but him." The words rang hollow, but he clung to them.

Having made his point and his allegiance clear, William turned to walk away. He would return Brienne to the village and set his men to prepare for his meeting with Lord Hugh. On the morn, he would seek out the king's counselor and discover the truth of the man's loyalty and plans. This lunacy, these weird and inexplicable events, would cease as soon as he returned to the king and received his grant of lands. By then this would all seem like a nightmarish dream.

"Sir William," Marcus said before he even took a step away. "There are several different bloodlines, descended from the ancient ones. Each one carries their power in their blood and is marked by it."

Facing the man, he noticed the sleeve of Marcus's tunic had dropped away from his wrist. There on his arm was a raised red area just like the one William had. He could not take his eyes from it. He reached for Marcus's arm and pulled him closer.

"The mark of my bloodline," he said. "We are priests. We stand for humanity before all the gods."

Simple words, but William could not comprehend it. The area on Marcus looked like a stick figure of a man while William's . . . He lifted his own arm to take another glance at it, but dropped it instead, not willing to reveal that he carried one, and shook his head. He wanted no parts of talk of heresy or deviltry. He wanted only to fulfill the king's request and get his lands.

"You are a warblood," Marcus explained. "Your

marking is in honor of Sucellus and his abilities as a warrior. A sword mayhap? Or a battle-ax or hammer?"

William could not stop himself from clutching the place on his arm where the skin bore exactly that. How did this man know? Before he could argue, Marcus spoke again.

"We have been raised with knowledge of the old gods and their ways, but you have not. You are a practiced warrior with the experience and knowledge that we lack. We need you, Sir William, as our leader. Someone to organize us and lead us in the coming battles."

"Do you know how mad you sound, with this talk of gods and the rest? 'Tis blasphemy or treason, or both!" he whispered harshly to the man who made such outrageous claims. "I am no leader in whatever your endeavor is. I serve only the king. I see to his orders now."

He ignored the recent things that had happened to him and turned to leave, convinced that his mind was playing tricks on his judgment. He could not let this get in his way.

"William," Marcus warned just before he stepped back. "Tell her nothing you do not want Lord Hugh to know."

William narrowed his gaze, studying the man. So Brienne was linked to Lord Hugh? He'd seen the fear in all the villagers' eyes and knew they feared their lord. Nay, they lived in terror of him. He'd thought this young woman would be no different.

"Roger. Gautier."

He walked over and held out his hand to Brienne to help her up. In spite of his recent rude behavior, she accepted it without hesitating and nodded to the woman sitting with her. They'd gone only a few paces back into the middle of the tents when the soft voice called out to him.

"Sir William?"

"She is called Aislinn," Brienne said as he stopped and faced the young woman.

Aislinn's green eyes grew bright as she approached, her long red hair worn in one long braid that swayed from side to side as she walked. A pale white light outlined her body. Her voice, when she spoke this time, seemed to come from farther away.

"Your father is in grave danger, William. Only by completing your part in this quest can you hope to save him."

"My father? Aislinn, my father is happily ensconced in his lands, drinking fine wine and eating heartily. He is in danger only if my mother discovers his newest leman." He laughed, or tried to, but her voice deepened and echoed, and her face changed into someone much older right before him.

"Your father will die, Warblood. 'Tis time to accept your destiny. Come to us. Come with us."

She held out her arm, and he watched as the crescent moon–shaped mark reddened and burned, as his did. He resisted clamping his hand down on it, but William noticed Brienne's hand move to her own arm. Did she have a mark as well? What was this?

"We must leave," Brienne whispered to him, sliding her hand into his. "I pray you, now."

He nodded to his men and they departed, walking to the hilltop and down, crossing the stream and reaching the main path to the village. When they did, Roger and Gautier continued on, leaving them alone.

"Go," he said softly. "I will wait until you are down

the path before leaving." He wondered if her mind was as full of thoughts and doubts as his was now.

Brienne began to walk away, but she turned and came back to his side.

"Do you think your father is in danger?" she asked.

In that moment, he realized that Aislinn had not been referring to his mother's husband but to his real father—the king. A cold, icy finger ran down his spine, and he fought against shivering.

"Any man might be in danger, Brienne. I have not been home in many months, but the last letter I received spoke of no dangers." He could not acknowledge the father who had never named him son.

"Why did they kidnap me?"

He let out his breath, trying to figure out how much she knew and how much he could tell her. "I told you strangers were arriving. They most likely saw us together and thought to use that to bring me to them."

"But why did they not simply send word to you?"

Suddenly he knew the answer, as clear as the blood coursing under his skin—Marcus wanted to see the connection between them. He wanted to force the beast that lingered beneath his skin and his soul out into sight. He wanted to discover if Brienne was his weakness. And he had accomplished his goals. William was a fool, for he'd let them.

"I know not these men or their ways." He nodded toward the path. "Go back to your village, Brienne. Think not on anything but your family and your usual life. Leave all of this, all these questions be." He said it softly, but hoped she understood the warning in the words. "Farewell, Brienne."

"Sir William?" Though her lower lip quivered in a

mutinous fashion so he thought she would argue with him, she simply nodded and then moved quickly along the path, disappearing into the woods. It would take her only a short time to reach her cottage.

He made his way back toward the encampment on the hillside, avoiding several watchmen along the way. On the morrow, he would see Lord Hugh and find out the truth of his nature and his plans against the king.

He knew he must first give some explanation to Roger and Gautier about what they had witnessed. William knew only that he had no words to explain the changes they must have seen, for he had no idea of what had come over him. He must trust his two closest friends to keep this secret, one more among many.

Brienne had witnessed and done more things in this short day than she had in her whole life. William's words of farewell and warnings should have scared her all the way home; instead she had more questions to ask and no one to answer them.

After disobeying Gavin's instructions about not leaving the village and not speaking to the knight, she could not go to him. She would like to speak to her mother about her feelings for William, but she knew that wasn't an option either for the same reason.

Once more, she was alone as she had always been. To fend for herself.

Now, though, so much was happening to her. Her powers were increasing. It took no more than a moment for her to create the fire from nothing in the cave and another moment to dissolve it. Luckily, she'd stood back in a small alcove in the rock when William had crawled back in or he would have seen her there. The mark on her arm moved constantly now, reminding her that she controlled the flames.

If that was not extraordinary enough, there was the moment when William had become something else, something more than a man. When she had watched him run into the strangers' camp, almost tearing it apart looking for her, he had changed. Taller, impossibly taller and bigger and stronger and faster, he moved with a lethal speed and strength.

The strangest change was the way his skin took on the color of the sky and markings she had never seen before moved across it. The others scrambled out of his path, for they read their deaths in his gaze. He seemed not to know how he'd changed and become . . . a weapon. Though she knew it was impossible, she could swear that his arm and his sword merged into one weapon.

Terrified she would be killed when they took her, fear for her life shifted to fear for those around her as William approached. She did not know what made her intervene; she only knew she could stop him. And she had.

His skin, stretched tight over huge muscles not there before, glowed an icy blue, changing much like her hands did when she brought the fire. His eyes were inhuman slits of glowing molten red-orange. His face retained only a slight resemblance to his own features, while his hair grew longer and more unruly.

As much as she did not want to believe such a thing, she accepted that the same could be said about her own power. How could a person, a human, be surrounded by fire and not be destroyed by it? And if they had these powers, who else and what other powers existed?

Was that his task for the king, then? For the king had

visited here in Yester some time ago, and rumors still whispered that he'd seen Lord Hugh casting spells before he left in a rush, with his retainers trailing behind him.

Brienne found her way to her father's smithy, and she stood by in silence as she watched him work the glowing metal. She looked around the hot, smoky chamber and noticed the number of swords, both finished and waiting to be completed.

"Swords?" she asked quietly. Her father mostly worked on farming tools and blades, repairing swords as they needed to be, but not often.

"Lord Hugh ordered more," he replied without taking his attention off the fire or the heated metal he pounded with his hammer. "Many more."

He worked in silence then, Brienne standing near the door watching as he perfected the metal to a killing edge. It was the thing he liked least to create, she knew. Weapons. But he served at Lord Hugh's pleasure.

"Why do you remain here? You are skilled. Any lord would be pleased to have you work for him." She'd never asked that question before and had not really thought on it. Gavin stepped away from the fire and put his hammer down. Wiping the sweat off his face with the back of his arm, he smiled.

"You, lass. We could have you only if we remained here and served him." Shocked at this revelation, she faced him across the fire.

"For me? I did not know."

"Fia could not bear a living child, and it broke her heart. My father, the last blacksmith here, had just passed, so Lord Hugh offered us what we wanted—a bairn to raise as our own child and a place to live and work."

"If you stayed?" she asked. At his nod, she shrugged. "But why did he insist that I remain here? I'm only his bastard, not important to—"

Gavin grabbed her by the shoulders and pulled her close, stopping her from finishing her words. "Never say that. You are the most important person to me and to your mother and worth whatever the price we paid to have you," he whispered harshly. Kissing her forehead, he held her to him, and Brienne savored the comfort of it. "And you must mean something to him, too. Otherwise he would have just let you die."

Brienne pulled back and looked in the face of the man who was the only father she knew. There was more to be told, but from the way he held his jaw and his mouth, she knew he would not say it. He thought to protect her, from the truth or from the coming danger.

"I think he knows what I do."

For a moment, his expression froze, and she thought he was going to lie to her. Instead, his smile turned sad and he nodded. "I think he knows, Brienne. I think he's known since you began to feel it happening."

The worst feeling flooded through her then, making her want to weep from despair. Looking at him, she knew.

"You and Mother must leave Yester. Go as soon as you can. Something is coming. You must leave and be safe," she urged. She could feel the doom approaching faster, and she knew that it would cause many people to perish. "Take James and his parents. Take whoever will listen to you and leave in the night."

"Hush, lass," Gavin soothed, wrapping his arms around her once more. "Nothing can change our destiny. Nothing can keep us safe if it is not meant to be. And your mother and I would never leave you."

"But you must," she said.

He did not answer then. He did not need to, for she knew her parents would never abandon her.

"Go, now," Gavin said softly as he released her. "Your mother could use your help with the laundry."

Brienne wiped the tears from her face and nodded. He picked up his hammer and went about his task without another word. As she left the smithy, she glanced back and had the very strong feeling that she would never watch him work the metal again.

CHAPTER 10

"**A**re you ill?"

Brienne smiled and shook her head. "Nay, Mother. I am well." She walked to the stream and knelt at her mother's side, taking the tunic from her and placing it on the flat rock.

"Then why do you come to help with this? I know 'tis your least favorite chore to do and you avoid it at all costs."

"Father suggested it."

Her mother laughed softly but did not say anything. They worked in silence for a short while, stretching the dirty clothing over the rocks, rubbing them with soap, rinsing them and hanging them to dry over branches. After everything that had happened to her this morn, the mundane chores soothed her.

She knew the steps of how to do these things. And for a short time, her life was the one she'd known it to be. It was almost as if she could step back and forget all that she'd seen and heard and learned and be the young woman she'd always been.

"Look at me, Brienne," her mother said. Lifting her

head up from her task, she smiled at the woman who'd raised her. "You are different somehow, I think." Only the shiny glimmer in her mother's gaze told her she was teasing.

"Different?" she asked, sitting back on her heels. "How am I different?"

Her mother studied her face and her form and then met her gaze. "You have the look of a woman who has been well kissed!"

Brienne could not stop herself from touching her mouth then, remembering all at once the sensations that had poured through her when William had kissed, caressed, and touched her. She'd never felt anything so wondrous, and she was caught in the web he wove around her with his hands and his mouth.

"Mother!" she said. "I have not—"

"Hush now, Brienne," her mother said, taking hold of her hands. "James has our permission to court you, and a few kisses are to be expected. What man would not try to steal a few from the woman he wants to marry?"

In the sensual onslaught caused by William, she had forgotten that kiss from James. It was nice, but would never come close to the heady, intense power of William's.

William had urged her to return to her life and to forget about him, but how could she stop her body from remembering the passion in his touch or her desire for more? How could she consider becoming another man's wife?

"From the expression on your face, daughter," her mother began with a knowing look on her own face, "you are not thinking on young James's kiss or his proposal."

She let out a sigh and touched Brienne's cheek. "Your father thinks you have been spending time with the strangers you encountered on their way here to Yester. A knight named William?"

"You know about them?" she asked. Her father had promised not to tell her.

"Your father and I keep no secrets from each other, Brienne. He worried about the attractive, young knight who seemed interested in our daughter. You cannot expect that he would not tell me of such matters and ask my counsel in how to best protect our daughter."

Her mother stood and walked over to a shady place among the trees, away from the other women who also washed there by the stream, waving her over. Brienne followed and sat at her mother's side. Her mother turned her and began to untangle and then make a new braid in her hair.

"It must seem exciting to have someone new, someone from outside the village, pay attention to you. And when that someone is a handsome, strong, young knight, it is difficult to keep things in order." Her mother's hands rested for a moment and then began anew, weaving the long plaits together in one braid. "Whatever brings him to Yester will also take him away. And your place will remain here. The excitement of the moment cannot replace a lifetime of commitment."

"Mother, there are things . . . "

"Hush now and pay me heed. He will leave. You will stay. And you will bear the cost if you allow him what you should not." She tied the bottom off with a strip of leather and patted her shoulders. "Sometimes we have no choice. I suspect the woman who birthed you had none. But do not allow the excitement and interest of such a man to spin your head until you make bad choices."

Her mother had never once referred to Brienne's parentage. She had never brought up the subject of Lord Hugh willingly.

"Men of power use and cast aside, whether that be women or tools or playthings they no longer want. Remember that, Brienne. Men of power use."

"Mother, I—"

"It is just a little advice for you, love," her mother said, standing behind her. "Now, let's carry the washing back to the cottage."

With nothing else to say, Brienne followed along, helping through the rest of the day but not without noticing the glances that her parents shared.

It was only in the dark of the night that Brienne allowed herself to relive those few moments of fearless passion. She knew she should have refused him and rebuffed his advances. She should have at least attempted to push him away.

She had not. Instead she'd allowed him to touch her and to kiss her and to hold her. Brienne knew there would be nothing between them, and no amount of hoping would make it different. Yet those few stolen moments of passion would be in her memory forever. If she had to give him up, if whatever was coming parted them, at least she had those memories to enjoy.

As she lay on her pallet on the night of the most strange and incredible day of her life, Brienne wondered at the path her life would take. Would all of this pass when William completed his task and left? Or would the growing danger she could sense rise up and claim them all? Though the door and window shutters were closed, a chill wind passed through the cottage, sending shivers of dread through her.

Danger. Danger was close and getting closer.

Brienne just never expected it to arrive so quietly at her door the next morning.

William sat near the fire, watching Roger and Gautier trying to accept all that he had shared. They'd seen him transform into something else when Brienne was threatened. They'd seen his arm become a weapon and yet still be part of him. And they both had told him how his body grew and turned blue, like ice, as he went on the attack.

"Berserker," Gautier had whispered afterward.

They'd all grown up hearing the legends of old, especially since their Norman ancestors began as Norsemen in the Viking north before moving to France's warmer shores. Berserkers were humans, taken over by the power of the god of war. They fought without thought or concern, often continuing to fight even when they had grave injuries. Some whispered that old priests gave warriors a nectar to make them change into these battlefield giants.

But William had taken no nectar or concoction. He did not believe in the old gods, be they Norse or the ones that Marcus claimed as his, the older Celtic ones. He was a warrior and not a berserker. And yet he did not remember anything that happened from the time he heard Brienne's voice in his head, screaming his name, until she said his name in Marcus's camp.

William drank more of the wine and waited for his friends to give their answer. He must move in the morning and wished to have them at his back. But after this morning and what they claimed they'd seen, he did not know that they would be there.

"Will you change again?" Roger asked, drinking the last of his wine down in one mouthful. "Into ... whatever you were?"

"I know not," he answered truthfully. "I know not how it happened, nor what happened."

"She caused it," Gautier said, nodding at both of them.

"Do not blame Brienne."

"I am not placing blame, Will. I think you changed because you knew she was in danger. The old berserkers needed the call of battle to enrage them. You, well, it looks like all you need is her."

William could not argue with him. He knew that both times he'd felt some change come over him had involved her. The first time, when he'd watched her and the young man from the forest. This second time when she'd called out to him somehow. Both times she'd needed to be protected. Both times he'd needed to protect and claim her. And each time the change pushed him further than the last. How far would it go?

"What did the old man tell you? When you spoke?" Gautier asked.

"He ..." William looked at each of them and leaned in closer so no one would hear their words. "He said they worship the old gods and that there is a war coming between good and evil. And they want me to lead them."

The silence was heavy and foreboding as it settled around them. It sounded even more foolish and maniacal when spoken aloud like that. How could a sane man believe any of it?

"She, the girl with the strange gaze, knew about your father," Roger said. "Your true father, the king. I know that was whom she referred to being in danger. Do you think it's true?"

"Do not speak of such things!" he warned. "I would not jeopardize what little chance I have by exposing it."

"Will." Gautier shook his head, then glanced over to the gathering of men near the tents and back at him. "It is the worst-kept secret at court. Those over there who know not the truth suspect it. Your mother was not the most discreet woman among the king's . . . favorites."

"You did not answer me, friend," Roger said. "Is the king in some kind of danger from this?" He motioned with his hand in the direction of Hugh's castle.

William had thought on that all day, while watching Brienne return to her village and while finalizing his plans. And he knew the truth of it—if the king suspected Hugh of some duplicity, it would not be difficult to imagine that Hugh knew of his suspicions. And if treason was in the air, the king *was* in grave danger.

"Aye, he is."

"So no matter if we understand everything at hand or if we simply carry out the orders the king gave you, his safety is part of this?" Roger clarified.

"Aye," he said, nodding at them.

Roger stood and dusted off his legs. "Then we have no choice but to carry out his orders and find out the heart of the matter. My mother's mother used to tell stories about the old gods, but I know not whether they exist. It matters not. The king's safety is the only thing."

When he said it that way, William's path became clear—meet Hugh, seek out his plans, and report back to the king. William stood and shook hands with both of them. A huge weight seemed to disappear from his body and soul now that he knew his friends would guard his back and be by his side in whatever happened.

"When do we go?" Gautier asked as he stood.

"I think midday. Four of us with the others at the ready."

"Will he invite us in?" Roger asked.

"I come from the king. Not offering us hospitality would be an insult. So, aye, I think he will. If for nothing else than to discover our reasons for being here."

"Do you think he knows we are here?"

William thought on the sight of Lord Hugh below in the valley, staring up at him and laughing. "Aye, he knows. Any man who controls his lands as Hugh does knows every time a stranger steps across the lines of his property. He knows."

"I will post extra guards," Gautier said as they walked to their tent. "And I think it should be Armand who comes with us."

Armand was the best fighter after William, even better in battle than Roger, Gautier, or Herve. He was better at seeing patterns in dangerous situations than Roger and able to use his head as well as his sword. "Very well. Tell him on the morrow."

The camp settled down for the night and a chill wind ripped through the tents, making some of the men shiver aloud. William felt it, and he needed no priest of the old gods or the one true God to tell him what his battle-ready gut could explain quite simply from experience—it was a harbinger of danger.

Even with so many unknown people and possibilities facing them, William slept well that night, as he always did before going into battle. His dreams did not show him battle plans though. Instead visions of a lass with black hair and amber eyes teased him through the long night. And the taste of her mouth, the feel of her soft flesh in his hands and against his body felt so real, he woke with his own flesh hard and ready to pleasure her.

Unfortunately, she was not to be his. And never could be.

As he rose and began to prepare to ride into Yester, he prayed that she was safe in the village and would stay out of his dealings with her lord. And he hoped that Gavin would keep her safe.

CHAPTER 11

Brienne walked back from the well and along the path and never noticed the man standing in front of their cottage. But others had. She heard the murmurs growing as she got closer and looked up. But no one would meet her gaze, and everyone appeared to be interested in something else.

The man, the warrior, standing at her door stared only at her. She'd seen him before, at Lord Hugh's side, both as they went about their business in Yester and whenever the lord rode out. Eudes was his name, and he bore a long scar on one cheek and down his neck, which added to his frightening appearance.

"You, girl," he called out as he pointed at her. "You are to come with me now."

Her heart pounded in fear. A summons to the castle was never good and usually deadly. Had Lord Hugh discovered she'd been with the strangers? Had someone reported her actions to him? Glancing around, she saw no one willing to help her.

"Why?" she asked, trying to delay in hopes that

someone would scurry off and find her parents. "Where are you taking me?"

The words were not enough to stop him. He walked over to her and grabbed her arm in his meaty hand. His expression showed his surprise that any person here would question his order.

"You will find out when we get there." Then, with a nod to others she'd not noticed, he pulled her along with him, his long legs covering the ground at a much faster pace than she could keep. Soon she was running, and when she could no longer do that, he dragged her as if he had not realized. Through the village, to the gates, and then over the bridge into the castle yard, they went at a relentless pace.

"Sir. Please." She tried to pry his fingers loose so she could slow down and catch her breath. "A bit slower, I pray you."

"My lord does not brook delays when he gives orders," he barked out at her. "He wants to see you now, and I will not answer to his anger if I take too long getting there."

She gave up then and found another soldier at her side, clutching her other arm and forcing her to keep up with them. None of the villagers even glanced at her as they passed by. Those living inside the walls of the castle and keep went about their tasks, taking no notice of the young woman being dragged within. As they passed the walls, doors, corridors, and stairs, Brienne knew she would never find her way out if she could escape. Then they reached what she thought was the third story in the farthest of the two sections of the keep and came to a stop.

When they released her, she crumpled to her knees, unable to breathe from both exertion and from the fear that was taking hold of her now. She'd been inside the keep a few times, coming with Gavin to deliver work to the steward in the great hall. But this chamber, on a high floor, was a place to which no one from the village was invited.

A few minutes passed, and no one attempted to help her to her feet or assist her in any way. The soldiers who'd escorted her stood in silence near the doorway, and Eudes stared out a window in the one wall. Pushing herself to her feet, she decided it was better to meet her fate standing than groveling on the floor. Brienne brushed the dirt from her gown and pushed the now-loosened tendrils of hair back out of her sweating face.

The chamber was small, but the rushes on the floor were clean and fresh. A large chair sat at one end of the room, opposite the doorway. No other furniture was present. She glanced around to see if anyone waited outside in the corridor. Now each passing moment added to her fear. What did Lord Hugh want with her? Why bring her to what looked to be the family's section of the keep? Eudes frowned at her when she moved.

Then, without warning, he was there, in the doorway. Larger than she remembered him to be and younger, as well. He entered with the vigor of youth and not the age she knew he must be. How had he changed?

"Girl!" Eudes barked out as he shoved her back down to her knees. "My lord," he said, as he bowed. "I brought her as you commanded."

"Eudes, help her to her feet and get out," Lord Hugh said in a softer voice than she'd imagined he would use.

Barely a second passed before she found herself standing alone in the center of the chamber before her true father. She kept her gaze down, not daring to meet his. He circled her slowly, and she felt his intense stare as though he touched her, gliding over her body and face.

"Come."

With nothing more than that, he walked from the chamber into the corridor and away. Her hesitation lasted a breath, and she followed him. No one else was present. The chambers they passed were empty, and the silence was interrupted only by the sounds of their feet moving along the stone floor. The chamber they entered was the last one before the stairway. Larger than the first one, this had a long table with many stools and chairs around it. But it was as empty as the first one until he clapped his hands.

All manner of servants came running with trays of food and cups and pitchers. They stood by the table waiting as he took a seat at the center, in the largest seat there.

"Have you broken your fast yet, Brienne?" he asked, pointing to the chair across from his. She shook her head. It mattered not, for he simply pointed and a servant came to her side. "Here. Sit. Join me."

He nodded to the servants, and she found a cup of ale and a plate in front of her. When they offered him cheese or bread or cold meat, they offered it to her. When he held out his cup for more, they filled hers. It would have been a pleasant meal if her stomach had not threatened to expel every bite she took. And if she could force her heart to slow from the brutal pounding pace it kept up. And if the man sitting with her did not have the power to destroy her and everyone around them with simply a thought.

She tried to study him since she'd never been this close to him before, but he kept meeting her eyes, causing her to look away in fear. His hair was black now, the gray gone, and his eyes were the same color as hers. He took a breath as though ready to speak, when a commotion began outside the chamber.

Two women entered, and Brienne recognized both of them immediately. Standing quickly and backing away to the wall, she bowed low before the Lady Margaret, Lord Hugh's wife, and Lady Adelaide, their daughter. Brienne dared not look at either one, for she knew not whether they knew her parentage. One did not remind a lady of her husband's bastards.

"Margaret. Adelaide," he said in a mild tone. "I am pleased you decided to join us to break your fast this morn. We have much to discuss."

Brienne dared a glance at her father's wife and her half sister and was surprised that they did not object to her presence there. More shocking were Lord Hugh's words.

"Come, Brienne. Take your place, and I will explain why I have sent for you." She did so in slow, measured steps. Once seated again, she kept her head bowed and eyes lowered.

Who was this man? This was not the same dangerous lord who rode through the village and whom everyone feared. He spoke in a civil manner; he saw to her comfort and invited her to join his family at table. Something was very wrong here.

"I have been remiss, Brienne," he said to her. She looked at him and found him watching her with a smile. "I have known about you for some time now, but have not done my fatherly duties toward you."

"My lord?" she said, shaking her head. "I do not understand." Speaking of such things had been forbidden for so long, it hurt her to even listen to him say it openly—and in front of his ladywife and daughter.

"You are my daughter," he said boldly. "I want you to live here now. Lady Margaret and Adelaide will guide you in the womanly pursuits suitable for a daughter of mine." A quick, furtive glance at the two women told her nothing, for they wore similar, empty expressions and said nothing.

"But, my lord, I . . ." She lost the words she wanted to say. How could she refuse him?

"I should have stepped in long ago, when you approached the end of your girlhood, but I was attending to other matters. Now, though, I think it time that we learn more about you and help you learn your place in the world."

For so long, her place had been in the village, as the blacksmith's daughter. Though she'd hoped and prayed for this exact thing for many years, now that he said the words, she found the words of acceptance stuck in her throat.

"I could not," she stammered out finally. "I cannot . . ."

"I do not understand, Brienne. Surely Gavin and Fia made the truth known to you—I am your father and it is my duty to see to you. They understood that you were never theirs to keep."

"It is a shock to her, my lord," Lady Margaret said. "Such a change without warning." She thought she heard sympathy and compassion in the lady's voice, but one look at her eyes and Brienne knew neither was possible. "She will learn to accommodate herself to your will, my lord. As is her duty as your . . . daughter."

"Why, my lord? Why now?" she asked, unnerved by the lady's acquiescence in a matter like this.

A lady would never allow her husband's bastards to be brought into her home, let alone be acknowledged and welcomed. They were a fact, unavoidable when most lords married for lands and titles and sought love and companionship from others. But to allow him to do this in front of her and their unmarried daughter was unthinkable.

From the time her parents admitted the truth to her, Brienne had been warned to stay out of the lady's view. To avoid being identified as Lord Hugh's get. Now he was insisting his wife accept her?

"Forgive my language," Lord Hugh said. "But even bastards have their uses, Brienne. And I think you have much to offer to me and to our family."

She cringed at his words, for her mother had warned her of exactly that—the ways of powerful men. He stood then and walked around to her.

"And there is much I can offer to you. A chamber of your own, servants, new garments—whatever you need or want shall be yours. Lessons to teach you to read mayhap?" he offered. "And you and Adelaide are of a marriageable age, so I can even arrange a suitable match for you. Many clamor to relate themselves to a man high in the king's regard. You will not marry the miller's son."

Brienne glanced at Adelaide and read the disgust in her eyes, disgust that she could not hide as well as Lady Margaret.

Although he made it sound as if she had a choice in this, Brienne understood there was none. If this was what she'd always longed for, why did it ring so hollow now that the option was before her?

"May I have time to consider your offer, my lord?"

The lady gasped at her request and shook her head at Brienne. "Foolish girl! Do you not know what your lord father is giving you? How dare you—"

"Ah, lady," Lord Hugh interrupted her angry, sputtering words. "As you yourself said, this must come as a shock to her." He threw a glance at Lady Margaret, who closed her mouth so quickly Brienne almost heard it snap shut. Then he turned back to Brienne and said, "I thought you might want to discuss this with Gavin and Fia, so here they are. Speak to them." He gestured to the hallway.

Brienne found her parents directly outside the chamber. She stood and bowed to the lord and lady and ran to greet them. Worry darkened their gazes and covered their faces.

"Did you know?" she whispered. They stood before her almost as strangers, not attempting to hold her or draw her close.

" 'Tis time for you to return to Lord Hugh. You were never ours to keep," her father, Gavin, whispered to her. "We had you to ourselves longer than we dared to hope."

"But you never told me this could happen," she said. "This has happened in such haste that I know not what to do," she admitted.

"Ah, lass," her mother said. "He offers you everything we cannot. How can you say nay to that?"

The words were spoken correctly, but everything in

their manner and expressions said that they did not want her to accept. Nothing about this felt right, and the only thing she thought was true was Lord Hugh's words about bastards having their uses. A strange tingling crept up her spine, a warning that all was not as it seemed to be.

She leaned over and lowered her voice. "I cannot trust him. I do not trust him," she whispered. "If something is wrong, seek out Sir William. He can help."

Their eyes widened at her words, and they surprised her as well, but they nodded and smiled and bade her farewell. With a nervous glance at Lord Hugh, they kissed her quickly and left. As they walked down the stairway, she felt as though her heart had been torn from her. Taking a deep breath, she prepared to face her future here.

"There now," Lord Hugh said from just behind her. "We shall make things right between us."

He placed his hands on her shoulders and squeezed them in what should have been a reassuring gesture. The feel of it made her even more nervous. Then, releasing her, he called out to his wife and daughter, who remained like statues at the table.

"Margaret, see to it that Alain arranges a suitable chamber and clothing and accoutrements for my daughter. Adelaide, show your sister around the keep so she will find her way."

Had she flinched at the words or had they? Brienne could feel their hatred even though they controlled their expressions better with each passing moment. As in the village and anywhere on his lands, no one disobeyed Lord Hugh's commands. He may be dressing his words and deeds up in politeness for now, but Brienne had no doubt that his true nature would show through very quickly.

Brienne did not doubt that she'd been brought here more for her special skill than for this long-ignored claim of fatherhood.

Those under his command worked very efficiently, for by the time they sat at table again for the noon meal, Brienne had been fitted for several new gowns, shifts, stockings, shoes, and any possible clothing needed. They assigned her a large, bright chamber, and Adelaide had led her through the floors of the keep, pointing out the places she would need to find.

From the impatience that simmered just below his control, an impatience she could feel growing, Brienne knew that Lord Hugh would reveal the real reason he had brought her here very soon.

While the chamber, the clothing, and the excellent food felt very comfortable to her, she wondered what the true price of this acceptance would be . . . and whether she would survive to enjoy these newly found comforts.

CHAPTER 12

William's horse grew nervous under him.

They'd been sitting at the gates to Yester Castle, waiting for a long time on what would be one of the sunniest, warmest spring days seen in many years. And that meant that sweat poured down under his heavy armor, soaking into the thick padding he wore underneath it. He urged the horse to settle once more and tried to ignore the grumbling of those who accompanied him now. Roger walked his horse up next to him.

"Is this done apurpose?" he asked, lifting his helm from his head. His hair was matted down as well, so William knew none of them was comfortable.

"Certainly it is," William said quietly. "I have no doubt we are being observed until Lord Hugh wishes to have us enter."

"But you come from the king! How can he . . . ?" Roger cut off his words as the gate began to open, and he moved back to a position behind William. He could feel his men tense as though ready for battle. This could be just that.

"Sir William," a man called out as he walked toward

them. "Lord Hugh apologizes for this delay and bids you to attend him in the hall. I am Alain, Lord Hugh's steward. Right this way."

They rode through the gate and across the bridge that had been dropped into place. There was a second gate before the walls widened around the yard. A tall, square stone keep stood against the south wall and another shorter building stood on the other side. William nodded his head at the smaller one, telling his men to take note of it and everything around them.

Yester Castle had begun as a motte-and-bailey type of construction, but that original part sat outside the walls, still surrounded by the moat. Fed by two streams and a river, the moat would make an attack harder, for it was wide and deep. It was a defensive castle and would withstand a siege for a long time if it had a water source within it. After they passed a well, he knew it would be almost impregnable.

They made their way up to the large keep. Dismounting, they handed their horses off to some boys waiting there and walked up the steps. Alain led them inside and up to the next floor and into a large open room. The great hall, no doubt. There, at the front of the room, in his thronelike chair, sat Lord Hugh de Gifford. As they approached, he stood to greet them.

"My lord," William said, bowing to him.

He remembered seeing Lord Hugh at court some years before and was surprised by his appearance now. Though he was a number of years older than the king, who was nearing three score, Lord Hugh looked like a man half that.

And there was something more.

Something different. A strange brightness about his

figure that shimmered as he moved. Trying not to openly stare, William studied the man as he could. When Lord Hugh held his hand in greeting to William and he accepted it, William fought not to lose his balance as the heat washed over him.

"Sir William," Lord Hugh said. His gaze narrowed and focused on him, watching his reaction to the strange sensation that had passed between them. "My apologies for such a delay in receiving you. A family matter needed to be seen to first." Lord Hugh peered behind him, taking the measure of his men.

"I will pray for the health of your family, my lord." William offered the polite reply, trying not to let his shock show. This was a feeling not unlike when he'd seen Brienne for the first time. But how could that be?

"Oh, aye, well," he said. "And what brings you to Yester, Sir William? My man did not say."

"I did not tell him, my lord, preferring to speak with you directly."

"Alain, see to Sir William's men."

Lord Hugh gestured for William to follow him to the table and they sat. Once servants brought cups and wine and they'd each partaken, William knew it was time.

"My lord, the king sends his greetings to you," he said.

"How is the king?" Lord Hugh did not flinch at his words.

"He is well."

"And the queen?" he asked.

"She is also well," William answered. "The king missed you at his Christmas court and wanted me to send you his greetings."

"Ah, well. The king has little time or attention for anyone but his lovely new wife, and I did not wish to distract him from his happiness over his new marriage. I have recently had news that she already carries an heir for the king, Sir William. Is that true?"

Though the king had revealed this to him, William did not know that this news was publicly known. Deciding that the king's closest advisers would have been told, William nodded. "Aye. The queen is *enceinte*."

If he had not been watching closely, he would have missed the shadow that crossed over the man's features. Lord Hugh was not pleased by the news of an heir to the throne of Scotland. Just then William's birthmark burned and his blood began to heat, much as it did when he was near Brienne. What was he reacting to?

"So, what brings you to this part of Scotland?"

"I have lands in the south and was going to inspect them," he bluffed. He and his lands were insignificant, and he suspected that Lord Hugh would have no knowledge of them. "The king asked me to stop on my journey and bring you his greetings."

"And you are his faithful subject—are you not, Sir William de Brus?" The man smiled then, and it made his skin crawl.

"As are you, my lord." The smile did not falter. Lord Hugh stood then, and William followed to his feet.

"You have been camping on the hill—have you not?" he asked.

"Awaiting your return, my lord." He would not deny it—Hugh knew he had.

"You must be my guest for a few days, then, Sir William. Allow me to show you the hospitality you would have received if I'd been in residence on your arrival on *my lands*."

"My thanks for your hospitality, my lord," he said, nodding agreement. He'd be better able to watch Lord Hugh from inside his keep.

"You should send word back to the rest of your men, so they do not think something has happened to you," Lord Hugh urged.

So, they had been watched, and Lord Hugh knew where his men were. He probably also knew how many traveled with him and about the others. William kept his expression at ease, trying not to give too much away.

"Would you like to bring them here or send them supplies?" he asked in a tone that made it seem like having bands of armed warriors outside your gates was not something of note.

"As long as they have your permission to hunt, they will be fine, my lord." William would assume that nothing was secret.

"Of course," he said, nodding to his steward. "Alain, find a suitable chamber for Sir William and a place for his men in the barracks. They will be staying with us for a short time. I have some matters to attend to, but we will talk more at supper. Your men may join us as well, if you wish." He gestured at Roger, Gautier, and Armand, seated a distance away.

"Again, my thanks for your hospitality. It will be a welcome change from living on the road."

His men stood and bowed as Lord Hugh passed them and then they came to him. The steward stood ready to show them to where they would sleep.

"I need to know how many he has here. And where

they are," he said quietly, never taking his gaze off the steward who stood just out of earshot. "And anything else you think important."

He turned to the steward. "Alain? When does Lord Hugh eat his evening meal? I have a matter to see to and do not wish to be late."

"At sundown," Alain answered.

"Roger, accompany Armand to your quarters. Gautier, come with me."

"Sir William, the gates close at sundown and will not be opened for anyone."

"Just so, Alain. We will be back by then."

They reclaimed their horses from the stableboys and left then, watching as Roger and Armand were taken to one of the smaller buildings farther inside the castle. This time they rode through the village, not trying to hide or be discreet. Now they were guests of Lord Hugh.

He slowed his pace as they passed the smithy. From the sounds and smells, Gavin was hard at work, making weapons for Lord Hugh. Glancing down the smaller paths and around the cottages and other buildings, William searched for any sign of Brienne and saw none. He hoped that was a good omen, that she was heeding his warning and keeping to her usual tasks.

After giving his men new orders, he sent one of them to Marcus across the valley. Nothing he'd seen there spoke of a knowledge of fighting or defense. From the man's own words, they had no skills and no soldiers among their group. But he knew that he must at least warn them of the possible danger of an angry lord in regard to the trespassers on his property.

Riding back toward the castle, William felt as though his true task for the king was finally under way.

The evening meal was uneventful and more pleasant than he had expected it could be. In spite of the fear that seemed to control the villagers, those living here in the castle seemed at ease. The lady and her daughter ate with them and retired early to their chambers, which William noted were not in this building but in a smaller one across the yard.

Lord Hugh did not remain in the hall, though his men did after his departure, offering some games of chance that lasted well into the night. Remarkably, when he returned to the room he'd been assigned, a young woman stood at his door, offering whatever *hospitality* he wished. Whether sent by Lord Hugh or Alain, it mattered not, for William would not partake of her favors.

Lying on the rope-strung bed that night, William realized that the one woman he would like to have in his bed was the one he would not ever have. He would not dishonor her by taking her virtue. And no amount of wanting or desire could make it so.

She'd taken her evening meal on a tray in her chamber.

Her chamber.

Glancing up in the light of the expensive wax candles that sat around the room, she could not believe the events of the day. The bed had a down-filled mattress over tightly strung ropes, which made it blissful to lay on. She'd let out a gasp and then a long sigh as her body sank into the softness of it. With plump pillows and a pile of blankets to keep her warm, Brienne knew she would be asleep in moments.

But now, an hour or more later, according to how far the candles had burned down, she could not sleep.

Pushing the bedcovers back, she climbed out and pulled on a robe. Unlike any garment she'd ever had, it was plush and thick and covered her from neck to feet. She did not know what the fabric was, but she loved the way it felt against her skin.

Walking over to the trunk in the corner, she lifted the lid and just stared at the costly clothing inside it. During the rest of the day, servants had come to do Lord Hugh's bidding—delivering gowns, shifts, stockings, shoes, and jewelry, the likes of which she'd never seen or hoped for before. Combs, veils, and circlets for her hair, and several belts and fine linen kerchiefs added to the amazing collection.

The most extraordinary arrival had been a young woman named Emilie. Emilie came from Lord Hugh's holdings in France and was some sort of distant cousin. And now she was Brienne's lady's maid and companion.

As someone who took care of herself and carried out her chores and performed errands for whoever needed help in the village, having a servant to see to her needs was too difficult to believe.

And Emilie, with guidance from Lady Margaret and Lady Adelaide, would help Brienne learn the skills a young woman of good birth should have. Music. Embroidery. Reading and writing—skills that had been ignored in her life because there were other more important tasks to be done. Now she would learn them.

She was shocked by the wealth showered upon her. It was not that she was unaware Lord Hugh was wealthy. She had known. But the chance that any of it would be shared with her was not something she thought in the realm of possibilities until now.

She walked to the window and carefully opened the shutters to peer out. From this height, she could see the village over the wall. The cottages seemed even smaller to her now, seen from this distance. Nothing moved in the dark. Gavin and Fia would be asleep by now, rising at dawn to face the new day's chores and tasks without her help. And James. It seemed so long ago that the boy had asked to marry her.

She let out a sigh. The bliss was beginning to slip a bit, and her sense of judgment crept back in. Brienne knew there was surely a price to pay for all this good fortune.

Nothing she'd seen in Lord Hugh over her whole life led her to believe he did this for her. Or that he was seeking to do the right and fatherly thing. He needed or wanted something from her, and all these luxuries were payment for it. When she turned back from the window, he stood before her as though her thoughts and questions had conjured him.

"My lord," she said, dropping into a curtsy the way Emilie had shown her. "I did not hear you enter."

"Your chambers. The garments. All are to your liking?" he asked.

"Aye. 'Tis more than I ever expected," she admitted.

"But what you deserve as my daughter."

She had no words to reply to his declaration, so she remained silent and waited on his reasons for calling so late in the night.

"Come." He lifted the latch on the door and opened it. "I would like to show you your heritage."

Though she hoped to see paintings or tapestries of ancestors or castles, Brienne did not delude herself. Her heritage was the power she'd inherited. This would be a test, and she had no doubt that failure would mean exile or death.

Unlike Adelaide, this one did not flinch under his gaze. Oh, he knew she was afraid. He could feel her terror, feel of the emotions pulsing through her right now, but he sensed her curiosity balancing out those fears.

As she followed him from the bedchamber, Hugh tried to remember who had birthed her. He paid little attention to which whelp came from which bitch unless it was his hunting hounds. Over the years he'd fathered a dozen or more bastards. He would ask Alain, who paid attention to these matters.

When she glanced up at him, he felt a flicker of recognition in the way her brow lifted and in the nervous smile on her lips. A wave of acid rolled in his gut then, and Hugh feared he knew the truth of her origins.

"Have I displeased you, my lord?" she asked softly as they walked to the other end of the smaller keep and then up the stairs. He shook his head.

"How many years have you, girl?" She must be younger than Adelaide, and if she was, then it was not possible. It could not be possible.

"I will be eight and ten when I mark the anniversary of my birth in the summer. At least that is what my parents—what Gavin and Fia—told me."

She'd been born on the summer solstice eighteen years ago.

A year before Adelaide. Before his marriage to Margaret, which had seemed so promising to his father. She'd been born to—

He forced himself to stop remembering the rest of it. Controlling himself was an action he'd perfected, and he enforced it now, pushing away any memories that would interfere with a millennia of plans. They'd reached the corridor that led to his chambers.

"No one comes down this hallway without my permission, Brienne. Do you understand?" At her nod, he guided her down the darkened corridor, causing the torches to burn brighter to light their path. There was the slightest hesitation in her step, but she continued at his side.

Promising.

As he lifted the latch on his door, he heard the slight intake of breath as she prepared herself for what would come. He smiled then. The wench had no idea what she would face.

Once inside, he closed the door and they stood in complete darkness. When one controlled fire, one did not need to leave candles burning, he thought. Now her fear began to overwhelm her curiosity, and he felt her begin to tremble.

"Go ahead, Brienne. Show me."

He liked this one, for she did not pretend to misunderstand him or his order. She took in a long, deep breath, and as she released it, Hugh found he was holding his.

If she was his daughter, if she inherited his power over fire, if he could bring her into his plans, their power would be infinite. So much depended on this unexpected turn of events, not the least of which was his own life. A sacrifice from the fireblood line would ensure Chaela's success and his survival. And he intended to survive.

The room filled with light and heat as she created fire in her outthrust hand. The flames burst forth and burned brightly between them. He smiled. A good sign. She was untrained but carried the power of his bloodline.

"Must you hold out your hand to begin it?" he asked, watching the intense concentration on her face. "Just bring it forth," he urged.

The room plunged into darkness for a few seconds as she dropped her hand and let it extinguish. Then once more Brienne made the fire burn between them. Hugh nodded and walked behind her.

"Larger," he ordered. She made it larger.

"Brighter." A human would have had to shield his eyes at the intensity of the light she brought forth. But he looked on it and into it, assessing the power she had, and smiled again.

She calmed then. He felt the tension leave her, and the fire became more intense and more focused. Walking to the other side of the room, at the edges of what she'd created, he took the next step.

"Aim it at me."

Darkness was her answer.

"I told you to aim your fire at me, Brienne. Do not disobey me now." He took a step closer.

"I cannot, my lord," she said in a whisper.

She thought he would be harmed! He laughed at that. But if she would not follow his commands and use the fire as he wanted it to be used—as a weapon that swords and daggers could not stop—then she was of no use to him. And he would not waste his time training her. Better to end it now before she gained more power and did not know how to use it.

"I find myself unusually disappointed, girl. I had such hopes for you."

Without any further warning, he unleashed his fire on her. She threw her hands up before her face to protect herself, as many had before her—but this time he found himself unable to prolong the torment he usually so enjoyed. He sent another terrible burst of fire at her to end it.

Danger!

William jumped from the bed and looked around the chamber.

Nothing. He was alone. The keep lay in heavy silence, and no sounds of alarm or attack could be heard. And yet . . .

His body began to shake and tremble and sweat.

His muscles tightened and grew, his head high above the floor. A bluish glow filled the chamber as his flesh changed and his vision filled with red.

His control was slipping away, and he was losing himself.

Brienne!

Then it was gone. The pull to that other being cut like a thread and he changed back to himself. He panted as the sweat poured from him and tried to gain some sense of what had happened.

She had been in danger; he knew it to the marrow of his bones. Just as she'd been before. But now he could feel nothing of her.

No fear. No sense of danger. Nothing.

Knowing they would not open the gates until the morning, he could not leave to seek her out. He lay back on the bed, still shaking from the changes in his body. Had he only thought his body altered? He'd been asleep and so possibly it had been a nightmare?

William listened to the unnatural silence around him. No nightjars chirping their songs. No sounds in this night at all, as though a heavy blanket had been tossed over Yester Castle, muffling any noises.

He waited for some sign of distress from Brienne, but all sense of her had been snuffed out like a candle.

CHAPTER 13

It burned!

Not like her fire.

This fire burned her skin and clothes and sent heated waves of air into her lungs.

The pain!

Her hands took most of it, flung up before her as though they could stop his fire from burning her. Then the power within her came alive and pushed forth, protecting her from the assault.

She hid within her flames so his fire could not harm her. Never had she wanted to send her fire at someone or even thought it a possibility, but he wanted her to. She could hear him urging her—daring her—to do it even now from inside the flames.

With little effort, she aimed at the shape of his body outside the flames and directed her power at him. He laughed as it struck him. Suddenly, she was no longer harmed or even slowed down by his assault. She thrust more and more at him until he was gone.

"Excellent, daughter of my blood!"

The words came from within the fire she'd created

around her, for he was there now with her. At first she thought Hugh had spoken, but the voice was a mixture of male and female or . . . something else.

"She has the power," the female said.

"She is ours," the male said.

"Ready her for us," the blended voice said.

"Stop!" Lord Hugh commanded.

Within a moment, all fire stopped, and she walked from among the flames. The lovely robe had burned to scraps in the first moments of his fiery onslaught. He reached for something on the chair in the corner of the chamber and tossed it at her.

Shaking from the physical cost of bringing forth such power, she collapsed as her legs gave out. Her father carried her to a chair and reached for a bottle of golden liquid, pulling the stopper from it before handing it to her. When she did nothing, for her body would not obey her now, he wrapped her hand around it and guided it to her mouth.

"Drink. Now," he ordered, as he pushed the bottle against her mouth until she leaned her head back and took some. The liquid slid down, coursing a molten path down her throat and into her stomach. "It is whisky." She tried to lift the bottle from her mouth, but he held it fast.

"Again," he ordered, tipping the bottle more and forcing her to swallow it. She tried again to draw back, but he shook his head.

"More," he demanded. Another and another mouthful until her stomach eased and the heat of the whisky spread through her. Brienne lost the will to fight him. "Good," he whispered as she drank once more from the bottle.

Dizzy now from the exhaustion and from the whisky, for she'd never had such a potent drink before, she fell back against the chair and felt her eyes closing. A moment or a minute later—she could not tell—the soft touch of a man's hand on her cheek woke her, and she forced her eyes to open.

"The goddess is pleased with you, Brienne," he whispered from in front of her. Crouched down so that their faces were level, he nodded and smiled. "Very pleased, as am I."

Then he wrapped the cloth around her and scooped her into his arms. Soon they were moving through the hall and down the steps. He carried her in silence. Too dizzy to keep watching, too sleepy to think on much at all, Brienne could feel them making their way in the chilled air of the corridors. One glance into his face and she closed her eyes and let it all fade away as he spoke once more.

"The goddess is very pleased."

She stumbled through the darkness, seeking a way home and finding endless black. Falling and falling and falling. Brienne called out for help, for Gavin and Fia. She could end this. She could end the darkness. She had the power. All she had to do was to make—

Nay! 'Twas forbidden. 'Twas secret. No one must know.

Dragged back into the nightmare, she fought it, fought its control and the terror. Lord Hugh stood before her then, throwing his fire at her, burning her and burning her until she . . .

She woke up trying to scream. Clutching her burning throat, she looked around and found herself in the middle of her bed in her chambers.

In Yester Castle.

"Here now, Brienne," said a soft voice. "You have been dreaming."

Emilie. A cousin. Her companion and maid.

"How long have I been here?" she asked.

"All through the night, I suppose," she said with a soft laugh. "Unless you went off cavorting after I put you to bed last night?" Brienne accepted the cup of cool water and sipped it as she watched the girl tug the bedcovers and smooth them around her.

No matter that she was considered family, she had no doubt that Lord Hugh wanted to keep her fire powers a secret, so she said nothing. Part of her thought she'd dreamed it, for there was no sign that she'd left her bed since she'd climbed in after her bath. Then she noticed Emilie searching for something.

"I cannot find the robe I left here on the bed last evening." Emilie knelt down and looked beneath the bed now. "Did you . . . put it away? Or pull it under the bedcovers with you?"

The memory of the robe burning off of her flooded her mind, along with the pain and fear. She shivered against it. Had it been real? She looked at her hands, the ones that had taken the full force of the fire, and saw no evidence of injury.

"No matter," Emilie said, going over to the trunk that held her new garments. "Here is another, though not as heavy as the other."

The girl held out the robe and waited for her to get out of the bed. Unaccustomed as Brienne was to dressing or undressing or bathing in front of another, she found it difficult to do without hesitation. So, she slid out of the covers, keeping most of her body beneath them until the last moment. Or she would have if Emilie had not pulled the covers off her.

"What? How?" she asked, tugging Brienne aside to look at the sheets. Black streaks marked what had been pristine linens. "This," Emilie said, rubbing a finger along one of the marks and smelling it, "smells like ashes. What did you do?"

Brienne knew that the ash was from last night, but how could she explain that? Searching for the right words, she was about to try to explain—something—when the door to the chamber opened and Lord Hugh walked in.

"Emilie," Lord Hugh said without even glancing over at her.

"My lord?"

"Do not ever think to question my daughter. About anything. Do you understand?" he asked. The way he stood with his arms folded across his chest and a very serious expression on his face made Brienne glad that she was not the one to whom he spoke.

"Aye, my lord," Emilie whispered, bowing to him. "Never." Now when the girl looked at her, her eyes filled with terror.

"You may leave us now."

All it took was that and she fled without looking back. Lord Hugh closed the door and faced her.

"I beg your pardon if I was expected somewhere, my lord," she offered.

"How do you fare, Brienne?" He walked closer and examined her closely. "Is your strength returned?"

"I am well," she said. Though she'd awakened badly,

now that the stupor of sleep had passed, she felt much better.

"I find that it invigorates me," he said, not taking his gaze from hers. All pretense was gone between them; she understood that now.

She shrugged. "I have never done that before. Never tried."

"And always hidden it away? From Gavin and Fia?" He sighed. "I did not know you had inherited the power of our line," he admitted. "From everything planned, it should have been Adelaide." He gestured for her to sit. She did so.

"And she did not?" she asked. Strange that her half sister had been raised with their father believing she would be the one.

"Nay," he said. "A disappointment in every respect. Never mind, though. Now I have found you." He smiled, and she was amazed at how his features softened when he did. "Will you stay and let me train you to use it? There is so much to show you."

The enthusiasm in his voice warmed her heart even though she tried not to let it. This was a strange new world, and she was lost in it. He could guide her to accept and learn about this awesome power they shared. And now that he knew, the fear of him discovering it vanished. She did not have to hide it. She did not want to hide it any longer.

If she accepted his offer, she would not have to.

"Aye, my lord," she said, nodding.

"Do not misunderstand, Brienne. The power that I have, that you inherited, has been honed and passed down through generation after generation. There is a purpose for it—a great purpose."

She shivered at those words. She'd heard something like that whispered among those who'd taken her that day.

Bloodlines. Generations. Powers. Destruction.

The young woman Aislinn had spoken only of the gods she worshipped and had not given her much information about those gods in the short time they had. Was that what he meant?

"Ours is a dangerous power that could destroy us instead of our enemies, so you must give me your word that you will follow my guidance and instructions."

"Aye, my lord. I wish to learn," she admitted. And it was the truth, for she had wanted for years to understand it—since the first hints of it had appeared.

He smiled again and nodded. "Speak of it to no one and remain within the walls, at least until you have learned to control it more. Then you shall take your place at my side. I will come for you this night after the others have gone to bed and we will begin. Rest this day. You will need your strength." He walked to the door and then turned back to her. "This pleases me greatly. You please me."

And then he was gone, as quickly and as quietly as he'd arrived.

Brienne knew somewhere deep inside that she should be suspicious of such a fortuitous change in her life, that this man had done terrible things to people she knew and to others she'd heard about. But bringing her here, accepting her and the power they shared, and inviting her to learn and be at this side—it tore down her resistance. For so much of her life, she'd long to be claimed, not to be the secret, not to be the one forced to live in darkness.

Now he offered her what she'd wanted.

How could she not grab for it?

William and his men rode out in the morning, invited by Lord Hugh to tour his lands. They spent much of the morning riding through the area around the castle, inspecting the moat and the canals that drained it. Lord Hugh was an amiable host, pointing out various improvements he'd made, instructing William in land management and offering suggestions about crops.

Watching for any signs of discontentment or sedition, William found none. At least none spoken of or whispered where he or his men could hear. And though the weapons he'd seen would arm a very large group of soldiers, they saw no more than would be expected to guard a castle of this size.

Neither did Roger, Gautier, and Armand find anything amiss in the barracks where the guards and others who served in the castle lived. No one talked openly, but they heard neither gossip nor tales passed around. If this man was planning a revolt against the king, there were no signs of it here in his principal holding.

Yet they had been in residence for only one day, so Lord Hugh could be hiding something. Someone good at deception could hide something for months, but there was bound to be a slip somewhere and sometime. A prickling under his skin told William that Lord Hugh was very good.

A messenger came for him, calling Lord Hugh back to see to a matter in the keep and he bade them to continue riding with Alain. William engaged the man in a discussion over the size of fields long enough to seem interested and then gave him leave to return to his duties. Circling the castle, he rode through the village, again looking for Brienne.

"You look for the girl, Will?" Roger asked as they rode side by side along the path.

"I have not seen her since that day. I . . ." He did not know what or how to say that he was concerned over what had happened to her.

"I've not seen you like this over a woman before," Roger said. "And I have seen you with many, many women."

"I find myself thinking about her more and more, even though I know she is not suitable for me once the king's grant comes through. I want to seek her out and speak to her and . . ." He shrugged. "I have not felt this way about a woman before, as you said."

"She is one of his villagers," Roger said, nodding his head toward the castle. "She is tied here by family."

"I understand all of that. I also know she is deeply involved in our mission. And I suspect it is much bigger than even the king suspected."

"Bigger than treason?" Roger scoffed. "What could the king fear more than losing his throne?"

Losing his life? Losing his soul? William dared not voice those suspicions, but they weighed heavily on him.

"Well, between what happened to you and those strangers," Gautier said, "and all of the peculiar things we have heard and seen, I know this is not something we have ever dealt with before. It will not be as simple as a battle or a fight, Will. There is something larger and more dangerous at play here now."

William nodded. "I think we will long for the days of simple fighting by the time our task is done, Roger."

William could not yet accept the things he suspected, but he knew the time was coming when he would question everything he thought and believed or pay for it with his life.

And knowing that, he prayed that neither he nor his men would pay that price.

CHAPTER 14

The weather outside remained sunny and mild for the second day in a row, and Brienne decided to walk outside and enjoy it. If the truth be told, she was bored at having no tasks to see to or errands to carry out.

The anticipation of what was to come this night made her shiver when she thought about it, and that brought attention from either Lady Margaret or Adelaide when they were with her. So she asked permission to walk and left the keep. She noted that her chamber was at one end of the building on the second floor as she followed a servant out. Trying to remember where Lord Hugh's had been, she studied the windows from outside, deciding that his was on the far end in the small tower.

She thought about leaving the castle grounds and going to see her—Gavin and Fia, but she'd said she would remain here until she gained control over her power. Looking about, she walked toward the far corner of the castle, where men trained. Drawn by the sound of cheering, she discovered that small groups of men were practicing their skills by fighting other groups.

She walked to the fence that surrounded the training area and watched as one of the groups, four men in each, moved effortlessly and won against each opponent. They did not use the longer battle swords yet, but first worked with the long wooden staffs and then shorter ones and then short swords and shields.

The crowd grew and the men became quite boisterous, calling out to their friends, though none seemed happy that the successful four soldiers were winning. One of the four outshone the others, moving expertly no matter which weapon he held. His steps were like those of a dance; he was sliding and shifting without watching and all the while engaging whomever he faced. Only when he turned and came out of the shadows did she recognize him.

Sir William de Brus.

Her breath caught in her body and she could not turn her eyes away from his every move and step. William seemed to lose himself in the battle, paying no heed to anyone or anything but the fight. A pale blue shimmer outlined his body, and she watched as it ebbed and flowed around him with each movement.

Knowing now that he held some kind of power, as she and her father did, she was not frightened as she had been the first time she'd noticed it. It made sense now that there might be others like her and Lord Hugh. What power had he? The way that he fought this day and on that other one, the way his body had changed as he faced danger and became one with his weapon, she thought he must carry some warrior's power.

She shrugged it off, content just to watch him.

Soon, too soon for her, the matches were over and the ground littered with his opponents, though none seemed to be injured. Their pride mayhap bruised, but all would live to fight another day.

Just then a cloud crossed in front of the sun, casting a shadow over William and his men. She shivered, knowing somehow that they would fight again and they would face Lord Hugh's men, these very men, again. The next time, though, it would be a struggle of life and death for all of them.

At that moment, William looked away from the men to whom he spoke and met her eyes. At first glance, she thought he did not recognize her, but then he nodded to her. With a word to his men, who also followed his gaze and noticed her, he walked toward her. He wore only breeches, and his broad, muscular chest glistened with sweat. He'd pulled back and tied his long brown hair out of his face, which just made the masculine lines and angles of his jaw more attractive.

When he reached her and smiled at her with a sense of familiarity, any words of greeting scattered in her mind. This was the man who had kissed her relentlessly. This was the man who had touched her so intimately. Though he said it was to teach her the dangers in being alone with a man, even she recognized the moment when he'd forgotten the lesson and simply kissed and caressed *her*. Her body blossomed with heat of a kind different from the one she could bring forth.

"Brienne, I did not think to find you here," he said with a glance around to see who was near. "Are you well?"

"I did not think to see you either, Sir William," she finally said. "Aye, I am well." He watched her as though he expected her not to be. That was puzzling. "So you have met with Lord Hugh as you wished to?"

"I have," he said. Confusion filled his eyes now. "What are you doing here in the castle?"

What could she say without revealing Lord Hugh's secrets? What reason could she give for being here, being dressed not as the daughter of the blacksmith any longer but as the daughter of the lord? Deciding simpler was easier, she gave him the truth, or part of it.

"Lord Hugh summoned me here."

It was not enough; that much was clear on his face. But just as he began to pursue it, one of his men called out to him.

Torn, he waved back and turned to her.

"I must go," he said. "I would speak to you, if you will be here later? Or do you return to the village?"

"Sir William!" He took a couple of steps away and waited for her reply.

She only shrugged and did not say.

"I will look for you, then." And he was gone. He did lift his head and glance at her a few times, until she walked away.

Brienne returned to the family's chambers then, ignoring the racing of her heart and the way she had responded to the sight of his strong body moving across the field. He was here, within these walls, so near and yet so impossibly far from her. Her father was watching her, or at least having her watched, and she did not wish to do anything to jeopardize her newfound position in the family. So she would not seek William out.

No matter that her heart wanted her to . . . or that her body could still feel his hands moving over her stomach and touching her.

She ate once more in her chambers and then waited for the sound of her father's footsteps outside her door, but instead, he simply appeared there and beckoned her to follow. With her palms sweating and her mouth dry, she trailed him without hesitation that night.

William looked down every corridor and hallway the rest of the day and evening. Lord Hugh did not appear for supper, so Lady Margaret entertained him. They came from neighboring areas in France and they had many common topics that kept the conversation going. But every time another person entered the dining chamber that sat off the great hall, he would turn to look.

And not find her.

Mayhap she was not here? Mayhap she had been there only on an errand between Lord Hugh and her father? Remembering the garments she wore, he doubted that. The gown was unlike any he'd seen her wear before. It was of a costly fabric, and the belt around her hips was fine-tooled leather. Again, costly and finer than the daughter of the blacksmith would have.

More like the kind a wealthy man gave to his mistress.

The thought of Brienne being taken to the bed of a man like Hugh turned his stomach. And it was not just Hugh's reputation. It was . . . It was . . .

Her.

He drank the rest of the wine in his cup, trying to rid himself of such thoughts and suspicions. And a servant filled it once more. Against his own limits on drinking strong spirits, he finished that cup as well.

Lady Margaret babbled on, not realizing his attention had turned. Lady Adelaide had retired earlier, claiming a sour stomach. Finally, he pushed his cup away and nodded at her.

"It is selfish to keep you here paying attention to only me when you must have things to see to before retiring, Lady Margaret. May I," he said, rising to his feet and holding out his arm, "escort you to your chambers?"

"Ah, 'tis later than I realized, Sir William," she said, glancing around and signaling those who served there at table. "No need to escort me. My maid waits outside for me."

Before she could leave, he asked her a question, trying to phrase it in a way that would not offend. "I thought I saw the blacksmith's daughter here earlier, my lady. Is she staying here now?"

The effect of his question was clear—the lady's face went blank and empty except for the slightest clenching of her jaw.

"There is no blacksmith's daughter in Yester Castle, Sir William." He would have asked it again, differently, but she gave him no opportunity.

"Very well, my lady. My thanks for the meal and the company. Until the morn, then," he said, bowing to her.

After she left, he comprehended that whatever task had brought Brienne here, whether an errand for her father or something else, Lady Margaret was not pleased by it. Her tone spoke of being treated with disrespect and not liking it.

Still, an errand for her father did not explain the expensive gown and belt, for the blacksmith would not ask nor expect such things in exchange for his work. Once again, his gut tightened at the thought of how those gifts came to be.

Although he did not believe the lady lied, there was something odd in her gaze and her words. As he strolled along the corridors, eschewing offers of help when servants offered, he took note of each doorway and chamber and the layout of each floor and also looked for any sign of Brienne. Once done with his task, which he had the others doing in the barracks, as well, he sought out his chambers.

The strange thing was, once there and once the keep's occupants settled for the night, he could not stay awake as was his custom. He'd had wine, aye, and more than his usual amount, but not enough to make him this sleepy. William sat on the bed, trying to regain his balance, and next, he was sound asleep.

She followed where he led, through the silent corridors of the keep. Such an anxious, needy thing; he fought to keep from laughing at her outright. It had taken little more than a few soft smiles and a few hollow promises and she was his.

As her power would be.

Hugh worked with her for the next several hours, into the darkest part of the night while everyone in the castle slept deeply, and he began to understand the potential within her.

Unexpected.

Unharnessed.

Unlimited.

Her dam could not have been of the blood or she would not have been discarded. He would have used such a carrier to breed more offspring so that he had the chance to produce children who carried his power. He would have watched a woman capable of producing issue with such power carefully and used her carefully. How could she have escaped his notice?

Or had she? whispered the mocking voice in his head. Memories flitted through his mind before he tamped them down, ignoring the taunting doubt. Instead of dwelling on it, he focused on showing Brienne how to hide herself in the smallest of flames. The girl learned quickly, absorbing all of his instructions and demonstrating skills he had not had at her age, even with training.

He would have taken a few moments to be proud of her if it wouldn't be a waste of his time. She would serve a purpose in the goddess's plan and then be gone. Once the portal was opened, she would be a powerful sacrifice and would make both him and the goddess he served invincible and unstoppable. The spells cast to exile the goddess worked only if all four gateways remained closed. If he could open one, she could escape its prison and then destroy the others, never to be bound again.

He turned his attention back to the girl and found her distracted. Closing his eyes, he opened his senses to discover the reason for it.

Fire was not the only power he possessed. Once he'd discovered the portal in the oldest ruins of the original castle—a window of a sort—the goddess shared more with him. He could work other spells, such as a sleeping spell like the one at work tonight. He could cover any sounds that others should not hear. He could sense, almost hear, the thoughts and fears of those around him, which was helpful in deciding how to sway them to his use. There was another power that he'd just begun using—one that would bend others to his will—and he salivated just at the thought of using it.

The image of the king's knight appeared in his mind.

"William de Brus?" he whispered aloud. The fireball she was perfecting dissolved at the words.

"My lord?" she asked, carefully avoiding his gaze.

"You know the king's knight?" Hugh studied her face as he waited for her to speak. "You spoke to him this day." Everything she did was observed. He trusted no one, not even his recently claimed bastard.

"Aye," she said. Nothing more. Hmm. Did she purposely hide something from him? It would not work, but she had not discovered that part of his abilities yet.

"You know him, Brienne?" he asked again, pushing against her mind with his, causing some amount of pain for her. When she gasped, he paused.

"I met him when we traveled back from Gifford."

"Who else was with you?" He pushed again, and she hissed against it, her face going pale.

"My father."

He decided he did not want her to think of Gavin again like that. Hugh spread the pain out so that her whole body felt it this time. She cried out then, her hands clenching against it.

"Who was with you?" he asked again. She looked at him with fear-filled eyes. "Call him by name, Brienne. And remember that you are my blood and not his."

"Gavin," she whispered. He released her, and she panted as the pain, once very real, faded. "I was with Gavin."

"So the knight has been on my lands for weeks now?" he asked, waiting to see if she would tell him the truth this time.

"Aye, my lord." She was breathing heavily now, part in fear and part in anticipation of the pain she knew he could cause. He reached over and lifted her face to his. Inhaling her scent, he knew something else now.

"He arouses you." He pulled her closer and inhaled once more. "He excites you and you want him." Interesting. She reacted like a bitch in heat at the mention of the warblood's name. He dropped his hold and walked a few paces away. "Are you a virgin, girl?" he asked. She did not answer immediately.

He knew the answer from the blush that rose in her cheeks. But he wanted her to answer him. This was about obedience, which he was enforcing as surely as he was building her skills with the fire. Hugh pushed.

"Aye," she called out, wincing as it hit her.

Untouched.

Another asset he could exploit if and when he needed to draw the others to his cause.

"Again," he said, pointing to the center of the chamber.

She walked to it and created the perfect sphere within seconds. Her mind was focused so closely on her creation that she did not see it coming. He blasted her from behind, throwing his power at her. The fire flared, filling the entire chamber before she pulled it back.

"Do not let it falter, Brienne. Keep the sphere before you," he ordered. He did not lessen his assault until she realized what he wanted and did it. "No matter what I do, keep it before you. Perfectly round and compact."

He moved around her, pushing her mind and throwing his own fire against her. Over and over, until she could both fend him off and focus on her creation. Hugh continued until he could feel her weaken and heard her scream out. He stopped.

A good effort for the first full night, he thought as she collapsed on the floor before him. With only burned scraps of clothing left, for the garments could not withstand the flames once she'd faltered, he let her lie there while he went to speak directly to the goddess.

The warblood was his next target. Sir William, the bastard son of the king, would be a triumph for Hugh, and he intended to bring him to his side of the battle. Oh, he'd known from the moment Sir William had crossed onto his lands that he was one of them. Those last few left who would try to defeat him.

He was also untrained in how to call upon or control his power—the power of the supreme and utter warrior. Because of his ignorance, Hugh was able to shield his power from the knight, so he would be unaware of his true abilities until it was too late. Since the others were just as ignorant of the prophecy and what they must do, Hugh would use his advantage of knowledge to conquer them, one by one.

He opened the secret doorway to the goddess's chamber, leaving Brienne. She would not wake for some time, for she lay unconscious from exhaustion and pain. Such was the price paid for using the power in their blood, at least until she learned how to use its rejuvenation properties, too.

As he walked down the steps, into the underground vault that sat beneath the old castle ruins, his flesh roused in anticipation of communing with *her*. Deep within the ground, surrounded by the buried stones that had been hidden away by his ancestors, he stood before her and prepared to be cleansed by her fire.

The shock of it as he pushed his hand through the wall that separated them forced him to his knees.

The heat as she approached shocked him in its intensity.

And then his body and soul burned in the heat of her pure fire.

"My goddess," he forced out. His jaws clenched as he held fast, fighting the urge to pull away from the agony of her touch. "I am yours," he pledged.

"She pleases me." The goddess's voice echoed through the barrier and across the stone chamber. "Power seethes in her veins. *My powers.*"

"Aye, Goddess. She is strong," Hugh said as pride tinged his voice now. Though she lay unconscious on the floor of his chamber above, she had been spectacular.

"The priests and the seer are near. And a warblood," she hissed, her form rearing back as she spewed more fire at him.

The goddess swirled in anger inside the darkness, shooting flames and screaming out curses. He had never seen her so and tried to placate her in some way.

"The warblood means something to the girl, my goddess. She could bring him to our side." Hugh dared a glance up at her. "And she will be the sacrifice to put an end to your enemies."

Her fury calmed then, and he heard the sound of her fluttering wings behind the barrier. She existed in that form there. But what would she be when he freed her? He shivered in anticipation and arousal.

"Use her," she hissed. "The warblood must be ours."

Hugh smiled and nodded. "She will do as I command her."

Chaela sent a burst of molten heat across the barrier then, and he felt her pleasure in the wave after wave of pain that sent him writhing on the floor. His body melted into flames and merged for a moment with her heat. Barely able to withstand such a joining, he fought to remain flames but could not.

His human body re-formed and burned anew. Hugh screamed against the pain, and then in the final moment of agony, he attained release. As he lay there, letting his own powers heal his scorched flesh, the goddess spoke in his thoughts.

Use her. She is ours.

Later, as he carried Brienne back to her chambers, he realized the more important connection—she would mean something to the warblood. Hugh must play on that. Time was growing short, for the priests had arrived, and if they could convince the other bloodlines to work together, it would jeopardize his plans.

"Girl!" he said, shaking her as he walked down the stairs and along the corridor. No one would hear him. "Girl!" He shook her once more. Her eyes fluttered open for a moment. Hugh held her closer and whispered to her, "Does the warrior want you? Does he lust for you?" When she did not respond, he used his thoughts to wake her.

"Aye," she mumbled, startled.

"Has he shown his power to you?" Another push, and she stared into his eyes. "Has his blood risen yet?"

All it took for her to answer was for him to narrow his gaze. Like a trained dog, she knew what would follow if she did not. "Aye, my lord. He changes . . . into . . ."

He pushed again, but it was too much. She fell unconscious, and he could not rouse her. Arriving in her chambers, he dropped her on the bed and walked out, disappointed that she could withstand so little before losing consciousness. With more training and more *encouragement*, he would teach her to endure longer. Pulling the door closed, he returned to his sleeping chambers, his body stronger and more vigorous for what he'd endured below.

Knowing he would see the goddess and that his condition would change after such encounters, he made certain that a wench waited for him in his chambers. As he'd ordered, she knelt next to his bed, naked, the marks of his last attentions still reddened and burned into her skin. Because of the spell he'd cast, she slept deeply, curled over herself with her face resting on the cold stone floor, awaiting his return.

No matter that she slept, he thought as he lifted her and laid her on her stomach over the edge of the bed. She would wake soon enough and scream the way he so liked.

As he had for his goddess.

They always did.

CHAPTER 15

"Brienne!"
   "Brienne!"
Her name seeped into her exhausted mind, and Brienne raised her head to find the source of the noise. It hurt to even think about moving, and it hurt when she finally forced her body to respond. The chamber spun around her as she turned to face . . . someone.

"Brienne, you must hurry. He has called you to the noon meal in the hall."

The frantic sounds of Emilie searching through the trunk and the slap of the tossed garments on her skin made her look around. She lay half on her stomach, half twisted on her side, across the bed. Wrapped in a gown she did not remember donning. On top of the bedcovers.

Memories flooded in then, and she groaned at the flashes of fire and burning and pain, inside her head and all over her body. Curling her legs up and holding them, she ached and her head throbbed.

"Are you ill? He did not say to excuse you if you are

ill. He said 'bring her to the table for the noon meal.' He ordered." Emilie continued her words, but they garbled into a slurred chant of endless words. "Brienne," Emilie said loudly as she grabbed her shoulders, "You must get off that bed and get dressed."

Chilled, she shivered as she sat up. She was never cold, but this morn she felt as though she would never warm. Emilie dressed her without pause, intent on doing what she'd been told to do. After last night and its "lessons," Brienne understood how she felt. She'd quickly learned that her father drew her in with enticements and appealing promises and then delivered brutal punishments if he was not pleased.

Emilie pulled her up to sit, and her hand slid down Brienne's arm. Jumping back, the girl grabbed at her hand and cried out.

"You are burning!"

Tugging her own arm free, Brienne looked at the place where Emilie had touched. Her birthmark. The flames, now vibrant red and moving freely, entwined with each other and separated, rippling on her flesh as though alive.

And the heat moved through her, reminding her of the power in her blood. Clutching her hand over it, she moved away from the girl and stood. "Give me my shift," she said.

Pulling it over her head, she covered herself and the mark. Though she could feel the heat through the thin fabric, it did not appear to burn through it. Turning back, she looked at the girl and a knowing glance gazed back. This was not something to be discussed with anyone. Nor was the presence of more ash in her bed and on her feet when she sat to have her stockings put in place.

A few wordless minutes later and Brienne stood dressed and ready to go to the hall. Emilie lifted the latch and opened the door. There in the corridor stood both Lord Hugh's wife and his daughter.

"My lady," she said, dropping to a curtsy.

"Are you ready? Come along, then," Lady Margaret said in a biting tone. Out of Lord Hugh's sight and hearing, she made her dissatisfaction with this arrangement very clear. As did her half sister, who simply did not speak to Brienne at all or acknowledge her in any way. Even now, she looked up and down, anywhere but in Brienne's direction.

Lady Margaret did not wait for a response. She began walking and expected everyone would fall in line behind her—which everyone did. Never having lived in a noble household before, Brienne marveled at the structure and rules that governed it all. Rules she would never remember. Emilie had pointed this out just about every moment of every hour since she'd arrived. They'd been called to the hall and Brienne knew that meant the large room over in the main keep, so she walked behind the others.

As they made their way across the yard, Brienne realized that she missed the friendly conversations that sprang up as villagers went about their daily business. Neighbors spoke to one another. Mothers called out to their children. Everyone was at ease among themselves. Here no one addressed anyone else. When the lady or lord crossed the yard, all motion and talking stopped. No one spoke unless they were spoken to first. A sense of unease pervaded Yester.

The sunlight could not break through the thick clouds that swarmed the sky above her this day. And just so, for the dreariness suited her well. Her head and body ached from last night. Having a power such as theirs and knowing his ways, she should not be surprised at his ruthless method of instructing her. Succeed or die was the message he gave, and she would learn it one way or the other.

She'd heard rumors about his abilities and his dark practices, and Brienne thought those who spoke of them must have some knowledge about him. From what she'd witnessed so far, the rumors were correct. He had power of fire. He could force people to do his bidding with only his thoughts and could read the thoughts of others. He could call forth the dark magic and cast spells.

She shivered then, remembering how she'd felt when she first woke up this morning. She had no memory of how she'd come to be there. The last thing she remembered was his orders to bring forth a sphere of fire and hold it before her.

Then a barrage of fire and pain had come at her and she'd fought to keep the sphere and protect herself. When her garments caught fire and burned her, she knew she'd failed and expected to die. Instead she'd awoken back in the bedchamber.

Now that she thought on it, it would make no sense to let her die. Lord Hugh knew she did not understand her power yet and was inexperienced in using it. He would not want to bring her here and then allow her to perish so quickly. So she would need to learn faster and better. To make up for lost years of learning and to gain the skill that he had and to control the fire in her blood.

Brienne knew that she would. For in the midst of it all last night, when she'd perfected that sphere, it had been pleasurable and invigorating. The fire raced in her blood and into the ball and back into her, a cycle that sent splinters of sheer bliss coursing through her. It was a feeling she liked, one she wanted to feel again.

After keeping it so secret and daring to let it free in only tiny bursts, allowing it to flow and directing its path felt right. She was a fireblood, he'd told her, and she made fire the way that others breathed. It was not evil or bad; it simply *was*. Brienne found the experience thrilling. She knew she needed to be able to release her power, and she wanted to feel it burn through her blood as it moved.

The winds picked up then, and the smell of rain filled the air around them. Lady Margaret began walking faster, and the others rushed to get to the keep before the rains came in earnest. Tilting her head down, she ran up the stone steps and into the keep. Once inside, she waited for Lady Margaret to lead the way.

They entered the great hall. It was the first time Brienne would be joining them for a meal. Brienne saw Lord Hugh coming toward them. Lady Margaret, apparently thinking he would speak to her, moved toward him. But her husband walked past her directly for Brienne, drawing her away to speak privately. When Brienne glanced over her shoulder, the lady's mouth hung open in surprise before she closed it with an angry breath.

"Are you well this morn, Brienne?" he asked in a low voice, releasing her as soon as they were far enough from the others. She might have mistaken his question for concern had she not met his gaze just then and saw the cold, calculating stare of a man with plans.

"I am sore and tired, my lord," she said.

"Too sore and tired to continue your lessons this night?" he asked. Again, coming from another, it would have been solicitous, but from him, she sensed he was already wondering if he'd overestimated her.

"Nay." She already knew she would suffer whatever she must to free the fire from her blood again.

"Nay?" he asked. She felt the pain that told of his displeasure, and she hissed in a breath at it. He did not like her to be familiar with him. She'd forgotten.

"Nay, my lord," she said, closing her eyes against the continuing pressure in her head. "I am neither too tired nor too sore to have lessons this night."

"Very well," he said. "I will come for you. Be ready."

He stepped back, and the pain eased against her mind. Thinking he was done speaking to her, she turned back to where the women waited.

"Brienne." She faced him and waited for the rest. "I have a surprise for you. A guest I thought you might like to see."

Lord Hugh would never have invited her pa—Gavin and Fia—here to the keep, so she could not think of who it could be. He walked back to the table, and she waited as Lady Margaret and Adelaide took their places. With a curt gesture, she was directed to the last seat on the end. Never having dreamed she'd eat a meal here in the keep, she did not mind. The servants, the ladies' maids, and companions who'd accompanied them took seats at the lower table. Glancing down the table, she noticed the one empty place to Lord Hugh's right.

Only a minute or two later, before cups could be filled or food served, a small group of men entered the hall and walked toward the table. Most of them stopped and sat at one of the lower tables, but one continued up the dais to the high table.

"My lord," he said, "my thanks for inviting us to share your meal this day." The tone was not precisely pleasant, but it was respectful. It was Sir William.

"Welcome, Sir William," Lord Hugh said. "Here is your place. I wish to continue our discussion about your plans for the king's grant of lands."

Once he took the seat offered to him, Brienne could see him but he could not see her, unless he leaned and looked past all the others between them. But she could see his men clearly and they her, and they recognized her immediately. Brienne watched as they talked among themselves, nodding in her direction.

He must have noticed, for he leaned forward then and met her gaze. She offered a smile and a nod before Adelaide kicked her under the table.

"My lord father will be displeased if you pay notice to a male guest," she whispered furiously without looking at her. "Look away, you little fool!"

Reacting to the orders of the lord's daughter as she had learned to do, she lowered her head and did not look back up.

What must he think of her now? What had Lord Hugh told him about her?

The food placed before her tasted like dirt, and she forced herself to eat enough that she would not gain notice by those watching her. She listened to Lord Hugh's voice, strong and confident, and Sir William's as they talked through the meal. Though unable to hear the words, the discussion sounded friendly. Then, as the plates and food were cleared from the table, Lord Hugh's voice called out to her.

"Brienne, come here."

William watched as she stood at the end of the table and walked to Lord Hugh. He'd been trying to watch her through the meal, but her placement made it difficult to see her. Then, as the meal ended, Lord Hugh called out her name.

"You seemed interested in the newest member of my household, Sir William. So," he said, motioning her closer, "here she is. Brienne, I think you know Sir William."

"Aye, my lord," she said softly. Why wouldn't she meet his gaze? And she trembled as though fearful of him. Why? He glanced down at his men, who watched the scene closely.

"Brienne told me that she met you on your arrival in Yester, Sir William. On the road to the village, I believe?"

He could feel her hold her breath as though she expected repudiation of her words. He looked at Lord Hugh.

"Aye, my lord. That is true. We wanted to know if you were in residence, and we met some of your villagers on their return."

"And what did they tell you?" Once more the tension thickened around the three of them, as though the other two waited for some misstep to occur.

"They could tell me nothing, for they were returning from some journey and knew not if you were here," William answered truthfully.

"You may go, girl," Lord Hugh ordered, and she walked away.

"I was surprised to see her here, my lord," William said. "I thought her one of your villeins." From her placement at the far end next to Lady Adelaide, he now thought she might be serving as the lady's maid.

"Nay, villein no longer. She is one of my bastards, recently claimed and brought here to live," he said, holding his cup up to be filled. "You understand how difficult it can be to keep track of a lifetime of bastards; do you not, Sir William?" Lord Hugh chuckled as he lifted the cup to his mouth and drank deeply from it. "But I am carrying out my fatherly duties now that I know of her."

William tried not to let his surprise show. He'd thought of many possibilities and relationships between Brienne and Lord Hugh and never once considered this bond. He forced himself not to look down the table at her where she'd returned to her chair.

The irony of the situation was not lost on him.

As one of the king's oldest counselors and guardians, Hugh de Gifford knew more than most about William's parentage—he knew the rumors and he knew the truth. His words were an efficient reminder of William's small place in the king's very large world. A large world that Hugh had influenced for years.

Unable to argue or make a sensible reply to his host's inflammatory comment, William drank from his own cup of ale. After last night's reaction to the wine, he would avoid that again.

"You trained with my men yesterday."

"I did. They are proficient, and it felt good to work

out after so many weeks of inactivity." The conversation backed away from personal insult to more acceptable topics between noblemen.

"I saw only a bit of it and would like to see more. Would you remain as my guest for a few more days and show me some of your legendary prowess as a fighter? Eudes, my commander, spoke highly of your abilities."

"If you wish, my lord," he said, giving the correct and polite answer. Welcomed, he could observe more and find out what was happening here. And now, with this revelation about Brienne, he wanted to speak to her, to find out more.

"Excellent. Eudes," he called out. The huge, brawny man lumbered his way forward to stand before the dais. "Sir William and his men will train our soldiers. Choose the best and give them orders thusly." Standing, Lord Hugh nodded at him and then left.

The hall emptied quickly once the lord left, and William watched with his men as the ladies, including Brienne, walked by on their way back to the family's building. She would not look at him now. He could feel the misery pouring from her and her shame at being exposed as a bastard. Remembering the first time someone had called him that, he understood how it must feel to her.

He would bide his time until he could talk to her. His blood pounded once more, but this time, he felt the need to comfort her.

He and his men walked out of the keep and watched the torrents of rain turn the yard into a quagmire of mud and puddles. It was too dangerous for men or horses, so they went to William's chambers to talk. For even as the day passed without discovering anything incriminating against the lord of Gifford and Yester, dark feelings swirled around this place, around these people and their lord.

And William knew this was the center of what was to come.

CHAPTER 16

B rienne stared out the window at the rain.

Emilie made some noise of displeasure again at having the shutters thrown open, allowing the damp air to enter the chamber. But Brienne had no intention of closing the window. The air from the storm might be moist and chilled, but it was fresh and somehow soothed her jagged nerves and heart.

For the whole of her life since discovering the truth of her parentage, she'd borne the sidelong glances and the careful distance most of those in the village served her. She'd accepted that being the natural daughter of Lord Hugh would keep her apart and separate from most of them. That James and his parents had overcome that and considered her for his wife was a credit to them, for none of the other families ever had.

But having Sir William know her truth tore her apart. She'd heard her father's words as she'd walked back to her seat and felt disappointment and shame bloom inside her with every step.

Mercifully, the meal did not last much longer, but her torment would, for her father had invited the knight and his men to remain as guests. So the chance that she would see him again was great. She would face the shame each time, for being the daughter of the blacksmith was more honorable than being a bastard of a nobleman who had discarded you until you were needed.

Now her black mood made her restless. The rains eased, but the sun was far from shining. She wanted to walk. She needed to get out of this chamber, this keep, this castle. Knowing Lord Hugh would not allow the last, she decided for the first two. But glancing down at the costly gown and shoes, she knew could not ruin them due to her own poor temper.

"Emilie," she said without facing the girl. "Leave me."

"But, Brienne, your father—"

"I know my father's orders and yours." She turned then and crossed her arms over her chest as she'd seen Lord Hugh do many times now. "Leave me." Brienne did not relent and did not drop her gaze until Emilie did.

"If—"

"If *anyone* asks, I am resting, as I will be," she said, giving the girl the excuse she needed. She was being watched at all times—he knew that—so she would need a little help in getting out unobserved. "Please send for some hot water. I wish to wash."

"A bath, Brienne?"

She shook her head. "I had not time to wash before the meal and wish to before I rest. A bucket of hot water will be plenty for my needs." It was a task that would require one kitchen maid and not an onslaught of servants.

Emilie left then, without argument, and Brienne reached behind the headboard of the bed, where she'd managed to stuff her one remaining plain gown, which she'd worn when she was brought here. It was accustomed to being in the rain. As was she. She undressed quickly, for she knew one thing about the servants here—they did as ordered very, very quickly. When the knock came on the door, Brienne was ready.

A few minutes later, a young serving woman left the family residence and walked toward the oldest part of the castle, where the ancient keep lay in ruins just outside the walls. And, there, tucked into an alcove near the stables and not far from where she'd watched Sir William, she breathed in the damp, wet air and did not care if the rain dripped on her head from the roof above.

"This is the Brienne I would recognize."

His deep voice invaded the silent cocoon she'd created to block out everything but the sound and the feel of the rain. She opened her eyes and found Sir William standing before her, outlined by a still-unworthy sun's light. He stepped back, and she could see the soft smile on his face.

"And which one do you recognize, Sir William?" she asked. Her dark mood remained in place, and she wished, against all reason, to hear his thoughts on who she, Brienne, was. He crouched down before her, bringing their faces level, and reached out to push a sopping-wet tress of hair from her face.

"This is the Brienne who haunts the forests and the paths of the village," he said quietly. "This is the blacksmith's daughter who fears no one, not even the king's knight."

Tears, damn her, filled her eyes then, and she looked away. Pulling her ragged edges together, she looked back at him. "Blacksmith's daughter no more."

"Blacksmith's daughter or lord's bastard, they will call you what they will. But you must know in your heart which one you are. Who and what you are, Brienne. And let no one take that from you." He touched her cheek and wiped a tear away. "No one."

She cried then, letting out the uncertainty and the pain and the fear. When there seemed no more tears to flow, she lifted her head and realized he'd slid in next to her in the small alcove and gathered her onto his lap, holding her while she sobbed.

"Better, demoiselle?"

She nodded her head. Now her own sense of mortification added to the shame she felt when this man looked at her. He lifted her face with his finger beneath her chin and shook his head. Brienne wanted to cry once more at the sympathy in his gaze.

"Hush now," he whispered. "Sometimes you must simply decide who you are and not let anyone tell you otherwise."

"Sir William," she said as she began to push off him. He held her with just enough strength to keep her there.

"William," he corrected her.

"I should go," she said. Her moments of self-pity passed, she knew she would be missed. But these next words stopped her from moving and nearly from breathing.

"I understand how you feel, Brienne," William whispered. "I, too, am a bastard." The puzzlement made her brows furrow as she thought on his words.

William had never willingly admitted it before. Those who knew did not hear it from him unless there was a dire need. The men in his hillside camp who would face the coming danger with him. Roger and Gautier. And that was the end of the list of those to whom he had disclosed his shame.

And now this young woman before him.

"My mother's husband was bought for her to cover the truth. She went to him already months into carrying me. It did not take long for the rumors and insults to begin in my life."

"But you are a de Brus," she said. "Part of a noble family. Raised as a nobleman's son. Claimed by him."

"You were raised by the blacksmith as his daughter. Now claimed as a nobleman's," he offered.

"That is not the same," she began. He shook his head and touched his finger to her lips. Her eyes, the color of the amber seen during sunset, widened at his touch.

"Nay, 'tis not the same. You were raised by a mother and father who wanted you. Raised with love and pride. Now your true father claims you and raises you to the position you should have as his." He could not keep the bitterness from his voice. His intention to ease her shame was quickly becoming something else.

"So," he said, pushing to his feet and allowing her to slide to hers, "that is my sad story. But the wisdom I would offer you, *chérie*, is to decide now, now that your life has changed because of your past. Decide who you are and stay true to it. For many others will try to determine that for you, whether you are called the blacksmith's daughter or Lord Hugh's get."

He could not resist her soft mouth, which beckoned to him. Leaning down, he touched his lips to hers and felt her sigh escape. He pressed and she opened to him, as though made for him and only him. This kiss was not to possess her or to claim her. He tasted her deeply.

When she arched up against him, pressing her lithesome body against the ridge of his already-hardened flesh, his desire slipped his hold and he kissed her as he wanted to. As he had in the forest. But the lesson to be learned this day would be his, for beneath the desire in this kiss lay her shame. Easing back from her, he stroked her cheek and then released her.

"I must go," she said. His body jolted when she slid the tip of her tongue along her bottom lip. But he wanted only to ease her pain and not begin something he, and he suspected she, would not want to stop.

"Here." He handed her the kerchief he found on the ground next to her. "Go that way, for now that the rains have stopped, men will be heading to the training yard."

She turned and took a step before facing him once more.

"William," she whispered as though the feel of his name on her tongue was sweet, "do you know who your father is?"

He stared away then, looking at the old ruins and the sky behind them. The words he'd offered her as advice came back at him, mocking him for his self-righteousness. After telling her that all that mattered was who you decided to be, William smiled at the irony of his plight and his quest.

"Aye, I do, Brienne."

"And he knows of your birth?"

"Aye, he does."

"And he has not claimed you? I do not understand."

"Worry not over my father, Brienne. I am making my own way, just as you will." He glanced over his shoulder as the sound of people approaching grew louder.

"My thanks for your kindness today," she whispered. Lifting up to her toes, she kissed the edge of his jaw before dashing off around the corner of the building. Leaving him unmanned more completely than he'd felt since he was a young squire seeking his first feminine conquest and failing.

He waited until he did not hear her steps fading away before stepping from the sheltered corner. Eudes began shouting orders for his men to gather and, when he saw William there, he nodded to him. Roger, Gautier, and Armand had followed as he'd told them to, and the four walked to the training yard.

The rains had turned it into a muddy mess, but battles were often fought on ground just like that. What began as dry earth could turn into a bog of mud, blood, and mess as men fell and bled their lives out onto it. Therefore, it made sense to train in just such conditions. As he climbed the fence, taking off his tunic as the others had, he watched Eudes choose his best and line up facing them.

Something tilted in his vision as the lines formed against each other, a sense—nay, the knowledge—that this would happen very soon and the intent then would be violent death and not civil practice.

The call came just after she closed the door to her chambers, pleased that no one had seen her sneaking back into it. Her body trembled from the pleasure of his kiss, and her heart was lighter—not for knowing that he was a bastard, but for the kindness and comfort William showed her. She dipped the kerchief in the now-cooled water to wash her face and hands and found herself on her knees, gasping against the blinding pain.

Come to me now. Now.

Rolling on the floor, she held her hands to her head, trying to block the screaming voice. When the waves of pain eased, she climbed to her knees and then to her feet.

Lord Hugh summoned her now without even being present.

Dizzy from the agony and from the pull of his call, she moved to the door and then into the corridor and through the house. With each step closer to his door, she felt the strength of his anger. Then, standing before it, Brienne realized she'd made a grievous error in seeking to learn about her power and for wanting to use it. Fighting the urge to vomit, she tried to resist him.

Now!

She crashed her body against the door as his power jerked the chain that connected her to him, unable to stop herself and unable to delay for even just the moment it would have taken to lift the latch and enter. Brienne tumbled into the chamber and skidded to the floor before him, scraping her hands and knees on the rough stone floor. Unwilling to anger him further, she stayed on her knees and watched as he walked to stand close enough that the folds of his garments touched her head.

Had word gotten to him so quickly that she'd met with William? That he'd held her and kissed her? Shared his secret with her? Did he think she would give her virtue away much as her mother had—to a nobleman who beckoned her to his bed? Whoring her-self for what?

This time, she heard him gasp.

And that was the only warning she got that he could tell what she was thinking. In the next moment, he grabbed her by the throat and slammed her against the wall.

"What are you thinking?" he demanded. "Why do you look like a peasant again when I gave you appro-priate gowns to wear? I do not wish you to be seen looking like a blacksmith's daughter again!"

And then her dress, the last thing she had to connect her to her previous life, went up in flames, the wet fab-ric first sending off sputters of steam as the water evap-orated, and then it burned. She cried out with the little breath he allowed her and tried to push him off, tearing at his hands and kicking out to free herself.

Only when the gown lay in ashes below her did he relent and drop her to the floor. Naked and gasping for breath, Brienne looked around for something to cover herself. Crawling over to the table, she began to pull the linen cover from it.

"Stop!"

This time the word was spoken so quietly that she thought she misheard. Glancing at him, she found him standing white-faced and shocked, his gaze transfixed on something on her back. Tugging the linen cloth around her aching body, she used the table to help herself to her feet. He was on her before she could take another step, pushing her down across the table and pulling the linen away.

Then nothing but the sound of their breathing filled

the ominous silence in the chamber. His hand was hot and unmoving where it lay on her upper back, holding her body down against the table as she struggled. Then she realized what he must see there. The other mark!

No one knew about it but her moth—Fia—who'd discovered it during her baths as a child. She'd forgotten it, seeing it only once, in a looking glass that belonged to her . . . Fia's friend.

Suddenly, he released her and she slid off the table. When Brienne gathered the linen around her and faced him, she found him sitting in his chair, staring off at the wall. Shaking and bruised, she waited for him to speak. Minutes passed and he did not. He did nothing but stare off, ignoring her.

She'd been thinking about her mother when he'd attacked her. And she could almost hear him thinking about someone when he stared at the dark, flamelike birthmark at the base of her spine. Was that something she'd inherited from the woman who'd given birth to her?

"Who was she, my lord? Who was my mother?" she asked. If he killed her for this question or another, she wanted to know this first.

Minutes passed again with no reaction from him. Then he stood and turned his gaze on her.

"Begin."

She shook her head at him.

Begin!

This time she pushed back, forcing at the word as it still echoed in her mind and thrusting it out. He startled then, and she knew he'd felt it. Nothing as strong or as painful as his had been, but her head did not hurt as much now.

"My mother," she repeated. "Who was my mother?"

Brienne felt his command this time before it entered her, and she pushed against it. His will was stronger and his art more practiced, so she knew she would fail, but she tried anyway. She looked away, finding it easier to battle his invasion when not looking at him.

Begin. Softer now. Not painful, more like someone tapping on her forehead.

My mother? she tapped back.

"She is gone."

She glanced at him then and found him studying her closely, as though awaiting her next move in some game of skill. No anger in his gaze now; she saw only curiosity and . . . searching.

"Was she your whore?"

He stood close enough that she could feel his breath against her face. When and how he had moved, she knew not. His anger was back now. And then, as though he pulled his control around it, his temper eased and he stepped back.

"She was no whore, so do not call her one."

The next question pushed forward and out before Brienne could control herself or consider the danger in poking an angry creature like Lord Hugh.

"What was her name?"

Silence was the reply as he walked back to his chair and sat. Brienne waited, hoping he would tell her, but those hopes were dashed with just one word.

"Begin."

She let out a sigh and cleared her thoughts of all her anger and hope. Thinking only on the power within her, she let it simmer in her blood until the heat pulsed through her as her blood did.

The sphere appeared between them.

The next hours passed with few words and less pain than the first lessons had, and when the sound of her empty stomach gurgling filled the silent chamber as she practiced creating and controlling the different forms of fire, he called an end to it.

"Return to your chamber. I will have your meal sent to you."

She glanced down at the linen that she'd wrapped around her, knowing that many servants and even the lady and her daughter would still be making their way through the building on the floors below them.

"Here," Lord Hugh said. He held out a silken robe to her, and she tugged it on. "Turn around." Clutching the robe to her, she turned, exposing her back to his gaze. She knew he reached out once more, but his hand never touched her. "Go," he said in a whisper.

Brienne tugged the too-long sleeves up and lifted the length of it from the floor. What the servants would think, she did not know. But she knew they would never question her or the lord about it. After curtsying to him and walking to the door, she lifted the latch and tugged, holding the edges of the soft, sliding fabric together in front of her legs.

"I remember not her name."

CHAPTER 17

She dared not look at him then, hearing the words and hearing the lie they were, too. The door closed behind her, and she stood in the hallway alone. She gathered her breath before she headed back to her chamber.

Brienne wondered why he would lie to her. He remembered her mother. She knew it. And yet he'd said he did not. Why? Who could her mother be that he would deny any memory of her?

The promised meal arrived and, thankfully, Emilie did not. The girl must be attending supper in the hall with the rest of them. Brienne ate every speck of food on the tray, even wiping up the sauce with the last bits of bread. With her hunger and thirst appeased and finally cleaned and clothed, she lay on her bed.

The sounds of the keep across the yard traveled through her windows, and she thought about what William had said about the choice she had to make. Lord Hugh's few clues about her mother only fed her confusion. She was the daughter of this nobleman who claimed blood back to the powerful families in Brittany and Normandy. She was the daughter of an unknown woman who had somehow known her father. As an infant, she'd been given over to Gavin and Fia to raise.

No matter their words before Lord Hugh, they had never planned to give her back. Even when they knew he'd noticed her, they still had not wanted to lose her. All of their words, actions, and love claimed her as their daughter.

And to William that love seemed even more important than noble blood. For his sad words revealed the pain of his upbringing—born of some liaison and not wanted by either or any of those he could name as parent.

So, who was she then? What person was she at her core? What part of her could no one take away?

She searched for that Brienne as she drifted into an exhausted sleep, one filled with dreams of William's kisses and the loving embrace of two women—one was Fia but the other one she could never see. She could only hear her voice and the soft song she sang to Brienne before she died.

When morning came, Brienne still had no idea who she was, but the ripples of power coming from beneath the castle and from across the miles told her she would need to know very soon.

Hugh stood on the battlements of the main keep, surveying his lands as the sun rose into a turbulent sky. The storms of yesterday had passed and yet the sky warned of more. He'd passed the night here, climbing to the heights and sending the guards away for the solitude he craved.

Thinking on the way the girl had faced him last evening, he tried not to feel pride in her. Beaten, bruised, exhausted, and frightened, she stood there and defied him. Smiling in spite of himself, he could see her face as she lifted her chin at him and fought off his incursions into her thoughts.

And all to gain the name of the woman who'd given birth to her.

He tried to tell himself it was stupidity on her part, to challenge him when her powers were so feeble and could never hope to beat his, but he felt something profound when she pushed back at him. A need so deep that it gave her more power than she should have. Hugh would usually have just destroyed someone for such an insult, such a challenge.

Then she fell against the table and he saw it.

There on her back was the same birthmark that Jehanne—her mother—bore.

Brienne was not just his bastard daughter—she was all that was left from the only time he'd defied his fate and the plans laid down for generations before him. His only failure.

He tried to remember how Brienne had come to be here in Yester and could remember only a wizened, old midwife arriving at the gates with a squirming, squalling bundle she said was his. She'd said the nameless mother died giving birth and asked what he wanted done with this one, the latest in a long tally of bairns born to women he bedded.

He remembered looking at this one and ordering her to be given to the blacksmith whose wife had just lost a child. For some reason, he had chosen to save this one rather than exposing her in the forest as he had other times. Even back then, in some way, he'd known that this one had meant something.

Now her power was a real thing, and he would mold her to serve the goddess in his plans to free her. She was either the prize who would push the balance to their side, or she was the seed of his destruction planted in the only woman he had ever loved. The woman for whom he had defied his father. The woman for whom he'd been willing to turn his back on his heritage.

In his father's attempts to breed a fireblood that would be more powerful than any before and lead the fight to free the goddess, he'd refused Hugh's request to marry Jehanne and forced him instead to marry Margaret. Jehanne, he'd said, was a mongrel, too much human and too little fireblood to allow her to taint their line.

His father had destroyed Jehanne to demonstrate that he could. And to show Hugh that anything less than complete commitment and compliance to his plans was futile. He'd torn Jehanne's mind in pieces and cast her body aside. Hugh had learned the lesson that night but did not know until now that she'd carried a child.

Now their daughter stood before him, and from the amount of power she carried in her, she stood as proof that his father had been wrong about her mother.

Would this girl be his downfall? When the moment came to sacrifice her in the service of his goddess, would he be able to do as his father had her mother? Or was she his last chance to save his own soul from eternal damnation?

The sun burst through the clouds then, shining

down on his lands and illuminating the fields and the hills around his castle. The followers were gathering, on his lands and near all four of the circles that needed to be destroyed to end the threat to Chaela forever.

Only days stood between now and his destiny.

He'd paid so much for the chance that was coming to him. Generations of his family had followed the goddess for centuries before him, believing in her and her right to rule the world, carrying out the plans that would reestablish her and place his family—and him—at her right hand.

A man rode through the yard below him then, leaving the castle as soon as the gates opened for the day. Peering through the shadows the walls cast, he opened his senses and felt the warblood moving away. De Brus went to visit those he'd left outside the village.

Did he know of his powers yet? Had the dampening effect of the stones and the bespelled chamber that opened into Chaela's prison beneath the ruins kept him completely controlled?

Unfortunately, Hugh needed William's powers unleashed to use them at the stone circle in Daviot. Fortunately, he had just the thing to draw the warblood into play. Hugh made his way back down from the battlements to break his fast.

There were many tasks he needed carried out to prepare to leave Yester. If the plans went as designed, he would never return here, to his lands or to these people.

So many things to do and now so little time in which to accomplish them. His blood raced with excitement, and he left his past and any regrets or doubts high above the castle.

*   *   *

William rode along the path away from the castle and was surprised to see the blacksmith waiting for him. He stopped and dismounted and greeted the man.

"Sir William," the man began, "have you seen Brienne inside?"

William heard the pain and loss in the man's voice and nodded. "I have. She seems well, Gavin."

"He will destroy her." Gavin met his gaze and continued. "And you as well." Did Gavin know of Lord Hugh's seditious plans, then?

"Why would he do that? What would that accomplish?" he asked, trying to draw the man out.

"He is gathering weapons here and men in his northern property."

"I've been inside the castle, the keep, and the other buildings, Gavin. I saw no weapons cache there, and neither have my men."

"They are here in the village. Every cottage. Every building. Ready to be moved soon, according to the command delivered yesterday."

William glanced around at the cottages, estimating their number and how many weapons could be hidden there.

"A score and ten," Gavin replied to the unanswered question. "Cottages and storage huts here. More in Gifford Village."

Even if only a handful of weapons were kept in each place, that meant that hundreds were at Lord Hugh's command. And if there was a man for each weapon, or close to it, that would be a devastating army to put on the field.

"Why do you tell me this?" he asked the man who'd made a great many of those weapons.

"She told me to come to you if there was trouble. Said to trust you." Gavin glanced over his shoulder and up the road. "Trouble is nearly here, and I thought you needed to know."

His task of meeting with his men forgotten in the face of danger to Brienne, William needed to get back inside before Hugh suspected he knew. He mounted and turned his horse toward Yester. Gavin grabbed his leg.

"You must protect her," he said. "I think you are the only one who can. In spite of . . . "

"In spite of what?" he asked, watching the man struggle to choose his words.

"She is Lord Hugh's blood, you know?"

"He told me so." Gavin still did not release him.

"She does not understand the power she holds, Sir William. She did not learn to control it."

"What power, Gavin?"

"She commands the fire, just like her father does." When William did not say anything, the blacksmith's astute gaze studied him. He could tell the moment Gavin knew. "You have seen it, then?" The man let out a breath. "I pray you can help her."

"Why do you think I can? I am but one knight against your lord, these weapons, and his men. And against the power that he and they have."

"I think you give yourself too little credit, sir," Gavin said. "There is something in you that is like them. But you are honorable. I will hold on to my hope that you care for her and that you will be her savior."

Stunned at this man's confidence, especially since he, more than most, knew the true resources his lord held, William could only nod. That the man who stood as father to her requested his help, knowing of his attraction to her, meant a great deal. He nodded then, accepting the task that his blood already had.

He could not do this alone, so he saw to his men, but all the while could not get the blacksmith's words out of his thoughts. Though he had little experience or knowledge in a world where unearthly powers battled with humans, he would never go into any battle unprepared. Knowing what he must do before returning to the castle, William made his way across the valley to the camp where the other watchers were. The man called Marcus walked out to meet him.

"Sir William, welcome," he said. "You look troubled. How can I serve you?" Marcus motioned to a log where he could sit. With a nod of his head, the man warned off several others standing close by, giving them privacy for this.

"What you said before," he began. "What happened . . . ? I need to know what happened."

"We are descended from an ancient people who were faithful to the old gods. Seven bloodlines from the seven gods, and priests to serve and guide them, William."

"What bloodlines?" William asked.

"You are of the warbloods; Brienne is of the firebloods," Marcus explained. "There will be five others—waterblood, stormblood, earthblood, sunblood, and beastblood. We know not who they are."

"You said you knew."

"We know the legends and the prayers, William. The

gods will guide us to those who carry the blood as they brought us here to you and Brienne."

"And Lord Hugh," William finished. "Is he a traitor, as the king suspects?" Marcus shuddered at his question.

"Lord Hugh is the truest believer of the goddess who was conquered and exiled. His family has worked and prepared for this moment for more generations than you could count. He knows more than any of us, and he has terrible gifts from the goddess."

"Tell me of this goddess." Marcus glanced around at the request, clearly nervous about speaking of this goddess.

"There were seven ancients worshipped as gods and goddesses. Six of them—Belenus, Cernunnos, Taranis, Sucellus, Nantosuelta, and Epona—banded together against the seventh when she decided she would rule over all," Marcus explained.

"And her name?" William asked.

"Chaela." Marcus grew more nervous as he spoke the name. "The goddess of fire and destruction and chaos."

Things were becoming clearer, but William needed more than a lesson in history. He needed to know about what had happened to him.

"What are the powers of a warblood, Marcus? How do I use them, if this is all true?"

"Your success at war is no accident, Sir William," Marcus said.

"Certainly, it is not. It is through training and experience that I have been successful on the battlefield. Years of training and years more fighting in elite battle groups across Brittany and here in Scotland."

"I meant no insult, sir," Marcus said, holding up his hands. "I meant that your blood runs strong and heavy with the skills you need on the battlefield. And more recently, your body changes when you face danger. When she faces danger."

William stood and walked away, considering this. He'd noticed it from the first sign of the changes. When he'd thought her threatened, his vision and sense of smell had sharpened, his blood had raced, and his body had grown in size and strength. Each time, the reaction was more pronounced.

"Is it linked to Brienne, then? Can I use this only when she is endangered?"

Running his hands through his hair, he wondered what kind of connection was growing between them. Oh, he was attracted to her, drawn by a desire the likes of which he'd not felt before. But there was more. Something deeper, something caring, already existed and grew stronger.

"I am sorry, Sir William," Marcus said, approaching him and speaking lower. "It has been centuries—nay, longer—since any humans have had and used these powers. We priests have not witnessed such things in a very long time. Though we have heard and studied the legends, I have never practiced making it work with a descendant of the bloodline."

William shook his head, frustrated that he could not learn what he needed if he was to use this power.

"Try to call it hence." He turned to look at the self-proclaimed priest of the ancient gods. "Come into the trees where you will not be seen and call upon it."

He followed the man through the small cluster of tents, already within the trees to a place deeper in the forest. Once they reached a clearing, he turned and faced Marcus.

"I will try to assist you."

"How?" he asked.

"By praying, of course. Calling on the ancients to lead us, to lead you."

The blasphemous thought that Marcus's words were no different from those of the Catholic priests when calling on God entered William's mind then. Shrugging, for he was no theologian or philosopher to debate such a thing, he walked a few paces away and faced Marcus.

Uncertain of what to do, William closed his eyes and thought about the changes he'd noticed before—his vision changing to red, his blood heating and racing within him, and his body growing stronger and larger. Though he felt silly, he called the warblood forth in his thoughts.

"William?"

He heard the priest speak his name. He opened his eyes and watched him take a step away and then another, nodding as he moved.

His vision held a red tint, and he noticed small creatures and the movement of the trees around him. Inhaling, he smelled the fear in the priest's blood and then the scent of a deer close by. Glancing down, he saw larger hands covered in blue-tinged skin rather than his. Flexing them, he ached for a weapon and watched as one hand began to change into . . . something else.

"Warblood," the priest said.

He could hear the pride and wonder in the priest's voice now. Crossing his hands over his chest, he smiled and nodded. He was the warblood.

And then, as quickly as a passing moment, it faded away.

"Sir William?" Marcus asked as he strode to him. "How did you make that happen?"

"I thought about becoming it, thought about the way my sight and smell and body had changed before, and it began."

Can it be that simple?

"It is only the beginning. Your power is just rising, so you should practice this," Marcus advised. "Come when you can and we will continue trying."

"I think I should bring Roger," he said. "For your protection if it gets out of my control."

"Sir William, should the warblood get out of control, it will take much more than one of your human warriors to stop him." Then Marcus shrugged and laughed. "Or one woman."

It all came back to Brienne.

"I will return as I can," he promised. Things were beginning to move now, and William felt the future pressing hard on them. He must be ready. He must learn.

He left Marcus then and rode back to the castle, waiting for Lord Hugh to make his move, all the while knowing he would. The invitation to share a meal with the lord and his family waited for him on his arrival back in his chamber.

CHAPTER 18

Brienne heard his call in her head, yet this time without pain. It was unexpected, for it was morning, and it was his custom to train her in the night. She left her chamber for his. Lady Margaret stood in the corridor outside the tower room and glared as Brienne approached. She curtsied before her father's wife and waited for the insult that always accompanied any encounter between them.

"He is waiting, girl. Hasten to him!" she hissed at her. Then Lady Margaret began calling out orders to the servants who scurried to her side.

Brienne rushed up the steps and knocked before entering. Lord Hugh stood at the window. The sun had won the battle over yesterday's storms, and its light filled the chamber through the costly glazed window in the wall that looked over the yard. For a moment, she did not see the feared lord but a man filled with regrets. But that was not possible.

"Her name was Jehanne. She was a year younger than you are now when we pledged our love."

Stunned by the admission, she said the name in her thoughts. *Jehanne*. Her mother's name was Jehanne.

"Our families opposed the match, and she was sent away. I was told later she died of a wasting disease," he said, his voice catching as he spoke. "I did not know you were hers—ours—until I saw the birthmark on your back. She . . ." He turned away and cleared his throat then. "She had the same one in the same place."

Brienne could not breathe. The truth of her past came rushing at her in a blur. Her parents loved. A forbidden love, stopped by their families. He had not known their connection and now did. Now she did.

Jehanne.

"We firebloods pass our power through our descendants, and my family was part of a plan to protect and preserve our line from ancient days, Brienne. I do not think my father realized your mother carried it as well. Now it is time for you to join our legacy and carry out the next step."

"I do not understand," she said. "Legacy? What about Adelaide? She is your legitimate heir and . . . "

"She cannot be part of this, for she has nothing in her blood but her humanity. Not like you," he said, walking to her and gazing at her with something she never thought she'd see—pride. "Be at my side; claim your rightful place as our plan moves forward." He held out his hand to her, and she stared at it.

Her heart beat so fast and hard, Brienne thought it would tear out of her chest. The pain of the past, being forgotten and shamed disappeared then. Everything she'd wanted was being offered to her. A small voice whispered in the back of her mind to have a care, but it mattered not.

"What is this plan, my lord? How can I be part of it?"

He led her to a chair and poured some wine into a cup. Much richer than the ale she usually drank, it was sweet and potent and reminded her of the wine William had offered her. She drank another mouthful and waited on her father's words.

"We are part of an ancient people, Brienne, descended from the gods whom the Celts worshipped before coming to these islands. We were blessed with their powers so that we could remain faithful to them. But over the centuries the old beliefs have fallen away, and now this other religion seeks to control all. In the north, my grandfather discovered the sacred place where the old gods could be called forth and hid it from those who would destroy it."

Old gods? Powers? Sacred place? Her head spun from hearing all of this. She was a simple girl, brought up to believe in one God, though now she realized that in her village, no one ever said so publicly. No priest saw to their souls, but she remembered hearing one mentioned from long ago. "Old gods?" she asked.

"Aye, the ancient seven," he said. A shadow crossed his face as he mentioned them, quickly gone. "Worry not over that now. I can teach you all about them as we travel north. We must gather our friends to us and go there, to protect it once more from destruction."

"North?" she asked. She knew Lord Hugh held properties in places all over Scotland even if Yester and Gifford were the only two she'd ever seen. She thought on the rest of his words. "But who knows of this and seeks to destroy such a place?" She knew the answer even as she uttered the question. "The king?" she whispered.

"Aye. I have been his closest adviser since his boyhood and knew he sought the place, and I have tried to prevent that. He knows that the legends were true and seeks to destroy what could threaten his control and his kingdom."

So many questions flooded her mind that she could not sort through them. And then she realized the part she'd missed. The king knew. The king sent . . .

Sir William de Brus, the king's knight.

"William is part of this, too?" At his nod, her heart fell.

"He is here to spy for the king, who suspects my part in this." She closed her eyes. "But I plan to explain this and ask for his help."

"You do?" She stood and walked to where he was. "Do you think he will? Mayhap if he understands?"

"He would be a huge advantage to have on our side. You have seen him fight," he said. "A warrior like him could help us."

"He is . . . ?" That little voice whispered not to give too much away. With what she'd witnessed, Brienne suspected he was involved in this more than her father let on.

"He is?"

"Very experienced? In war and fighting?" She shrugged then. "I have not met many men outside the village, my lord. I have nothing to compare him to."

He nodded, watching her now. Did he suspect what she did about William, or did he know?

"Ah, I forget you have not seen more of the country or the world outside these walls and lands. Aye, he has fought before, in France and here, too, I think. And he is skilled."

They remained silent for a few minutes, and she

thought on everything he'd said. She wanted to be part of her father's family. She'd longed for such a thing, and now he was offering it to her, asking her to join him in this strange endeavor.

"Is there anything I can do, my lord? To help you?" she asked, making her decision. There was much yet unknown in this, she knew, but she took this step now. He smiled at her, and once more pride was there in his eyes.

"I think if he sees that you are at ease here and part of the larger plan, he might see reason. I will speak to him about specific things, but if you are welcoming to him, it could ease the tension between us."

"But, my lord," she began. "It is not my place to do that. Lady Margaret or Lady Adelaide . . . "

"They will be leaving on the morrow to travel to our holdings in Brittany." He shrugged then. "My wife failed in her duty, giving me neither a son nor a child of the blood I needed." Stunned at such a revelation, she gasped. He shook his head and laughed.

"Worry not over them, Brienne. Both will be well compensated with lands and gold. A marriage has already been arranged for Adelaide. They go now to see to it."

Though she knew of such things, that nobles married for titles, lands, and gold, because she knew the warmth of love, the coldhearted sound of it shocked her.

"So, Jehanne's daughter, it is good to know that you will be at my side in this grand effort to right past wrongs." He walked toward the door, and Brienne followed. "We will begin our campaign to bring Sir William to our side at supper. He will dine with us in the family hall. Prepare yourself well."

With that, he lifted the latch and opened the door, allowing her to leave. She practically floated down the stairs and along the corridor, ignoring the servants and the noises and everything.

Jehanne's daughter, he'd called her.

William followed the servant from the main keep over to where the family and closest retainers lived. His men would eat with the others in the hall. He felt naked, wearing only his eating dagger and no other weapon, and uncomfortable. Though with the number of armed guards scattered around every step of the path they took, unless he was mounted and armored, he would stand no chance of even surviving if they turned on him.

He nodded to several soldiers he'd trained with over the last few days here. Lord Hugh had a core group of warriors who would be formidable in a battle, and William hoped his premonition that he would be the one they fought was wrong. But he'd long ago learned to trust that sense, and it had saved his life many times.

He climbed the steps to a higher story and down a corridor. The chamber they entered was a large one, holding one long table and several smaller ones. This night, only the long table was prepared for use. He'd been escorted to his seat when Lord Hugh arrived . . . with Brienne at his side. His surprise was even greater when Lady Margaret and Lady Adelaide entered behind them. If anyone thought this unusual, they did not show it by expression, glance, or gesture. A few higher servants and companions of the ladies took their places, and everyone waited on Lord Hugh to sit.

William discovered that because it was such a small

group, they were seated on both sides of the table instead of all along one side. And it placed him where he could watch and speak to Brienne.

Dressed in a simple but costly gown that nearly matched the shade of her unusual eyes, she was a treat to watch. It was hard to believe that just a week before, this young woman had lived in the village. She spoke quietly with two of the women who served as companions to the women in Lord Hugh's family. He could not help but smile when her face lit in delight at something she heard.

The meal began and continued through several servings. Heavy platters of roasted meat and fowl, pots of stew, wheels of cheese, and loaves of bread filled the table until he swore it buckled in the middle. Servants paced, quietly and efficiently, around them, assisting with the food, offering wine and ale, until everyone had eaten their fill.

Through it all, William watched her. A few times, he answered her questions about other places in Scotland or in France. He listened to her throughout supper and enjoyed her curiosity about what lay outside Yester's boundaries and outside Lord Hugh's dominion. For a moment he thought about taking her and escaping these lands, going back to France and showing her the sunny fields where grapes grew. Or to visit his mother's family holdings near the coast, with its turquoise waters and warm, sandy beaches.

He ached to have her to himself, away from the king, away from her father, and away from all the intrigue and danger that festered around them. But wanting could never be having.

"She has blossomed, has she not, Sir William?" He

turned to Lord Hugh, who watched him with much interest, almost as interested as he'd been in Brienne.

"She is lovely, my lord," he admitted.

No one with eyes that could see would not agree with that now. Garbed as a lady instead of a villager, she seemed at ease with it all. Lovely and more to him, she yet glowed as no other woman did in his sight. There was something between them that pulled his attention back to her, over and over. He wanted to sit and watch her uninterrupted by duty, by honor, by any other demands on him.

"Lady Margaret," Lord Hugh said, a bit louder. "Are the arrangements made for the morrow?" William glanced down at the lady, who stopped her conversation and nodded to her husband.

"Aye, my lord. As you ordered," she replied in a low, respectful tone. "We leave after we break our fast in the morning."

"Very well," he said. "Adelaide, you are accustomed to this betrothal?"

"Aye, my lord," came the reply from the young lady, who sat motionless next to her mother. "Certainly, my lord."

"Then mayhap you should retire early so that you are well rested for your journey?"

Stools scraped back along the stone floor, almost in unison, as they obeyed his suggestion immediately as the command it truly was. He and the other men stood and watched as they left. The servants cleared the table of the remnants of the meal and placed trays of sweet pastries and cakes before Lord Hugh.

"Come, Brienne," he said then to the only remaining

woman in the chamber. "You need not sit over there by yourself. If you are not too tired, stay with us."

Instead of the stern, unfeeling voice with which he'd ordered his wife and daughter away, he spoke to her softly, inviting her to stay.

William waited for her to sit, now in the seat next to him to the right, and then he sat. Eudes and the captain of his guards sat on the other side of Lord Hugh. Alain, his steward, faced his lord, seated to William's left. As Lord Hugh's discussion about travel arrangements continued with his men, William turned to Brienne.

"You seem more at peace, Brienne," he said quietly.

"I am, Sir William," she said, smiling. "I thought on your words and their wisdom. And I thank you for your friendship at a time when I needed it most." She touched him then, resting her hand on his. "This is where I wish to be."

Though his body reacted to just this slight contact, he tamped down the feelings that coursed through him.

"I wish I could follow my own advice," he said, keeping his hand still so she did not realize she yet touched him. "I am always so much more proficient at sharing my wisdom than in learning from it myself."

She laughed, and for a moment he forgot where they were. He'd seen her in fear, in passion, in the village, and here in the castle, and yet he did not remember hearing her laugh aloud like that before. He glanced over to see Lord Hugh's reaction, but he was engrossed in the discussion with his men.

"So," he said in a low voice, "Lady Margaret is leaving in the morn? And you remain?"

"Aye. Apparently this betrothal requires a visit, and so the lady is seeing to it. I was . . . not invited to accompany them."

"You do not look disappointed in the least," he offered, watching the delicate skin around her eyes crinkle as she smiled and shook her head.

"I would prefer not to leave here," she admitted. " 'Tis the only place I've known."

He wanted to pass on word from Gavin but feared upsetting her. Her next words gave him the opportunity he needed.

"I know you have been through the village. Have you seen . . . him? Them?" she asked.

She smiled, but it was forced, the trembling in her lower lip exposing her vulnerability to anyone watching or listening. He stopped his thumb from touching her lip, as he wanted to, tucking his hand under his leg to keep from raising it to her face.

"Aye. This very morn," he said. "I saw Gavin on my ride through the village to the hills. He asked about you."

"How does he fare?" she asked. "Was my moth—Fia—with him?"

She had stopped calling them mother and father already. From the way her gaze flitted over to Lord Hugh's as she mentioned them, he suspected it was her lord father's decision to end that custom.

"He seemed well," he lied. "He wanted to know about you and your new life here in the keep." That part was true. "Has Lord Hugh forbidden you to leave the castle?"

"Not forbidden, nay," she replied. "He asked me to

remain here until I learned . . . until I learn what is expected of me as his daughter."

He heard the hesitation in her voice and, from what Gavin had told him, he knew the reason—Lord Hugh was teaching her how to use her power over fire.

"And you agreed?" he asked, watching for signs of truth or lies in her answer.

"I have agreed, though sometimes I simply want to wake in the morning and find myself back in Gavin and Fia's cottage."

"He is a hard taskmaster, then?" He leaned back, enjoying the few minutes of conversation with her.

"Aye, very," she admitted. "But I have so much to learn and so little time in which to do so."

He was about to ask her about that, and he suspected it had to do with the bad feeling he had, but Lord Hugh interrupted then.

"Sir William, excuse my poor manners," he said, standing. William and Brienne did so. "I must give Eudes a document from my chambers. Brienne, please keep our guest entertained in my absence."

A blush crept up her cheeks at his request, and she nodded, clasping her hands in a way that showed how pleased she was to be asked. Within a few moments, all of the men followed Lord Hugh out of the chamber, leaving him alone with Brienne.

"Are you truly well and pleased by this change in your circumstances, then, Brienne?" He sensed something deeper in her that he could not name. Some ambiguity clouding her joy. "No regrets?" He would be leaving soon and wanted—nay, needed—to know she would be well.

"I do miss them," she said. "I miss Gavin and Fia, I miss telling them of my day, asking their advice. I miss knowing my place and what is expected of me." She glanced around and leaned closer. "You noblemen have so many rules to follow."

"*We* nobles," he corrected. "You have joined our ranks now, Brienne." He watched as she thought on that.

"Oh, aye." She nodded and glanced off over his shoulder for a moment. "Who could have thought that a simple word of acceptance from one lord could have changed my life so much?"

And that sentiment described his life as well, for with one word from the king, one acknowledging word, William's life could be as he wished it to be. He noticed she was now watching him closely.

"That could be said for you—could it not, William?"

Had she read it in his eyes? Or just known the secrets of his heart? "Aye, it could be, Brienne."

He had never spoken of his bastardy to a woman before, never exposed what he considered his unworthiness as he had to her. Another connection he felt that tied them together in some way. And yet he would be leaving soon to report back to the king. Leaving her here.

"But your father has raised you and mine will not."

"Who is he, William? Who is your father?"

Any temptation to reveal it to her—and his heart wanted her to know his truth—stopped at the sound of steps down the corridor outside. He waited to see if Lord Hugh returned.

"Sir William," a servant said to him with a bow. "Lord Hugh is detained with matters he must see to and wishes you to remain at your pleasure here." Then the man turned to Brienne. "Your lord father bids you to see to Sir William's comfort and to escort him to the yard when he has finished."

With the extraordinary message delivered, the man left, and as his footsteps and his presence faded, William understood that this was planned. A battle strategy, plain and simple, for no nobleman would leave his unmarried daughter alone with any man not related by blood and rarely with one related by marriage.

And yet here they sat. The bigger question was—did she know? Brienne stood in the heavy silence and brought a pitcher of wine over to fill his cup. He covered it and shook his head.

"I have had enough wine this night. But my thanks."

She placed it down and returned to the seat next to him. "Have you eaten your fill? These"—she picked up a small, sticky, folded pastry and held it before him—"are my favorites."

"Here only a few days and you already have a favorite?" he asked.

"There is a chance I will discover something more pleasing, but for now this is my choice."

She nodded and brought it closer to his mouth, offering it to him. He opened and took a bite, careful not to touch her fingers as he did. There was an intense burst of sweetness, and then a spicy flavor filled his mouth. He could not identify the flavor, but it was quite good. He watched her eyes as she brought the rest of it to his mouth. This time his lips touched her fingers as he took the rest of it in.

He grasped her hand, holding it to his mouth, and licked the rest of the sweetness off her fingers, one by one. Her mouth dropped open and her eyes widened as he suckled first one, then the next, then the next.

William knew that the sweet flavor of the pastry was not the one he wanted to savor—he wanted the woman sitting next to him. He tugged her closer and kissed her mouth.

She leaned in to him then, her hand sliding along his arm and up onto his shoulder to steady herself as she kissed him back. Her tongue slid along his lips, and she murmured her surprise at the sticky coating that remained from the pastry on his lips.

"Sweet," she whispered against his mouth.

"Aye, sweet," he whispered back, plunging his tongue deeper inside her mouth.

Their tongues played and swirled, and he sucked hers into his mouth. She learned quickly, for she did the same thing to his, and he savored the taste that was only her. A mixture of innocence, curiosity, and desire.

He took her by the shoulders and pulled her across his legs, never breaking the touch of their mouths. She wrapped her arms around his neck and returned his kisses until they both were breathless. Drawing back, he watched as she lifted her hand and traced down his cheeks and along his jaw.

"You terrified me," she admitted to him. "When you first arrived here, you were so stern and forbidding."

"When did I stop terrifying you?" he asked, curiosity now his to suffer.

"I think I still am a bit," she whispered, pressing her mouth against his. He tilted his head and kissed her again.

"You do not look terrified," he teased.

"You were the first man from outside the village and castle who spoke to me. You are a man of war. You come from the king. All of those were good reasons to fear you," she explained. All the while her finger teased his skin.

"You do not look frightened now, Brienne." She looked well kissed and bolder than any woman he'd kissed before. "When did you stop?"

"When you came charging after me when those men took me, no matter the danger to yourself." She stroked along his jaw and outlined his lips. "When you tried to tell me about the dangers of men like you." Her finger slid along his face and circled his ear, making him shiver. "When you touched me."

Her body arched against his, and for a moment he wanted to lay her on the table and finish what they'd begun that day in the forest. To peel off the layers she wore and taste every inch of her skin until she opened for him. His breathing became even more ragged, and the battle for control was nearly lost when she slid her hands into his hair and pulled his face to hers, kissing him with abandon.

"But mostly when you held me in the rain," she whispered when she could speak again.

The footsteps coming down the corridor finally reminded him of their location and stopped her—stopped him—from moving forward. Instead he lifted her from his lap and put her back on the chair. Standing, he adjusted his breeches and walked a few paces away, as though retrieving the pitcher of water had been his intent all along and not the utter and complete ravishment of the lord's newly claimed daughter.

The person turned in to a chamber before this one and he let out his breath. Though the cockstand that never disappeared when he was near her would argue, the moment, the madness, was over.

"Brienne," he began. "I apologize for my behavior. I . . ."

How could he explain it to her? She was an innocent. Though if she continued gazing at him with her luminous eyes and well-kissed mouth, he might not be the man of honor he proclaimed himself to be.

"I should return to my chambers. I am certain you will be awake early and be asked to help the lady prepare for her journey."

She stood then and nodded at him. "Let me show you how to reach the main floor," she said as she walked from the chamber.

He took her hand and pulled her to a stop then.

"Brienne, I will be leaving soon, returning to the king and then on to my lands."

"You must leave?" she asked. "My father . . ." She did not finish her words then. It was the first time he'd heard her refer to Lord Hugh as simply her father.

"I will not leave without speaking to him first," he replied. She nodded. "I wish . . ."

He might wish and he might want, but he would not burden her now with the promise or hope of something that was impossible between them. Not now that she was claimed and recognized and would be a great heiress regardless of her illegitimacy. He did not finish the words he'd begun. He just pulled her to him and kissed her gently. A farewell, for he knew he would leave soon after Lady Margaret and her entourage did in the morning.

They walked wordlessly, the silence growing heavy between them. When they reached the stairway that would take him down to the main floor and to the door to the yard, they paused.

"You know that you need only send word if you need me?"

She searched his face. "So, you are leaving?"

" 'Tis time, Brienne. You must get on with your life, and I must with mine."

"Your father? You will seek his acknowledgment now?"

"I am beginning to believe that is not the most important thing."

"Then what is, William?" she asked as he took the first step that would separate them.

"I think I need to know who I am no matter what others call me." The smile was both sad and knowing, and the tear that tracked down her cheek was nearly his undoing.

"Ah." She nodded. "Words of wisdom I have heard as well."

He left then, turning and forcing his feet to move away, step by infinitely harder step. The door closed behind him, and he continued across the near-empty yard.

As he reached the main keep and entered the side door, William realized that for the first time, it had been just them—just William and Brienne, a man and a woman, with no concern over powers or dangers or threats or positions or others.

He realized that he would miss that most of all when he left.

William reached his chambers and closed the door behind him, never realizing he was being followed.

CHAPTER 19

Brienne knew full well what Lord Hugh was doing. He'd asked her to make William welcome so that he could persuade him to join their endeavor. If allowing a man access to his unmarried daughter would be that persuasion, Lord Hugh would allow it.

And he had.

As much as she'd like to think that her virtue would be too high a price for his cooperation, men like her father cared little for anything so insignificant as his daughter's honor. She had no doubt that he thought of her in the same cold and calculating way in which he thought of Adelaide. Her sister's betrothal would bring him something he wanted or needed, and so she'd be sent off to accomplish his goal.

She watched William walk back to the keep through the crack in the doorframe and knew that no matter what her father intended to offer him, he would turn it down if it meant betraying his king and his honor.

Even if her father offered her as the compensation for breaking his oath to the king.

Lord Hugh had left them alone. He'd sent someone

to interrupt at just the most inopportune time, thwarting any attempt to seduce her directly. She also knew with a certainty that he would offer her as bed play to the knight soon. She'd seen the whores who offered their services in the village do the same thing to increase the gold or trinkets that they got in return. Build a man's lust until he would pay the price. This dinner and Lord Hugh's timely absence played out just like that.

William was not the only one who would expect to pay the price for his father's approval. Brienne had entered into this night knowing full well that her father manipulated her. Something so keenly desired would have a dear price, but after years of waiting and wanting, she was now willing to pay it in order to excel at her fire powers. At first she'd decided she would allow this one expense, for there was still so much to learn before she could understand it all.

But there had been a moment during the meal when she'd decided that this night would be for her and not her father or anyone else. William had been watching her throughout the meal—also part of her father's planning—and she watched him as he described his visit to the west of Scotland. His face lit and the smile softened his features until she wanted to reach out and touch him.

Which she had done, once everyone was gone.

Her body throbbed from his kisses and the strength in his embrace. Her blood heated, from desire not from the power in it. The taste of his mouth and the sweet she'd fed him lingered yet on her tongue. She wanted to feast on him, to touch more than just his hand or his face. She wanted . . .

Him.

For herself. Not as a pawn in some plan.

Looking around, she saw no one. She listened and silence greeted her. Everyone, including the servants, had retired, knowing the busy and early morning they faced. Peeking through the crack once more, she saw that he'd reached the steps of the keep.

If she could not have him forever, could she instead have him for this night?

She was across the yard, using the shadows to cover her movements as she went, before she realized she'd made the decision. He'd gone in the side door, so she followed, not wanting to lose him since she did not know her way around the main keep yet. Creeping along the edge of the hall, she passed by those who slept here, careful not to wake anyone.

He'd already entered the chamber when she reached the floor above. She watched as light escaped underneath the door and knew which was his. Brienne waited for a minute or two before his door, gathering her courage, then lifted the latch as quietly as she could and slipped inside the chamber.

He stood naked by the bed.

She must have made a sound, for he had his dagger in his hand and turned to face whatever threat had entered in seconds.

He stood naked in the light of a sputtering candle.

Brienne could not have looked away if her life depended on her doing so. She'd seen him clothed and seen him fighting in only his breeches. But to see every muscle and limb, defined and covered only by the flickering shadows of the candle, took her breath away.

He was magnificent. His brown hair barely touched the wide shoulders that tapered to a thinner waist and hips. Strong, muscular thighs rippled as he moved. Curly, dark hair covered his chest and narrowed as it formed a pathway down past his waist. And that part of him that hung between his legs was as well formed as the rest of his body.

And when it began to thicken and rise, she knew she'd felt it when she'd sat on his lap in the alcove.

"Demoiselle, what are you doing here?" he asked.

He made no attempt to cover himself, and she was glad of it. If nothing else came of this night, she would have the memory of him standing like this forever. But she could not put words together while he stood there naked.

"You should not be here," he said, walking to her and reaching for the door. "What if someone saw you?"

"I was careful," she explained, finally able to speak.

He opened the door a bit and peered out into the darkness as she watched and waited.

"I will dress and escort you back," he said, grabbing the garments that lay in a pile at his feet.

The movement made the flame of the candle flicker and threaten to go out, so she took care of that, making it burn a little brighter so she could see every inch of him. He glanced at her and then the candle and back again as though he suspected something, but he turned back to dress.

"William," she said, walking to his side and touching his shoulder. It was warm beneath her fingers. And strong. And hard muscle. "I did not wish this night to be over yet."

"Brienne, this is not a good idea. There will be hellish consequences if you are discovered in my chambers. Hellish for me, worse for you, I think."

He did not pause in trying to pull on his breeches, so she did what she needed to do to distract him. She lifted her hand and kissed him instead. His skin was hot, and his indrawn breath let her know he was affected by her kiss. He spun away and shook his head.

She did not let it stop her. If pain had not stopped her from pursuing the truth of her beginnings, pleasure—or the promise of it—would not stop her now. So she used the truth now.

"You will leave on the morrow, and I will be left here to live at my father's whim and will. I just watched him toss Adelaide into a marriage that she had no say in," she began. "I understand it is a daughter's duty to obey and accept his wisdom, but I am not accustomed to his ways."

She took a step toward him again and lifted her hand to touch him, this time his chest, outlining the ridges of muscle down to his stomach with her fingers.

"I pray you, William, be with me tonight. Let me make the choice before my father takes it from me."

She could see the desire and the wanting flare in his eyes as though he controlled the fire. His fingers curled into fists and released, over and over, as if he was trying to keep from touching her.

"Brienne," he whispered, his voice full of longing and hoarse with passion. "You know that I want you. I have wanted you from the moment I saw you. There is something between us I cannot explain."

She could. She could tell him what she knew. She could do it now, but she knew her father planned to on the morrow. Brienne wanted to have him this night before the knowledge of their fates was known.

"Shhhhhh," she urged, placing her finger over his lips. "Kiss me. Kiss me now."

And, like a storm, he did. Overwhelmed by his touch, she let him have his way with her. He slid his hands into her hair and shook it free of the braid. Then he brought her to his mouth and kissed her until she was breathless and unable to speak. Brienne held on to him, sliding her hands over his skin and feeling the way his body responded to her touch.

She felt him tug on the laces of her gown and stood in his embrace as he pushed the gown off her shoulders and down to her hips. Her shift followed, exposing her breasts to him. When she tried to cover herself, suddenly shy about him seeing her, he laughed.

"Oh no, *chérie*," he said, gently lifting her arms and caressing the sensitive tips of her breasts with the backs of his hands. "It is only fair that I get to see you as you have seen me." He eased her gown and shift down over her hips then and let them fall to the floor. "Ah, *magnifique*! As I thought you would be."

For a moment, Brienne's boldness skittered away, leaving her trembling. Then his hands began their magic, and heat flowed through her. This heat was the one he created as he cupped her breasts and lowered his mouth there. Her breath escaped in short gasps with each touch of his tongue. But when he began to tease with his teeth and then sucked on the tips, her knees buckled and she fell against him.

William caught her, sliding his arm beneath her legs and carrying her to his bed. He laid her on top of the bedcovers and climbed up next to her. Now his body touched hers from shoulders to feet and everywhere in between. The hard maleness pressed against her hip now, and she felt its sleek flesh against her skin. She reached out, curious about how it would feel in her hand, but he stopped her.

"Not yet, Brienne. Touch me anywhere but there."

She thought this was her choice, but her body quickly fell under his control. Her body ached and throbbed as his fingers explored and caressed every inch of her. He teased her skin, kissed her breasts and her mouth, moving, always moving and giving attention as he did. When he suckled her breasts, the heat and moisture gathered between her legs, and she arched against his hand with each inch he moved closer to touching her there.

When he drew circles with his fingers, gently touching across the top of her thighs, onto her hips and across her belly, she cried out. Everything within her tightened, tightened, tightened until she could not breathe. Her legs fell open and she grabbed his hand, needing it . . . wanting it . . . there.

"Do you want something?" he whispered against her ear. "Should I touch you . . . here?" he asked as he finally slid his fingers into that place, and she let out a sigh of relief at his touch. "Ah, so hot, so wet for me."

Relief turned quickly to something else as he explored the folds of her flesh there, with his finger and then fingers, rubbing slowly, then faster. Just as she thought she would burst somehow, he would ease the pressure until she moved away from some edge.

He praised her in his language with words she could not understand. His mouth and his tongue never stopped, and he moved them at a pace that had her arching against his hand and his mouth, begging for something. Whatever lay just . . . there . . . out of her reach.

He arched against her hip, sliding the length of him at the same pace, and she wanted to take him in her hand and hold his flesh, but every intention fell away when he slipped one finger inside her. Her body thrust up, trying to take him in deeper, but he laughed and withdrew it. Then he moved it in a circle, from outside to inside, harder, then softer, faster, then slower.

She was going to die. She was going to explode in the flames of passion he stroked.

"Please," she begged.

"Now?" he asked before licking his way back to her breasts. His hand did not stop its torment, and her hips lifted off the bed, begging as she had.

All it took was one slight rub against some small place in the folds between her legs and it pushed her to the place that waited. Her muscles tightened and then shuddered, the channel leading to her core spasmed and throbbed, and everything in her let go until she fell. She released the scream trapped within her throat, and he caught it with his mouth, kissing her and thrusting his tongue as he did his finger until she was . . . empty.

The first thing she realized was that his breathing was now normal and even against her ear.

The next thing was that she had not fallen at all. She had flown in his embrace, for his arms held her securely against his body as they lay on his bed.

The last thing she noticed was that he was still hard against her hip.

She tried to turn and found her body would not

obey her commands. So empty and so tranquil, all the longing and desire that had filled her was satisfied.

"*Magnifique*," she whispered, imitating his accent of the word.

"Aye, you were," he said. "Like fire in my hands."

She opened her eyes and met his gaze then. Had he meant that?

"You have not . . . You did not . . ." She glanced down at his flesh between them.

"Nay, Brienne," he said, kissing her face as he leaned back and looked at her. "As much as I want to, you are not mine to claim. I could not take what is meant for another."

They lay in silence, and Brienne savored the feel of him on her skin. A few minutes passed, and she felt him slide away from her and climb from the bed. The candle had sputtered out, unnoticed by either of them at the time. Now he lit it once more and dressed in his breeches and shirt. She watched his every movement, fighting the urge to touch him again. He did not try to hide or turn from her as he did so, allowing her to gaze on his body as he slowly covered it with his garments.

"Come," he said, holding his hand out to her. " 'Tis time for you to return to your chambers before they know you are not there."

Knowing she could not stay the night did not lessen her reluctance to leave him now. They'd had their moment of passion and pleasure and, if he did leave on the morrow, she would remember it.

He handled her as though she was a precious thing, and she allowed his care as he helped her with her shift and gown. Looking down, she laughed then, seeing that she still wore her stockings and shoes.

"You were in some haste," he teased.

Soon she was dressed and her hair gathered in a loose braid. Too soon. He snuffed out the candle and opened the door to check the corridor before guiding her out. They just missed being found by one guard on the main floor; only his quick action of pulling her behind him into the shadows in the corner and shielding her with his body saved them.

Brienne stopped him before he could follow her out of the keep.

"I will go the rest of the way alone, William. I will not be seen."

"If you are certain?"

"Aye." She took the first step away and then turned back to him. "It was more than I imagined it could be."

"You are such an innocent," he whispered, stroking her cheek. "Have a care as you go, Brienne."

She ran down the steps and across the yard, pausing as a guard crossed several paces in front of her. Then she opened the door slowly and slipped inside.

Brienne almost floated to her chambers, ducking and hiding a few times when a servant passed, but she arrived in her room unseen. Once she caused the torch high up on the wall to flare brightly, drawing one servant's attention so that she could sneak past him.

Minutes later, she lay in her bed, thinking on all that had happened between her and William this night. As she drifted to sleep, she realized the failure in her plan.

She'd gone to him simply to seek pleasure and some memories she could hold on to in the coming days. She'd come back in love with the man who honored her even when she did not.

*   *   *

"She is back, my lord."

The servant's whisper at his door was the word he waited on. He opened the door and dismissed him with a wordless wave of his hand.

Brienne and the warblood. Neither one could see what was plain to him—they had fallen in love right before his eyes. That mattered not. Though her virginity would have been an added gift to the goddess, using it to gain the warrior's cooperation was worth it. Once he'd taken the maidenhead of an innocent, his own honor would demand he protect her.

So that when Hugh took her north, the warrior would follow and do anything to save her. Even forfeit his claim to lands and his duty to the king. Then he and his powers would be Hugh's to command.

The girl was easy enough to manage—a few soft words and the name of her mother and she'd fallen into his hands to be molded and moved as he needed. Tonight had been the result. He knew she thought it her idea to pursue the knight, but a few subtle pushes and suggestions and she'd gone after him like a bitch in heat. Seeing the warrior's desire for her in his gaze, Hugh knew that he would not reject her when she followed him.

Hugh held the image of the torch outside her chambers in his thoughts and became that fire, re-forming there in the corridor. Opening her door, he walked in and stood over the bed where she slept. As he watched her sleeping, she murmured words in a whisper. He leaned in and tried to discern what she said, but they were slurred. Her body moved then, sliding on the sheets and arching. She was dreaming of sex. When she uttered the warrior's name, he nearly laughed aloud.

He left her chambers, using the candles in his chambers to draw him. Then he released his mirth and satisfaction. She had done her part and given herself to the warrior. On the morrow, he would invite William to join them—for a willing warblood would be easier to handle.

But, willing or not, virgin or not, William de Brus would be in Hugh's control and Brienne would be sacrificed once the gateway was open. Nothing else would matter after that.

William watched her leave, waiting until he saw her enter the family's residence before retracing his steps back to his chamber. Once in his chambers, he closed his eyes and remembered the expression on her lovely face when she'd seen him standing naked before her.

Most young women would be shocked or embarrassed, but not Brienne. He smiled then, thinking on the way she just studied him as though trying to commit his form and appearance to memory. Then she'd touched him and he was lost.

'Twas a miracle he had enough control to not ravish her. The way that her lithe, young body responded to his mouth and his hands challenged that control, but he won even as he lost. She became an extension of his touch, moving with him, following his caresses, opening to everything he stroked. Then she had been like fire in his hands, exploding in waves of heat and wetness as he brought her to completion.

Never in his life had he wanted to be inside a woman more than he had wanted with her. He'd wanted to fill her as she screamed out her pleasure. He'd nearly spilled his seed against her body, so close was he as she shuddered and rocked on his hand.

Even now, his cock reminded him of his failure.

But his heart knew the truth.

He could not take her virtue until she gave it to him. And she would not be ready to give it to him until her soul was her own and her heart was his. As he saw to his own needs in the silent dark of the night, he also knew the worst of it.

His heart belonged to her already.

But whether or not they would survive long enough for him to tell her was another matter.

CHAPTER 20

"Marcus?" She called out his name as she left her tent.

Marcus has not seen Aislinn since dawn, and he suspected she now had more to tell him. Her dreams came fast and strong now, tearing her from her sleep as the danger came closer with each day. From the terrible expression in her eyes as he walked to her, he knew it would arrive sooner than any of them had realized.

"You have been to the warrior's camp?" she asked as he reached her.

"They had to be warned." Marcus looked at her then, understanding that she knew. "What did you see?"

"It begins now. The firebloods rise. The evil one wakes. Many will die."

"William?" he asked, walking at her side as she glanced around their camp.

"The evil one tries to claim him. The firebloods are divided, but it may be too late for that to help."

The signs had been clearer, and this was more than she'd seen before. As he watched, her eyes rolled back and she rocked from side to side, raising her arms toward the sky. The words of an ancient prayer flowed through her, and she whispered it into the air around them. Even he could feel the amount of power flowing in this area, from Yester. Some was good, some evil, but all of it fed and strengthened her power to decipher the prophecy and find the location.

"We must be ready. We travel north, across the water north of Edinburgh. Into the lands to the northeast of Scotland. That is where the first circle lies." A frantic nervousness filled her then, and she began to shake. Dropping her arms as her eyes cleared, she cried out, "He knows! He has been there!"

"Aislinn!" Marcus took hold of her and held her by her shoulders as she watched something in the air or in her thoughts pass before her eyes.

"Blood had been spilled at the circle. The evil one pushing her power across the barrier meant to keep her in exile," she whispered, shaking her head. "So many centuries of waiting and it has begun."

"Aislinn, breathe now," he said, shaking her.

She clutched her hands over her ears, as though trying to block out some sounds. Aislinn could not help the warriors of destiny who would face the ancient one if she did not gain control over these visions, much as the warriors had to control the powers in their blood. He'd taught her such control, and together they prayed to the ancient six to aid her in her task. Finally, the shaking calmed and she faced him.

"Better, lass?" he asked, stroking her cheek.

She'd fallen to the ground, and now the rest of the priests surrounded them, drawn to the power of her prophecy. The horror in their gazes revealed what they'd witnessed. Aislinn tried to stand, but her legs would not support her yet.

"Give yourself a moment or two," he urged, even as he steadied her and helped her up.

"We must head north, Marcus, everyone." Those gathered looked to Marcus, who nodded.

"Pack and ready yourselves for the journey north," he said, pointing to a few of them. Then he spoke to the rest of them. "*A Warrior seeks the truth.* That is the first bloodline mentioned in the prophecy, and I believe we must wait for Sir William. He will lead us north."

They were neither worldly nor human warriors and would need someone with experience in fighting and planning to lead them. Though he still questioned their history and his part in this, William's blood had risen. The huge, blue-skinned, single-minded warrior who'd crashed into their camp when he thought the fireblood in danger would be their protector—and *hers*. In spite of their attempts to teach him, it was his own self-doubt that held his powers at bay.

"Aye, Marcus. William will lead us once he comes to us. Be prepared to do what he tells you to do," Aislinn confirmed.

The others scattered to do as she and Marcus bade them, and she stared off at the castle in the distance. In spite of some spell keeping it muted, it was no doubt the center of the evil one's power. It would begin there and spread out, evil trying to snuff out that which opposed it. He sent up prayers that they would all be strong enough to carry out their parts in this quest.

It began now, and by the time it was finished, the world could be brought to its end.

Gods have mercy.

*   *   *

William watched as the very large group began its trek out of Yester Castle. He counted more than three score soldiers escorting the lord's wife and daughter on their journey back to their lands in France.

"So many?" Roger asked from over his shoulder. "Do they travel through some hostile area I know not?"

"My thoughts as well," he said. "Return to the camp. Send a man to follow them." William turned to Roger. "Not to be seen."

Roger nodded and left.

"Gautier and Armand, you both remain here until the castle is returned to its usual condition and then make your way back."

"Will . . . " Gautier began to argue.

"I plan to follow. We must get word to the king about the weapons cache even if I do not know its purpose yet. And I want you both well away from here."

The strangeness increased with the dawn. A rumbling kind of sound, which he could feel around and within him, had woken him. He could feel it in his chest and with every breath. From the ashen faces of those around him, he was not alone in the experience.

"Get everyone ready to leave."

"And go to . . . ?" Gautier asked.

Will shrugged. "Just be at the ready. Arms and armor," he added.

It took some time for the large group to travel out of the yard, over the bridge and through the gates. As the carts, horses, and men on foot trickled out, William saw Gavin and the boy who'd kissed Brienne being led in by several guards. Tempted to follow, he stopped when Gavin met his gaze and shook his head slightly.

Bringing Gavin and the boy here, to the family's residence from their path, meant only one possible thing, and it was not good. He knew how men like Hugh controlled—through fear and pain. Pawns to be played. Was Brienne resisting Lord Hugh's plans, then?

A servant approached with a summons to meet with Lord Hugh, and William knew he would find out more. With a nod, he released Gautier and Armand, who would leave as soon as they could.

Following the servant, who kept glancing behind himself nervously, William paused inside the family residence. He looked down the corridor and listened for signs of the men, but found no trace of them. Lifting his head, he inhaled and knew they had been here.

Instead of going to the large chamber where they'd dined the night before or some other Presence Chamber, the servant trotted ahead, beckoning him to follow, up several stairways to a chamber on the top floor. They walked to the last chamber, and the servant knocked lightly, whispering his lord's name before he ran away.

The door was framed in a wood William had never seen and intricately carved with symbols and images. Most were unknown to him, but one caught his attention. It was the same battle-ax shape that was now burning in the flesh of his arm. But the one symbol used most often to decorate this frame was fire.

Brienne had some power over fire, which seemed to have come from Lord Hugh. Where did William's power come from? His beliefs in the world around him shifted in that moment as he finally accepted what Marcus had tried to tell him. It was not a good feeling.

If he had this power, then who else did? Who bore

the other symbols on the doorframe? And what powers did they carry?

The door opened and Brienne greeted him and bade him enter with a shy smile and a pale pink blush. She stepped back to allow him entrance.

Gavin's scent was here. He could smell it. Will glanced around the chamber and saw only Lord Hugh, sitting in a chair that was not unlike a throne. As he moved farther into the chamber and Brienne closed the door, the overwhelming odors assaulted his senses and he fought not to show his shock.

Pain and fear permeated the chamber and even the walls. Will had not imagined that those two things had scents, but he knew them now. Glancing toward Lord Hugh and attempting to approach him was nearly impossible due to the stench of dying and death. As he crossed the chamber to bow before the lord, the smoky smell of burning flesh and wood filled his nostrils and his gaze began to edge toward red.

And yet Brienne was unaffected.

Meeting her eyes, he knew that was not true—she was fighting something as well. Her mouth gave it away, her lower lip trembling as it did when she was nervous or afraid. In that moment, he knew he must get her out of here to safety. He must take her . . . now.

"My lord," he began, as he rose from the bow. "I know this is precipitous, but I would offer for your daughter's hand in marriage."

Brienne's shock showed immediately on her face, but before she could react, Lord Hugh's loud laughter filled the chamber.

"My bastard for the king's bastard, then, Sir William? Do you think it a good match?" Lord Hugh stood and walked to Brienne's side, lifting her face as though examining her skin. "She is fetching—is she not?"

Will did not respond. His vision began to redden, and he took in a slow, deep breath, trying to force it out. He needed to be calm now. He needed to be in control. For her. For her.

"Was she what you expected in your bed? As fiery and lively as her mother was in mine?"

Brienne gasped and pulled from his grasp. "You knew?" she accused. "You knew I went to him?"

She did not deny or explain what had happened between them. She only studied her father's face, and then the realization of the extent and methods he used to control her crossed her lovely features. She raised her hand then, swinging toward Lord Hugh to slap him.

And froze in place.

When Will tried to reach her, he could not, for something—someone—was in his thoughts, stopping him. Every attempt to move resulted in crippling pain. His vision began to narrow and grow more red as he could only watch the scene before him.

No words were spoken between father and daughter, but some battle raged on between them. If Hugh was using the same pain against her, how did she survive it? When she crumpled to the floor at Hugh's feet with a cry, he knew the victor. Lord Hugh walked in front of Will, exerting his power against him to keep him immobile.

"You want her, William Warblood? She is yours. And you need not bind yourself to her in marriage, since I know you hope to find a more suitable bride to establish your line. Take her; use her; keep her or discard her when you finish with her."

Hugh circled him, now chuckling, as Will tried to force his hold off. He'd used the same word or name that Marcus had in describing him—warblood. So Hugh knew.

"You need only to give yourself and your powers over to me and she is yours. But there is so much more at stake now. You can have your own kingdom. Establish your own bloodline and dynasty. Take what you want from the humans who will serve us. Take who you want. It can be yours with a word, Warblood."

William continued to fight for control and failed as Hugh walked around him, taunting him, teasing him, tempting him to join this growing evil.

"Oh wait!" he said, a sarcastic bite in his voice. "It appears you cannot move." Suddenly, the pain in his head increased, and he screamed against it . . . but no sound came out of his throat. His lungs would not take in air.

"You have a decision to make, William. You can accept your destiny and be at my side in the great endeavor to right an ancient wrong," he said, continuing to walk around him. When he stood directly before him, he said, "Or you can watch her die before you do."

The pain holding him there was so great, he could not even move his gaze to see her on the floor. His body shuddered and shook as he tried to change and could not. He could not even breathe. Some force held him in place and kept his warblood from rising.

"This is bigger than your quest for lands, King's Knight. This is bigger than your father the king or even Scotland. And by standing with me, you will gain more than you ever imagined you could. She is the least of it, but she can be yours."

Then he was free, and he fell to his knees on the floor, dragging in huge gasps of air and forcing his lungs to breathe. Will tried to reach for Brienne who still did not move, but Hugh stopped him, stepping between them and dragging him back to his feet.

"Join me. Join us. I will show you how to use the power of your warrior blood as we travel north to accomplish our holy quest," he whispered in the voice that every evil temptation used. "We will be invincible." Then Hugh thrust him away toward the door and watched him through veiled eyes with his arms crossed over his chest.

"You have two hours, Warblood. Send your men packing and stand with us or fall with them." Hugh lifted his head and nodded toward the hillside where Marcus hid.

"And Brienne?" he asked, unwilling to leave her behind. His senses told him he had no choice.

"She is alive until you make your choice."

William knew he was lying, but he could not take the chance to challenge him on it. If she was alive, it was because Hugh needed her for some purpose, for some part of this "great endeavor" of which he spoke. Alone, he could not defeat this man who held such inhuman powers. He needed help and needed to get to them now. Will lifted the latch and was pushed through the door. When it slammed behind him, he could not open it again.

He ran, grabbing his horse and riding as fast as he could out of Yester Castle, with the terrible stench still in his nostrils. Brienne was in danger and he must find a way to get back to her and help her.

By the time he reached the hillside opposite his own

camp, he could barely keep his vision clear and his blood from seething through his body, changing it. But he would, because right now in this moment, it was the only way to save her. He jumped from his horse before it had even stopped and stood before Marcus and the young seer.

"Tell me more. Tell me what I have to do."

CHAPTER 21

"Brienne." The voice was like a whisper, slipping into the darkness where she existed now. "Brienne, sweet, wake up."

"Father?" It was Gavin's voice that spoke to her, calling her toward him.

Pain! More pain struck her and she fell back.

"Brienne." He called her once more. She forced her eyes open.

She lay on the stone floor of a chamber she'd never seen before. Gavin and James knelt next to her, staring down at her. They helped her to stand, and she remembered battling her father over William. Turning around she saw Lord Hugh there, standing before a wall, staring at it.

"What is this place?" she asked, brushing the dirt from her palms and pushing her hair out of her face. She could see and feel the terror in both Gavin and James. He answered instead.

"This is the first sacred place my grandfather discovered here in Scotland. An ancient circle of stones buried deep in the ground. The king at the time gave my grandfather these lands, never knowing of the kind of power that existed here."

He lifted his hands and touched the wall, almost caressing it, as he slid his hands carefully over its surface in a circular motion. She shivered just watching him.

"Are we belowground now?" The dampness and cold spoke of a cavern or a cave that sank deep into the bedrock.

"Aye. This chamber was the first one built by the goddess," he replied. He faced her now, but never lost contact with the wall. "Chaela sent her power through to my grandfather, and he used it to build this," he said, glancing around the chamber. "Now that you are awake, you will feel it."

And she did.

Her blood carried it through her body. Every brick in this chamber had been touched by evil. And she had been, too, since the same power of this evil flowed through her blood. She knew what was about to happen, so she flung herself away from Gavin and James.

And became fire.

A body of living, breathing, moving fire.

She could see the horror and shock in their faces but paid them no heed.

The fireblood was free now, and she reveled as its power pulsed through her, burning and surging stronger each moment. She walked over to where her father stood and reached out with hands of fire to touch the wall as he did, trying to glean the source of its power. Instead she felt something moving toward them from the other side.

"What comes?" she asked in a whisper of heat and sound. She knew it was a being of immense force and it approached from behind that barrier. The fire that she was now could not resist its call.

The wall disappeared to nothing. Her fiery hands passed through the opening and she waited. It was coming.

Chaela was coming.

Her father's laughter grew louder, and she sensed that it was coming from a place of desolation and emptiness. An instant later, the searing touch of another fire melded with hers, and she screamed in agony and ecstasy as they merged. This was nothing like what she'd felt when her father had touched her or punished her.

She fell back then, swirling and burning and screaming from the inconceivable power and pain of the one. Gathering her fire, she moved closer to the goddess. Peering into the place beyond the barrier there, she watched and waited and saw something so magical and ancient that her human mind could not comprehend it. It flickered inside her thoughts, but she could not hold the image there.

"This is our goddess. This is—"

CHAELA.

The voice screamed it so loudly that every brick and stone in the chamber shuddered. Gavin and James fell unconscious at the sound. The pull of it, the call of it, drew her once more, her flames silently sliding toward the opening.

"Our power flows from her, daughter. Chaela is the source of all firebloods. Worship *HER* now and forever."

She could no more refuse than she could change her form back to the human she used to be. She moved across the chamber and lowered herself to the floor, sliding her flaming hands back into the barrier in obedience. She waited for the terrible torment to strike.

Daughter of my blood. Daughter of my fire, Chaela said, as the goddess caressed Brienne's hands with scalding, molten heat until she lost herself to it, screaming at the unending anguish. Memories of betrayal and exile flowed between them through this fiery connection. She saw the ancient ones. She watched their attack. She felt their powers against Chaela and saw her defeat.

Released a moment or an hour later, she crawled away from the barrier and lay on the floor.

"Brienne!" her father said. Opening her eyes, she watched as he crouched down next to her and put his hand into the very heart of her flames. "Come back now."

She pulled the fire back deep inside her, gathering it back into her blood so that her human body returned then. Her skin was singed black and smoking while the birthmark on her human arm still blazed. The pain of it mixed with something else. Some feeling like the pleasure that she felt at William's touch filled her body and blood then. Waves of pain and pleasure blended as her skin cooled and healed.

Lord Hugh took her by the shoulders and gazed at her with pride.

"Now you understand?" he asked, caressing her cheek and smoothing her hair over her shoulder. "The gift you have been given? The honor paid to you?"

Brienne's thoughts were a jumbled mess. The memories of the goddess in her moment of defeat mixed with the horror and fear of her own mind, and she struggled to figure out what was real and what was not. She glanced over at the wall, where something unspeakable had happened and saw nothing there now. But she felt the power, now banked, waiting.

"The goddess is so pleased with you, daughter," Lord Hugh said, stroking her arms and placing his hand over the burning brand on her skin. She hissed as his fire touched her skin. "We owe her much for the power she has given us. So much."

He turned his head and looked at Gavin and James, who now stood in a haze of terror and disbelief in the corner. She tried to go to them, to explain that she was still . . . she was . . .

What was she? Truly, she did not know at this moment. Her father held her in place for a moment until she stopped trying.

"She is in need, Brienne." He gazed into her eyes until she realized what he meant.

Them. The goddess needed them. Just as in her vision, a human must be offered.

"Sacrifice is the supreme way we worship her." Once more she could not move. He walked over to the two men who had meant so much to her—one who'd raised her and loved her as his own and the other who'd accepted her when no one else would. "Choose, Brienne. Choose the best sacrifice to show the goddess how we are her servants."

Lord Hugh came back to her, kissing her forehead and her mouth and whispering in her ear, "Go and bring one of them to the goddess. Your willingness to choose one of the humans shall please her."

Her mind emptied itself. Nothingness filled it. She could not think of such a thing. She stood there mindless, stunned by such a horrific choice. It jolted her back to the true Brienne hiding within. And William's words were the first she could hear there in the blankness.

You must know in your heart which one you are. Who and what you are, Brienne. And let no one take that from you.

She was Brienne, daughter of Gavin and Fia. She was human.

When Lord Hugh eased his hold on her so that she could make her choice, she did, choosing to throw herself at the opening in the wall. No one would die for her or by her hand. But the barrier held, and she hit it hard. Flung away by the impact, she tumbled to the floor.

"Stupid bitch!" he yelled, slapping her with the back of his hand and then flinging her at the wall. "Too damned human still. I will teach you the way of this," he said.

She turned to flame and attacked him then, throwing every bit of what she'd learned in those hard lessons at him. She also needed to protect the two who watched. Lord Hugh disappeared and formed again behind her, wrapping himself around her flaming form and forcing her toward Gavin and James. Though Gavin stood firm, James backed away until the wall behind him stopped him. Lord Hugh grasped her hand, still flames, and reached out toward James.

Brienne fought him. She pulled away and tried to free herself from the fire she was, but his power encircled her and made her reach for the terrified James.

And Gavin stepped in front of him.

"Take me, Lord Hugh. Leave the boy," the man who was her father said with a quiet braveness. His selfless words gave her the strength she needed to change to her human form.

"Nay, my lord," she begged. "What do you want of me? Do you want me to obey you? I will," she promised, kneeling before him. "Do you wish me to use my powers as you say? I will." She put her head down at his feet. "I swear. Just let them live."

Minutes passed as she prostrated herself before him. She prayed with all her soul that he would relent.

"Ah, the sight of my obedient daughter abasing herself before me has moved me to mercy," he finally said. "Rise and take your place at my side, daughter."

She pushed herself to her feet and wiped the tears out of her eyes with the back of her hand. Lord Hugh's expression was empty as she walked to stand beside him.

"I should thank you, Gavin, for raising her to respect her father's words," he said. "But I think she learned to be willful from you and the bitch you married."

Before Brienne could stop him, Lord Hugh slammed Gavin into the wall with his power and held him there. Then, grabbing her hand in his, he pointed at James, who stumbled toward her in spite of his struggles not to. When the terrified young man stood within arm's length, Hugh placed their hands, now flames, on the center of his chest and forced him back to the opening in the wall.

"Next time, you will obey me," he warned her, as they pushed the screaming man through the barrier to the goddess.

Hugh released her, and she reached in, trying to grab James and pull him free. She heard his screams and then a roar before she lost her grip. Falling back, she wrapped her arms around her head, trying to block out the sounds as he was sacrificed within the darkness. Brienne fell to her knees and retched until she could only heave an empty stomach.

She had killed him. Killed James. And he knew it as she pushed him in to be destroyed by whatever lived on the other side of the barrier. Rocking back on her heels, she wanted to die.

When Lord Hugh released Gavin from his hold, she expected he would be her next punishment. She had no strength left to resist him and would not be able to save him. Sobbing, she curled into a ball on the floor, unable to watch her father die because of her.

"Get out," Lord Hugh said quietly.

She lifted her head to see him directing Gavin to the steps. And she knew he would not leave her behind.

"I pray you, go now," she begged him.

Then she lay back down and gave up the fight.

William would have liked nothing more than to laugh off every word that Marcus had told him that first day. Ancient gods and goddesses. Gateways. Stone circles. Prophecies and spells. And he might have if only . . .

If he had not seen the power of the fireblood.

If he had not felt the warblood bubbling within him.

With time racing by, they needed to take positions to stop Lord Hugh from escaping Yester. They must not let him get to the stone circle that sat somewhere in the northeast of the country. Having traveled to that region, William knew that there were countless standing stones and circles all over Scotland. Without knowing specifically which one it was, they would be wasting valuable time.

From what William could tell, none of the people with Marcus had any fighting skills at all. They would be worthless in a battle, except he knew this would be no ordinary battle. And William would not remain an ordinary warrior for long either. He would be able to call the warblood to rise and fight, but whether he could control such a power was the unanswered question.

The most elite of Lord Hugh's soldiers would be the biggest concern for his men. And considering the cache of weapons hidden in the village, there must be more fighting men that Hugh had at the ready. Mayhap they were on the way from Gifford even now?

As his two hours came to a close, one of his men raced back to him from the village.

"They are not far behind me, Will," Emery called out as he took his place within the line of horsed warriors behind him.

A burst of light filled the sky, and he peered in the distance toward the castle as fire rose above it. Then it was gone and he heard the sound of approaching riders. Had there been an explosion of some kind? Had Hugh destroyed the keep or castle behind him so that none could use it?

A few minutes later, the riders broke through the edge of the forest and he faced Hugh de Gifford on horseback. As he expected, Hugh held Brienne before him. Ashen and in a stupor, she looked exhausted. What had he done to her?

His blood roiled and raced and his vision began to narrow. This time he did not fight the changes though that did not make it easier. His muscles stretched and grew, his arms strengthened, and his legs grew longer.

"Keep your attention on her, William," Marcus urged from behind. "Do not lose yourself as the power takes over."

As Hugh's forces lined up across from his men, William became the warblood that lived within him. His vision, red and ringed, could see farther and better than his human eyes could. He could smell each of those around him and differentiate their own separate scents. His right arm became a war hammer and his left a huge sword. Now towering over the men, he leaned his head back and let out the war cry that simmered in his blood.

"Take them," he ordered in a voice he did not recognize.

His legs ate up the ground beneath him, and he crossed the open space between the lines before anyone else could. And he ran right for her. Hugh called out a word, and many of his warriors ran in front of him, blocking Will from getting to her. Hugh pivoted and began to ride away, and the warblood could not allow that.

Swinging the hammer and thrusting the sword, he cut down the first ones who tried to stop him. Turning in a circle, he killed several more, parrying and thrusting, swinging and pounding, reveling in the blood that splashed and the bodies that exploded under his blows. They dared to stand between him and the fireblood who was his.

Swing. Hit. Dead.

Slash. Cut. Dead.

Over and over until his opponents fell before him. It felt good. It felt wondrous. It felt . . .

Her scream pierced the air and drew him from his deadly dance. Turning to where Hugh held her, he saw her pointing at the forest, a look of sick horror on her face before she screamed again.

"William!" Marcus called to him. The priest used some voice that reached through the fog of war to him. He looked at the forest, and even the warblood in him was horrified. He pulled his power back, thinking of it going back into his blood, and his body shifted, but not all the way back. His weapons remained where he needed them.

He'd wondered where the soldiers were that would use the swords Hugh had stashed at the ready. Coming through the forest was Hugh's new army—the villagers. William recognized many of them, but they were different. Men, women, even children, carried swords or daggers before them. Walking at a stinted gait, they were lifeless. They were creatures with glowing eyes and no will of their own. Worse, Gavin led them forward.

"He has bespelled them!" Marcus explained. "They will fight and kill because they cannot resist it."

"Well, priest, what the bloody hell do we do now?" Roger called out to him. His men were trained fighters, but to kill these people was wrong.

Brienne screamed again, struggling with Hugh, who nodded again and called out some word he did not understand. But those under his power did, and they began to run now, growing closer very quickly.

"Gavin! Father!" she screamed, but the man who used to be her father did not even blink at the sound.

"Roger, Gautier," William called out. "Tell the others. Knock them down. Do not strike them unless you must!"

He had expected a diversion. Any good battle commander would. However, this was not what he'd expected at all. A counterattack mayhap. More men attacking from a different direction. But not this depravity. Now he watched as Gavin turned and stalked him.

"William." She called out his name once, and when he looked at her, she fainted. Hugh mocked with a salute and rode off carrying her unconscious body with him. He had barely turned back when Gavin launched his attack.

Being a blacksmith, Gavin had the strength and experience to wield a sword well, and he did it in spite of whatever spell controlled him. William felt his blood rise as he faced the challenge, but he forced it back, preferring not to slaughter this man. Using his own skills, he pushed him back and back until one of his men came up from behind Gavin and hit him on the head with the hilt of a sword.

He joined his men, and they did the same all over the field, though fighting children was the most sickening thing he'd ever faced in battle. Finally, after more than an hour of fighting, they had prevailed. A number of villagers had been wounded and a few of his men as well, and it would take time to see to them. Roger approached as he spoke with Marcus about the spell used on the villagers.

"Gavin is . . . awake and would like to speak to you, Will," he said. There was a distance in his friend's tone that bespoke of trouble.

"Is aught wrong, Roger?" he asked, following him to where the blacksmith was tending to his neighbors.

"I just look at you and see that . . . warblood creature. How?" Roger let out a breath and stopped. "Do you have any idea what you look like when you change?" He shrugged and shook his head in reply. "I thought I was prepared. I thought I'd seen it before, on that day, but Sweet Christ, Will! You turned into a seven-foot-tall, blue berserker before our eyes."

Roger raked his hands through his hair and shook his head.

They'd faced so many shocks this day, William had no doubt they all wanted to leave and go back to their customary existences.

"And I will again, Roger. From what Marcus tells me, I will often, and I may not have seen the full extent of whatever my powers might be. And there will be others with other powers."

He noticed the others were listening and decided it best to sort this out now.

"This is unlike anything I have faced before in my life, and it is not over," he called out to his men. "We are being called to a purpose unlike any we can imagine. Some of us will survive and some will not. In good faith, I cannot force you to keep your pledges of service to me now that this has been thrust on me." He met the gaze of each of his men and then Gavin's. "But I must answer this call. I must stop this man—this monster— who would destroy everything that is good.

"So, each of you, examine your own consciences and make your decision. Those of you willing, those of you able, we leave in two hours. Those of you who cannot commit your lives and souls to this endeavor are free to leave with my blessing and my thanks for your service."

As he walked over to where Gavin sat, he heard Marcus's words to Aislinn the seer.

"As you told us, the prophecy said the warrior will lead us."

It struck him then—he had not considered the

priests and their pivotal role in this. Marcus spoke of chanting at the stone circle and reading the signs, but if they all knew . . .

"Marcus, do all of your priests know the signs? Do they all know how to chant at the circles?"

"Aye, William. They share the visions and the dreams, though Aislinn is the most powerful and will be the one to close the circle."

"And you sent one of your men after Hugh?"

"Ahead to watch and follow," he said, nodding.

"What troubles you, Will?" Roger asked, listening to the exchange.

"If they all know, then they each know," he said.

"What do you want us to do?" Roger asked, understanding the problem.

"I fear there is nothing we can do for the one sent ahead, but we must guard the rest of you."

The problems and challenges piled up in front of him with every passing minute. His only hope was that Hugh wanted him to follow to rescue Brienne, because if he did, he'd keep her alive. He hoped that Hugh would find the prospect of luring Will to her pivotal right now. Marcus had explained that either she or Hugh could be used in sacrifice to open the gateway, but chances were that Hugh would sacrifice her. And William knew he would do anything necessary to rescue and claim her.

He just prayed Brienne could do what she must to stay alive until he could reach her. Once she was safe in his arms, he would claim her heart and let the warblood inside tear Lord Hugh de Gifford apart with his bare hands.

CHAPTER 22

Cold misery seeped into her body and soul as they crossed the miles away from Yester and away from William. Her last memory, watching her father, mother, and all the other people from her village turn into mindless pawns to attack trained and experienced warriors, sickened her even now. Worse, she had no idea if they had survived.

She would never think of Lord Hugh as her father again. He'd tossed her to a large, hulking man on a huge warhorse, who carried her before him. Having little experience riding on a horse, let alone one this size, she feared death at every moment. They called him "Brisbois" and his usual task was as Lord Hugh's torturer. He'd come over from France to carry out whatever his duties were. She expected rough treatment from such a man, and so his gentle handling of her when he did not need to be so surprised her.

Yet something was wrong with her, for no matter how hard she tried, she could not shift into fire. She'd tried when she gained consciousness and watched Yester Castle disappear into the distance. She'd tried on the field when she saw her friends and neighbors come out of the forest armed and empty-minded.

How could she face them now—any of them, those who lived in the village, her parents, William or his men—now that she had killed an innocent man with her power? She'd never felt so soiled or low.

But it had taught her a valuable lesson—never, never, ever trust Lord Hugh. It was just terrible that it had cost a man's life to discover that truth.

"Here. Drink this," Brisbois ordered, handing her a skin of ale. So very tired and thirsty from hours of relentless riding north, she accepted it and drank deeply.

Though her hands were tied at all times, she was permitted to walk when they made short stops along the road. If Brisbois did not hold her leash, another of the warriors did. She'd heard Lord Hugh order that none speak to her, so she traveled in silence. She handed the skin back and watched as Brisbois returned it to Lord Hugh.

Her stomach turned then as she realized he was putting something in the ale! Her mouth went dry, and she was tempted to force it back up her throat. She gagged and coughed but kept it down. Whatever it was, it was not poison, for she continued to live and regret every moment in her life when she'd longed for her father to claim her.

They stopped for the night a few hours after sunset. The men were accustomed to traveling like this and did not require tents or other comforts. A few blankets were thrown on the ground for her to sleep on and another to cover her. Every bone in her body ached from the hours in the saddle. And yet they had days of travel ahead, from what she'd overheard.

Once sleep descended over the camp, she found it impossible to do so. She feared the nightmares she knew would follow her after witnessing such terrible things. Her body ached on the hard ground. Just as she began to drift off, screams filled the area. She started to get up but was pushed back down by the soldier guarding her.

Glancing around as best she could, she could tell the sounds came from the other side of the camp. Loud voices. Lord Hugh's was one of them. There was another scream and sounds of a beating followed. And then it all was repeated.

They'd captured someone. One of William's men? And he was being tortured. Her stomach rebelled then as she tried to shift. The only thing she could do, it seemed, was set a bush on fire nearby.

She wanted to cover her ears, to block out the sounds, but the way they'd tied her hands around a cart so she could not escape kept her from doing that. And the sounds continued on and on through the night.

Brienne did not remember falling asleep, but suddenly someone was kicking her hip to wake her. The sun barely peeked above the horizon and already most of the camp was packed. She stumbled into the bushes when Brisbois came and released her. Then she gobbled down a crust of bread and a piece of cheese before Brisbois tied her hands once again and led her to his horse. When he held out the skin to her to drink, she hesitated.

"This is mine," he said in a quiet voice. She met his gaze then and glanced at the skin. "I know you are thirsty, girl. Drink now." So he knew she was being drugged by Lord Hugh.

"My thanks," she whispered as she took several mouthfuls of the water in it. Only as she handed it back did she see the traces of blood along the edges of his nails. Her eyes met his as she realized he had been the one torturing the unfortunate through the night.

She looked away, knowing that she had done Lord Hugh's bidding as well. How could she hold this man any guiltier than she herself was?

They were on the road soon after. Not long after that, storms struck, slowing their pace to a crawl. Brisbois pulled a thick tartan blanket out of his pack and covered her with it as they rode along. Clearly, some rain and wind were not enough to make Lord Hugh stop. The bigger surprise came when the lord handed her some strips of dried meat.

"Why?" she asked, accepting them and hiding them beneath the blanket. He ignored her question and kept riding, following the others.

"You have to keep up your strength," he said. She lifted her face to look at him, ignoring the rains.

"Why?" she asked again. He gave her no answer and rode on.

Hours passed, with fewer stops now, and she heard orders passed back through the riders that they were heading for the coast. Though she'd dreamed of visiting the sea as a child, her first view of it was certainly not as she'd hoped. Afraid she'd be sleeping in the rain that night, Brienne was surprised when Brisbois led her to a small barn near a larger stone house.

"Lord Hugh is their guest and sleeps within," Brisbois said as he saw her settled in one corner of the unused building.

He left for a short time, and another man guarded her from the doorway. When he returned, he carried a bowl and a cup, which he held while the other guard released her from her bonds and left. He handed her the bowl, in which she found a portion of plain stew, still steaming.

"My thanks for bringing this," she said. "Do you want some?" He shook his head and went to sit by the door.

She dipped the spoon into it and ate it too quickly. He produced a small loaf of bread from one pocket in his jacket and tossed it to her. Then he pulled a skin from inside it and filled a battered cup to the top before bringing it over to her. Brienne drew her legs up under the length of her gown and sat cross-legged, eating and drinking until every morsel of food and every drop of water was gone.

He grunted when she handed him the bowl and cup back empty, and she thought it was one of satisfaction.

"Have you eaten, then?" she asked.

"Aye, with the others."

She leaned against the wall and pulled one of the blankets around her. The sound of the rain on the roof soothed her, and she could feel her body sinking into sleep, but there was one thing she needed to know.

"That man. Is he dead?"

He did not pretend to misunderstand. "Nay."

"Will you kill him?" she asked, watching his surprised expression. "Or just torture him?"

He ignored her question then, closing his eyes as though trying to sleep. She knew he would not, for he'd not yet bound her hands or feet to secure her for the night.

"Is he one of Sir William's men?" she asked softly. It was what she feared the most.

"Nay. He is from the west," he replied. She let out her breath at his answer. Not one of William's but one of Marcus's group. He must have been following them when he was captured.

"Is it difficult for you to torture or kill someone?" To plan something like that was unthinkable to her.

"You ask too many questions about killing," he said. "You have no need for such knowledge."

She stopped asking and leaned her head back. Closing her eyes, she confessed her darkest sin to the man who killed for his living.

"I killed a man yesterday. A friend. A man who had asked to court me," she whispered. "He made me kill my friend."

The tears flowed then, silently, and she turned away so he could not see them in the light of the lantern between them. Sorrow filled her as she remembered all the good things about James.

"'Tis his sin, then, no' yours, lass."

She slept restlessly that night and thought someone stroked her hair, comforting her as her mother used to when she could not find sleep. In the morning, the sun broke through the clouds and she saw the sea for the first time.

William did not waste time trying to follow them to the coast. Instead he took his men at a brutal pace back to Edinburgh and the king. The king was not there, staying at Dunfermline Abbey over in Fife instead, so William met with his Exchequer and got what he needed based on the king's previous orders. Leaving a message for the king's private secretary about increasing the number of guards on him, William led his company to Leith, to the cog the king's man had ordered made ready for their use.

From what Marcus and Aislinn could tell him, the stone circle they sought was north and west of Aberdeen, so they would sail there and go by land from the coast. Though those from Far Island were experienced sailors, his men did not fare as well on board the small ship.

Marcus and the others continued to teach him more about the ancient gods whose powers passed down to him and others and about the prophecies. But their worried expressions warned him that their friend was in danger.

"Do you know if he yet lives?" Will asked them as the ship moved along the coast, north of the firth.

"He lives," Marcus answered.

"How do you know this? Tell me of this connection you share. Is it because of your training?" he asked, sitting on a bench near the front of the ship.

"Aislinn is the strongest connection we have. She dreamwalks and sees him."

"Dreamwalks?" he asked, looking to her for an explanation.

"I cannot exactly explain how it works, William," she said. "I sleep. I dream. I walk and find those I know."

"And your man? You found him?"

"Aye. Corann has heard me." He waited for more, but when she did not go on, he asked.

"Will he break, Aislinn? Will Hugh find out the method to open the circle from him?"

"He is not practiced at deception, William. And he is not a warrior. He . . . will break . . . soon."

If Hugh knew what Corann could do—read the signs, chant the prayers—he might keep him alive. If he did, it could give them time to rescue him when they took Brienne back.

"Can you find Brienne in your dreamwalk?"

"I do not know. I have never sought someone not a priest," Aislinn said, glancing at Marcus first. "I can try though. You could help me find her since your connection to her is so strong."

"How? Tell me how."

"We must wait until nightfall. We will try then."

The next few hours were the slowest in his life, but finally, the men and women on the ship settled down to sleep for the night. William gathered with Marcus, Aislinn, Roger, and Gautier at the front of the ship, where a tent had been erected. They waited until dark had fallen completely and then began the task of finding Brienne.

William floated. His body remained on the ship, but his mind drifted above them. Aislinn spoke softly to him, pushing him to let go and sleep. He could feel her words and thoughts as though they were touches, nudges, pushing him this way and that.

Lord Hugh pushed his thoughts but not like this. He overpowered with his, while Aislinn gently led.

"Bring Brienne to mind now, William. In your thoughts, make her image clear and strong."

He smiled as he did it, for the image he had of her was lying naked on his bed, in his arms, as she found her release. Her head flung back, her skin glistening with sweat, his hand buried between her legs, stroking her until she screamed.

"Mayhap not that clear," Aislinn instructed as both she and Marcus chuckled.

William opened his eyes and looked at them. "Can you see her as I do?" he asked. Brienne would never forgive him for sharing such an intimate moment with them.

"Nay," she said with a soft laugh now. "But the way you feel about her is very strong."

Oh God. Can they tell I am aroused from the memory of her that night?

"Aye."

Will opened his eyes but she had not, still sitting next to him, eyes closed.

"Take a deep breath and try once more."

He let the motion of the ship on the water, its gentle rocking as it skimmed over the surface, lull him closer to sleep. This time he saw Brienne as he had the first time. Standing behind Gavin before peeking out to look at him, the colors of her standing out against the duller shades of everyone else and her eyes meeting his.

"Brienne," he whispered.

"Again."

"Brienne . . . Brienne. Where are you, *ma chérie*?"

"I see her," Aislinn whispered, her grip on his hand stronger now. "A small flame in the darkness, I am walking to her now." A few seconds passed in silence. "Say her name and speak to her. In your thoughts."

Brienne, are you there? Are you well?

"She is well." She squeezed his hand again.

Why do you not escape him?

"He is giving her something that mutes her powers. She cannot shift to fire now." William heard Marcus curse at this news.

"Ask her about Corann. Before I lose her. And ask her to see where she is."

Brienne, is Marcus's man Corann with you? Is he alive?

"Aye, though she did not know his name. They have tortured him. They are torturing him now. She can hear his cries."

William felt her hot tears fall on his skin at such a revelation. This time he gently squeezed Aislinn's hand.

He knows how to open the circle, Brienne. Tell Lord Hugh of his worth.

He felt her reaction then through his connection or Aislinn's—fear, anger, sorrow. Then he saw the young man James's death and felt her heartbreak.

It could save Corann's life, Brienne. Keep him alive until we reach you both.

"Ask her if she knows their destination."

Where are you heading, love? Have you heard any words or directions?

"Aberdeen. Inverurie. Oldmeldrum. Though she knows not where those places are." Aislinn patted his hand now. "Let her sleep. I can feel her exhaustion."

Rest now. Worry not, love. We are on our way to you. Do not lose heart.

"She's slipped away, William. I cannot see her any longer."

She released his hand, and he opened his eyes. Her gaze filled with knowing, she smiled at him then. Had she heard his words? She stood and whispered with

Marcus before leaving the tent without another word to him.

"We can land near Aberdeen and travel from there," Marcus explained. "Would you tell the commander, Roger?"

Roger made his way out of the tent, observing them with his usual silent regard.

"Do you know the area, William?" Marcus asked.

"Aye, dozens of standing stones and even circles strewn all through that area. Some large, some small. All ancient. How will we know which is the true gateway?"

"Worry not on that," Marcus advised. "As two of the bloods approach the circle, the goddess will try to break free. You, Brienne, Hugh, and the rest of us will know the true circle then."

"And if she breaks free? Can she escape?"

No one would speak of that. What was this goddess, and what would happen if they failed?

"What is she?"

"She is the destructor. She is chaos. She is fire. Very simply, her escape will be the end of the world as we know it. Death and fire will rule over man and reason." Marcus shuddered as he finished his words.

"Beginning with us?" he asked.

"Aye, we will be the first to die. But if she escapes, that could be merciful for us considering what the rest of humanity would face."

From deep within him, in his soul, William understood the danger. His ancestors had exiled this goddess once, and he must ensure that she did not escape the prison that held her now.

But could he save the woman he loved from a madman who would sacrifice anyone and everything in his quest for power?

Hours later he still paced the small confines of the ship, trying to sort out the endless possibilities ahead. With the dawn came no clarity of anything except his purpose.

To save Brienne.

CHAPTER 23

She walked slowly around the ship with Brisbois only a step behind her. The ship's rise and fall as it moved across the smooth sea made it difficult to keep her balance as she did. It was her first time on a boat, and this was a large one that carried many. Gazing across the water, she saw the other one a short distance away.

They did not bind her, for she could not swim and dared not try to escape. And since no man there would touch her, she had more freedom on the ship than she'd had on land.

On the third time that she'd circled the ship, she paused close to the unconscious heap of broken flesh that was a man named Corann. Though his face was beaten almost beyond recognition, she thought he might have been one of the men who'd taken her that day in the forest. Brisbois pushed her shoulder, so she continued past the man, trying to come up with a way to do as William had asked her.

She had dreamed of him!

She'd expected nightmares to haunt her sleep. Instead she could see and hear him as though he stood before her. She thought him just a dream until he asked her questions about that man and about their journey. He'd asked her to save Corann by sharing a vital piece of information with Lord Hugh—that he knew the priests' method to open the circle.

Lord Hugh would keep him alive then. At least until they reached the stones. At least until William could reach them as he promised. She smiled then, remembering his words to her as he'd promised to reach her.

As she approached him once more, she said his name loud enough for others to hear. Stopping before him, she repeated it.

"Corann?"

"Move along, girl," Brisbois ordered gruffly, nudging her shoulder to push her on.

"Does Lord Hugh know who this man is, Brisbois?" she asked. When Lord Hugh approached from the place where he stood in the front of the ship, she knew he'd heard her. She felt his presence behind her before he even said a word. Would there ever be a time when she could not?

"Brienne? You know this man?" he asked. He pushed Corann, forcing the huddled mass to his back, where she could see him more clearly. She could not help herself. Her gaze went to Brisbois, who looked away.

"Aye, my lord," she answered. "He took me to their camp some days ago. To draw the warblood, much as you do now."

Oh, she knew his intention. From what she'd heard, he needed only one fireblood in the circle to open it, and it would be himself. She was only the lure to bring the other one needed to it—and to ensure that he would do as ordered—so that he could open it for his goddess. Lord Hugh's expression changed from surprise to anger to amusement in just seconds.

"And he knows about the circles."

"Not as stupid as I thought," he said. "Are you speaking the truth though?"

She felt him trying to slide into her thoughts, to find the truths he wanted. He took her chin and held so that their gazes met as he pushed and probed. He thought her compliance was assured by whatever he put in her ale, so she thought of only what William had told her.

This priest can open the gateway.

This priest can open the gateway.

Over and over, she repeated it in her thoughts, and she began trying to push him out. Feeling more ability than she should have, she used only the barest bit of her power to resist.

"He can open the gateway?" he asked, staring at her. She tried to pull away from him. "This priest can open it? Tell me, Brienne. Now!"

The crushing pain in her head nearly blinded her. She collapsed on the deck next to the tortured man. "Aye, my lord."

His laughter echoed across the ship and the sea, and every one of his minions was drawn to it. For a moment she imagined that every soul in Scotland and beyond cringed at the evil sound.

"See to him then, Brienne. Keep him alive." Lord Hugh kicked the man, who roused and peered through a slit where one of his eyes should be. "She is your savior, Corann."

He walked off, still laughing, calling out orders to

get her what she needed. Brisbois stood over her, watching her every move and expression.

"Let me die," Corann rasped out, grabbing her with his bloodied hand. "I beg you, let me die."

She wanted to comfort him and tell him the truth, but he could confess it if they tortured him again. When Brisbois handed her a skin of fresh water and she held it to Corann's mouth, he refused it. Brienne cleaned his wounds and bandaged his broken arm as best she could. A blanket appeared, as did some watered-down porridge from their last meal. He refused that as well, determined to die with his knowledge.

Brisbois stood silently by through the rest of the day, saying nothing but missing not a movement or word she spoke. Lord Hugh stood under the tent on the high platform at the front of the ship and watched everything. From time to time, he would walk over and stand beside her. She waited for him to invade her mind, but he did nothing but watch.

They traveled north along the coast, always north, and she spent some moments watching the smaller boats of fishermen and merchants glide by, though none came too close. The sky remained clear that day and the sea calm, and soon they passed by a huge castle sitting on a rock cliff at the sea's edge. Lord Hugh's attention was drawn to it as well.

There was a low humming tone within it, as though some power sat beneath the castle in the rock itself. Was this a place of power, a sacred place, as he'd called it? It took some time and distance before the sound disappeared. Is that what would happen at the circle? As it had in his demonic chamber belowground? Did evil have a sound?

"What will happen?" she asked, against her own decision not to speak to him. She needed to know.

"At the gateway?" She nodded. "You will enter the circle with the warblood. He"—he nodded at Corann—"he will perform the ritual and open it. The goddess will be freed."

Remembering the sound and shape of the being behind the barrier made her shiver. She had no doubt that anyone in the circle would be dead once the goddess was free and had all of her powers back.

"You think to survive this, then? That she will let you live?" she asked.

A sense of peace filled her as she realized there was no question of her survival—she would not. She only hoped that she could get William and the others away before she died. Lord Hugh strode up to her, grabbing her face and bringing it to his.

"She has promised me great rewards for my loyal service," he whispered harshly so only she could hear. "I will be at her side, Brienne, as you should be." He released her. "You are almost out of time to choose the right side in this. Stand with me or be destroyed with the rest when she reigns."

"But what of the king? You were his guardian and regent, one of his oldest friends and counselors. Will he not fight for his kingdom?"

"His death will make it that much easier to take over."

She looked away and took a deep breath. So his plan included the king's death. William's father. She must warn him somehow, but she could not dare to anger Lord Hugh further.

"Now get back over there and see to that priest."

He called Brisbois as he walked back to his place at the front. As he spoke to his torturer, the man gazed back at her. She tried to ignore it, but she wondered if he'd just been given his orders to kill her.

Brisbois came now and stood over her once more. She tended to Corann as best she could, squeezing drops of water into his mouth and waiting for him to swallow. Awake, he fought her. Asleep or unconscious, she could get a few precious drops down his throat.

"You frighten him." Glancing up at the huge man, she was puzzled. "You scare him as no other has ever," he repeated with something that resembled a smile.

"What makes you say that? His powers are so much stronger than mine. He has knowledge and abilities that I have no idea even exist. How can I frighten him?" she asked.

He shrugged. Sometimes his wordlessness frustrated her. She thought about what she'd seen just now.

"Will you be my executioner?" she asked with a boldness she did not quite feel.

"When the time comes, aye." The man's piercing gaze did not move from hers. "I will make it a quick one, girl." She turned back to Corann when he spoke again. "As I hope you would make mine if the chance came."

Stunned by his admission, she could not speak. Then, remembering James's death, she thought that their tacit agreement might be a good thing.

Will did not believe in failure. The warblood who lived within him now did not either. Even so, he took no chances, reviewing their plan over and over as they crossed the miles north into countryside outside Aberdeen.

In Edinburgh, he'd sent a group of his men and some of the priests ahead by horse overland. The seas were untrustworthy and could send a ship miles and weeks off their course. He could not chance that. The king's gold paid the way north. Landing south of Aberdeen, he knew she was near.

He did not need to dreamwalk as the seer did—the warblood's connection to his fireblood was strong and clear. Apparently, the love they felt for each other bonded them in some elemental way he did not yet understand. But he knew that all he had to do was unleash his desire or need for her and the warblood would seek his mate.

Marcus informed him that more of his priests would join them at the circle, even though only one was needed to complete the ritual. Aislinn said little or nothing now, spending most of her time in between dreams and spell-weaving.

Insulted when Roger said the priests were worthless, worse, a burden to protect, Marcus cast a spell that took away his voice. And, he promised, there would be other spells, more powerful ones, to hide them from their enemy and to aid them in sealing the gateway forever.

One thing did give him pause—he discovered that none of them knew the actual ritual—they needed to be ready to read the signs at the circle. But it involved spilling the blood of the two on the altar stone. More than that, blank expressions were the only answers he got from them.

Part of him could still not understand this strange new world in which he now existed. The human warrior in him liked solid ground and strategic plans. That part of him liked knowing that his superior fighting skills would tip the balance of any battle. But this new world with beings of great powers and unknown abilities threatened to undermine his confidence and that of his men.

With every mile closer—to the circle, to the goddess, and to Brienne—William felt his own power growing and strengthening. When they stopped to rest the horses or to eat or take their ease, he practiced his, letting the power rise in his blood until his body changed. Pushing it further and stronger each time, until he became the weapon himself. At his command, at his will.

When they stopped for the night south of Inverurie, a village of some size, and gathered for one more time to finish their plans, Roger—with his voice restored—and Marcus came to him with a plan of their own.

"You say you can sense them—Lord Hugh and Brienne?" Roger asked. At Will's nod, he continued. "So they can tell you're coming closer?" Roger looked at Marcus. "And the priests? The same?" Marcus nodded.

Aislinn joined the group then with word that the other group of soldiers sent by land had arrived and that the priests of Far Island were not too long off. And that Lord Hugh and Brienne were only a mile or so from the circle. She looked exhausted from seeking so much knowledge in visions. Haunted and pale. She accepted a cup of ale from him and sat by his side.

"Then it must be us who get Brienne out of there. And it must be before they reach it."

"Us?" Will asked.

"Us, men—humans only," Roger said. "He can't sense us coming the way he seems to sense you. . . ."

"But he will know. He will expect such an attack."

Any good commander would, and from what Will had witnessed, Eudes had much experience and skill.

"Aye." Roger nodded. "So Marcus and his lads will . . . ?" He waved his hand, waiting for Marcus to fill in the correct word.

"Cast," Marcus filled in.

"Cast one of his fog spells to cover our movements. One group goes straight in, and the other goes for the girl."

"And Corann," Aislinn added. "He is so weak that he prays for death so he will not betray his duty to us and to the gods."

"Marcus? Will it work?" he asked.

"Only the gods know that, William, and they have not told me yet." Will smiled at his attempt to lighten such a grave topic. "I think that it could. Lord Hugh will be experiencing the same thing you and Brienne and we are—a sudden change to the powers we have. So if you approach, it could draw his attention away from their"—he nodded to Roger—"attack."

"This is something we must do soon," Will told them. "The longer we are here, the more time he has to prepare for us. We do not know how many more he has called to his side to face us."

They added details, each one using their own skills, talents, and experience to perfect the plan until they all agreed. They would travel the last few miles toward the circle before dawn and make their rescue at day-break.

Something in the pit of his gut made him call his men together to outline their alternate plan if anything went wrong in the rescue. Then he walked the perime-ter of their camp, watching as some of the priests set spells to keep out intruders and others prepared for the morning.

As he lay on his blankets, he tried to reach Brienne on his own, not using Aislinn's power. He could not see her, but he sent his thoughts out to her. By this time on the morrow, their quest would reach its conclusion and, just as they'd done with the priests, the gods had not deigned to tell him if they would succeed.

Or if evil would be unleashed on an unsuspecting world.

CHAPTER 24

Brienne shivered herself awake in the cold mist of the morning. The *haar* was so thick she could not see more than a foot or two away from her. Corann shivered his sleep. She felt him and heard him, but he did not wake. Brisbois had given her a potion for him he said would ease the man's pain, and it held him in sleep's grasp now. As she tried to pull the blanket over him, the rope around her wrists kept her from doing so.

"Brisbois? Can you untie my hands?"

She peered through the heavy, moving fog and listened for his reply. Nothing. Had he moved away then, called to some duty by Lord Hugh? Then she noticed the unearthly calm that the fog seemed to cause, for she could hear no one and nothing.

Then it came. His war cry split the silence, and her blood surged at the sound.

William was coming for her!

She needed to free herself and help Corann so they were ready when he got to her. Scrambling to her knees, she tried to loosen the knots. Brienne could still not see into the fog, and it seemed to thicken around her.

"Brienne?" a soft voice whispered from a few yards away.

Before she could answer, the attack began, or attacks, for she could hear fighting in three directions. Men rushed through the camp with torches, trying to defend their lord.

"Brienne? Are you here?" It was Aislinn, the girl from Marcus's people.

"Aye, and Corann," she whispered back. "I need help getting free. Where is William?"

Aislinn reached her side, cutting through the rope and checking Corann. "We must hurry. His distractions will last but a short time."

"Aislinn, what are you doing here?" A man joined them then, grabbing the girl and moving her aside. "Does Marcus know?" he asked as he uncovered Corann and knelt next to him.

"He needs me," she answered back.

A wind began then, whipping the fog into swirling shapes.

"Get him!" Aislinn looked at her. "We must get away now."

Brienne stood, ready to follow her to William. The man gathered Corann and put him over his shoulder. Standing, with Aislinn helping him to balance Corann, the man pointed in the direction they must go. She'd taken one step when flames of fire came for her. Moving at an incredible speed, the living fire seemed to hop from torch to torch, growing and changing until Lord Hugh stood before her, illuminating the area around her.

Aislinn was exposed, too, so she grabbed for Brienne's hand when the fire landed at her feet around her. Shocked by Lord Hugh's ability to move from flame to flame, Brienne screamed out in pain, for she still could not change and knew she would die. Lord Hugh shifted partly to human form, maintaining a burning grip on her. Since she could not overpower him, she watched in horror as he called out more orders to men he clearly had at the ready.

"Brisbois! Take her now!"

Brisbois stepped from the shadows and grabbed Aislinn, wrapping his huge arms around her and tightening his hold until she could not move.

"She is more valuable than the half-dead one," Lord Hugh said. "My thanks to your warblood for providing me with one of the most powerful priests I have ever encountered."

Brienne watched helplessly as Brisbois dragged Aislinn along with them. Lord Hugh's men gathered behind them, protecting them as they mounted their horses and rode to the circle. The sun broke over the horizon as they reached it, and Brienne could see the field where Lord Hugh's men already were in position to defend. He rode through the line, and they closed behind him. Reaching the lower of two circles, he dropped her to the ground and dismounted.

The same low hum she'd heard as they'd sailed past the castle on the coast was here, too. But it grew louder with every step they took up the hill. And her power flickered within her, too, unable to resist the call of the stones.

Brisbois stared at her as she allowed it to rise through her skin. Lord Hugh shifted to his fiery shape and continued to surround her, controlling her, but as she watched Brisbois, she remembered what he'd done for her. He'd stopped giving her whatever Lord Hugh was adding to the water to keep her powers from answering her command. Mayhap he hoped she would remember her promise to make his death a quick one?

"Is Paulin within the circle?" Lord Hugh called out.

"Aye, my lord," Eudes replied, grabbing the reins of their horses. He handed a torch to Brisbois.

"Brisbois, take the priest to him. Make certain she reads the signs and is ready when the warblood arrives." His torturer dragged Aislinn, crossing into the circle and taking her to the altar stone.

"William will not open the gateway for you," Brienne said. "He will sacrifice himself before he helps you bring . . . HER . . . into this world."

"Ah, sweet Brienne." He laughed as he dragged her closer and closer to the stones, which began to glow and hum louder. "He would not do a thing to save himself, but for you and the seer and his father, he would go to hell and back. And that is exactly what I intend for him . . . and you."

He used little force against her, believing her still compelled by the magical potion he'd been feeding her. Brienne allowed it and did not reveal that her strength and power and ability to change were back and were even stronger because of the stones that seemed to be the source of it. She waited, giving William a chance to save Aislinn before she would take Lord Hugh through the barrier in the heart of the circle and let their fireblood seal it over them.

Brienne had seen it in the memories of the goddess when they'd merged and melded in the barrier. Her blood and his, the last living firebloods, would forever close this gateway, preventing what he was trying to do. She could bring an end to the possibility that their bloodline would rise again.

Now she peered into the circle and saw Aislinn there, at a stone altar with Brisbois at her back and another man at their side. Lord Hugh was focusing his efforts on making the perimeter of the stones a hell. He set it all on fire so that none could pass. Chanting, he walked around it, casting more fire until the stones were almost invisible among it.

"Warblood!" he called out in a voice too loud to be human. "I will destroy them both if you do not do my bidding now."

It was a voice that combined male and female—Hugh and the goddess spoke. Brienne felt the ground trembling and knew she was attempting to force herself through the barrier that was the center of the circle. All it would take was a slight rupture and she would escape into this world. *Their* world.

She was held, burning and not being destroyed, against the tallest of the stones. It towered over her and seemed to grow taller by the minute. All the stones did, stretching and groaning and changing. Symbols appeared, being carved before her eyes like metal in her father's fire pit.

Flames. War hammer. A horse. A tree. A sun. Water moving. A stick figure of a man. A bolt of lightning. Carved, glowing, and disappearing. Again and again, across all the stones.

Then she heard the clamor of fighting coming closer and saw William striding toward her. Her blood roared and her powers soared as he approached.

He was enormous, almost as tall as the stone at her back, with huge muscles. His limbs were weapons that no man could have wielded. His eyes were huge and red, and his skin was the color of the sky and ice. He was death walking, and he was aiming at Lord Hugh.

He paused before her, and his eyes were William's for a moment, as was his voice.

"Brienne, my love," he said. He reached through the flames that surrounded her and stroked her cheek. She watched the skin on his blue hands begin to burn and still he did not pull away.

"Save Aislinn. She cannot survive the fire," she urged him.

He stepped back, the warblood once more, and faced Hugh.

"'Tis not just the one, Warblood," Hugh called out to him, and he pointed to the other side of the circle. Marcus's priests were surrounded by the flames. "I will kill all of them now or feed them to my goddess later," he threatened, "unless you open the gateway."

Hugh set one of the priests aflame to demonstrate his power and his determination. But William understood that Hugh would kill every last one of them if the warblood became his pawn. He watched every second of the priest's torment, honoring his sacrifice as others would honor his, for he could not allow the gateway to be open.

He pulled the power into his blood, urging it on, forcing his body to push to a new size and strength. Then he turned his hands into flat hammers. With one last look at Brienne, the woman he loved, the fireblood he would never claim, he ran, aiming at the stone next to where Hugh held her. The pain of the impact of his body against the stone was immeasurable, but so was the pleasure at feeling it move.

Hugh did not realize his intent until he did it a second time . . . and a third. The warblood's bones crushed and healed, crushed and healed with each impact. If he could bring down this stone and destroy the altar stone behind it, the integrity of the circle would break and no spell could be cast there.

The stone began to wobble. The warblood smiled and prepared to hit it for the last time.

And Hugh screamed and attacked him.

The fire swarmed him, burning his skin, burning his lungs, and driving him away. All it would take was one more blow to knock it over, but the heat and torment of the flames directed at him forced him to stop just a few paces from the stone. He laughed then, for Hugh had forgotten he needed the warblood for the spell and was destroying him on his own. Either way, it would end here.

And Brienne would survive.

I love you, Brienne.

If he died saving her and the rest of his world, so be it. The warblood closed his eyes.

She was there before him, a shield against the flames her father aimed at him. He felt Brienne but saw the fireblood around him.

I love you, William, she whispered in his thoughts and in his heart.

Hugh screamed again, and it sounded like a roar around and in him. Brienne did not relent, surrounding him so that nothing touched him.

Go, get Aislinn. Save them. Trust me.

And he did.

As she spread herself into a wall of flames, wider and longer over him, a path opened for him into the circle. He ran to get the priest but found her waiting for him. The warblood looked back and saw that the flames battled each other now, Brienne trying to keep her father out of the circle while he was in there.

"Hold up the torch," Aislinn said to the soldier who had carried her there. He was one of Hugh's men and yet he followed her orders without hesitation. The other lay dead on the ground. "Your hand, Warblood!"

He rushed to the altar stone and held his hand over it. Aislinn cut across his wrist, and his blood, blue now and glowing, flowed onto its surface. Then she held her breath, grabbed his hand, and did the same to her wrist. He watched as her human blood, rich and red, mixed with his.

"Call her now, William! Now!"

BRIENNE! He shouted it with his voice and his thoughts and his heart and his soul.

In horror, he watched the firefight outside the circle between Brienne and her father end in a flash—one second she held him back and in the next she disappeared. He heard Hugh's victorious laugh ring out. If Hugh entered the circle now and completed the other ritual with his blood, the world would end in fire and destruction.

In the next instant, before he could breathe or move or think, Brienne materialized from the torch that Hugh's man held. Still fire, she held out part of her and it became her hand and arm. Aislinn grabbed her, joined the three, and cut her wrist over the pool of their blood, adding the molten-gold colored blood to theirs.

The marks of their bloodlines lit up on their skin,

and suddenly the stones vibrated, sending out a sound unlike any he'd ever heard before. Chiming bells or singing stones? A barrier formed between the stones, keeping them inside.

And Hugh was outside.

"We are not finished yet, and he still has the power to destroy those outside," Aislinn said. "The stones must be marked and sealed."

The warblood turned and saw a great chasm form in the center of the circle. A roar emanated from deep within it.

"The goddess will try to escape now. Find the stone carved with your symbol and"—she smeared some of the gathered blood onto her mark—"and place yours on it."

He dipped his hands into the blood and smeared it on his arm, covering the mark in blood that boiled and swirled with the mixed colors and powers of the three of them. Brienne did the same, and they ran into the circle to the stone carrying their symbol.

The roar from the center of the circle increased, and the warblood saw talons and glowing eyes there. And fire, long bursts of fire and molten streams against whatever held it captive. The ground shook and the stones' song grew louder and louder.

He found his stone and waited for the fireblood and priest to take their places. When they did, they raised their marks and placed them in the carvings at the same moment.

The sky above them glowed and swirled, creatures or beings appeared over them, and the stones melted and reached for that sky before bending over to touch in the middle, over the abyss. The altar stone cracked in two, and the pool of blood flowed onto the ground and dripped into the void. Screams of rage and agony erupted as the pit sealed from the edges into the center. Then it was gone, all of it, leaving them in the middle of an empty field, the stones buried once more deep in the earth.

The warblood, the fireblood, and the priest were gone, and only William, Brienne, and Aislinn remained.

But Hugh de Gifford was only defeated, not dead.

William took Brienne in his arms and kissed her hungrily, then stepped away. There *would* be time for them, but first he needed to deal with the threat to his men, their people.

"Come, my love," he said to Brienne, holding out his hand to her. "There is still much to do." Pointing to Aislinn, he ordered the man who'd witnessed it all, "Protect her."

Then, with his mate at his side, he strode toward the fighting.

CHAPTER 25

Hugh the fireblood laughed when he vanquished his daughter.

Now all he must do to complete his quest was enter, destroy the altar stone, and join his blood with the warblood over the barrier to break it and free Chaela.

She would be glorious! Freed after centuries, eons, she would rise above them and destroy all who opposed her, who opposed them. They would rule the world together. Gathering his form, he turned to enter the circle.

And could not!

The stones changed and glowed and kept him out. He tried as a fireblood and then in his human shape, but a force greater than he'd ever encountered, stronger than anything the goddess had ever produced, kept him out.

Gazing into the circle, he watched as his daughter materialized from the flame of the torch, a power he did not know she possessed. Pride would not stop him from destroying her now and destroying every one of those who had helped her.

"No!" he screamed as she spilled her blood with the others. "NO!"

She could not do this. She could not stop him, stop the one who gave her the power in her blood!

He became a fire of immense size and strength and tried to burn his way through whatever kept him out, but it did nothing. He pushed himself through the air, circling the stones, burning and forcing against it until a terrible noise filled the air from within it, a cry of suffering and anguish so deep that it shook the earth.

When the stones bent to join in the center, he knew he'd lost.

Hugh did not waste his time or the men he had left. He changed his plan and called out orders to Eudes and the others to gather. Creating a wall of fire, he sent it out at the attackers, forcing them away so that he could escape. Riding away from the site of his first defeat, he offered up his prayer and pledge to his goddess. He knew it was not a complete failure, for he'd taken steps to begin the chaos that the goddess would finish.

Now that he knew how the priests communicated and what knowledge they shared, he grabbed one of them as they rode past. Not seeing Brisbois, and realizing he would die at the warblood's hand in the circle, Hugh tossed the priest to Eudes, who would now have to extract that information that his torturer would have.

With the priest, he could gain the location of the next circle, his next chance to free her and destroy their enemies. As they reached the top of the ridge, Hugh opened his senses, trying to get some idea of where they needed to go. Ripples of power echoed to him from the north. The priest Aislinn would discern the specific location from signs inside the stones, and their prisoner would share that with him.

Brienne walked at William's side toward the mayhem. Her blood felt different now. The power coursed more strongly through her, and she could feel some abilities she did not know she had before. Jumping from fire to fire was only a small part of them. If she became fire now, she could travel in that form through the air.

And William must be feeling the same changes within him.

She could not believe the powers he had nor the size he had become in that circle. And yet he never lost himself to it all. That was another change to them—they did not lose their humanity even as they became something else.

By the time they reached the battle, it was dissipating, for Lord Hugh was already retreating, escaping with those of his soldiers still alive, riding north over the hills. The wall of fire evaporated as he took his attention from it to save himself.

"There are more circles," Aislinn said from behind them.

Glancing back, she saw Brisbois standing guard at the priest's back.

William turned and nodded. "And you know their location? How to find them?" he asked.

"I read the signs on the altar stone before it was destroyed and await the prophecy that will complete it."

"When will that come, Aislinn?" Brienne asked.

"As and when the gods allow it."

"We should see to the wounded and organize ourselves for the journey," William said, tugging her hand. She smiled as she realized that he had not let go of her since they survived the ritual a few minutes ago.

They began to walk toward the people who gathered around the field, but she tugged William to a stop.

"Give me a moment. I wish to speak to Brisbois."

From his darkening expression, neither William nor the warblood in him liked the idea. He gazed at her, and she let him know all was well. He kissed her hand and released it, walking at Aislinn's side a few paces ahead of them.

"Why did you do it?" she asked the man whose actions had saved her and Aislinn, and probably ensured their success over his master.

He gave her that look, the one that said he did not wish to discuss such matters, and continued walking. Then he spoke quietly.

"You frightened him, girl. No one has done that before. And better than that, you defied him."

"And you have served him for a long time?" she asked, knowing nothing of how or why this man had become Lord Hugh's torturer.

"From the moment of his birth," he said, drawing back the sleeve of his tunic to reveal the same mark that she carried. "We shared our mother's womb, but only one could have the power. He was firstborn and inherited it. I became his to command, since he was the heir."

Brienne stopped and stared at his face then. She'd never looked for nor seen the resemblance before and yet it sat there in plain view.

"Brienne?" William called out to her, sensing her distress. She waved him on and faced her . . . uncle.

"Twins?" she asked. His face had been changed over

time and from injuries and hadn't been influenced by the goddess's power into something different from his brother's. He nodded. "And now?" she asked, unsure how she could be certain of his loyalty while Lord Hugh yet lived.

"I am still in service to the heir," he said gruffly. He went down on his knees in front of her. "If you will have me." Holding out his arm to her, Brienne stared as the mark they shared glowed. Stunned by his words and his offer, it took her a moment to accept both.

"I am the heir?"

"Aye, girl. The only one."

"Then I accept your loyalty and your service."

She placed her own mark on his, and their skin melted, allowing their blood to touch. He hissed as the power touched him, but he did not pull away until the marks separated on their own. By the time William returned to her side, Brisbois had regained his feet.

"What are your orders, my lady?" he asked.

The thought of having someone at her command unnerved her. William took her hand and nodded, understanding that this man had pledged his loyalty.

"As William said, guard Aislinn always, until I say otherwise."

"As you command, my lady." Her uncle nodded, this time with a wink at her, and followed Aislinn as she made her way to where the priests gathered.

"Your first warrior," William said. "And your first order. How did that feel?"

"Not my first warrior and not my first order, William." She rose onto her toes and kissed his mouth. "You were my first." Another kiss. "And my first order was for you to kiss me."

He wrapped his arms around her, pulling her up against him, and she felt his body respond to her. And he kissed her. More than a kiss, he claimed her. She tasted the passion in him as he possessed her. Lifting his mouth from hers, he smiled at her, and it warmed her as no fire could.

"I cannot promise obedience, but I pledge to be faithful and to always be at your side," he began. "And to love you, Brienne. If you will have me?"

The love in his gaze was all she needed to see before giving her answer.

"Aye. I will *have you*," she said, emphasizing the last words. He laughed and kissed her, hearing it.

"First, things to see to. Then the *having* will begin."

Marcus watched as the priests gathered, forming a circle around those who had fought the battle. Then, nodding to the couple, he watched as they came forward together, hands linked as they'd been since the ritual.

Though this was not a duty he'd performed often or recently, he'd agreed to witness the giving and receiving of vows, joining the lives of these two whose souls and blood had been united already. Now it was time to give their hearts.

As they spoke the words that would make them husband and wife, Marcus smiled and guided them, just as he had before for others in his care and would again. These two had taken on the mantle of leadership, the first two of the bloodlines to rise and the first two to be proven in battle against the evil one. They would lead the journey as they sought the next circle and lead the struggle as some lived and some died.

He could feel not only the love between the two of

them, but also the way it sparked their powers even more. They would be more together as one than the sum of them separately would be. Something they would learn very soon.

As they spoke, tiny glimmers of light appeared and floated above them in the air, sparkling and shimmering, forming shapes and signs that only he and Aislinn could see. Their gazes met, and she smiled, for they bore witness to the blessing of the gods they served.

It was right. It was blessed. It had been foretold.

His own powers surged, letting him know that the prophecy they needed would be given soon.

After the ceremony, they shared a simple meal before seeking rest. This endless day had proven a success—the one whose name he dared not speak remained imprisoned in the timeless chasm and one gate had been sealed. They needed rest and healing so that they could begin the fight anew.

As William and Brienne walked out of the camp toward a more private place for their first night together, Marcus summoned the priests. They needed to pray and offer thanks to the gods. And they needed to wait for the words to be given to them.

Rest would have to wait on the gods, even as they did.

CHAPTER 26

The path wound down the hill and through a small copse of trees until it ended near the stream. The night grew chilly, as the beginning of spring in Scotland was never warm. It mattered not to him, and from the becoming flush in her cheeks, his wife did not notice it. He lifted the torch to show the path. Aislinn had whispered of preparations, and then she'd blushed, knowing what this night would bring.

William had been living in a constant state of arousal for Brienne since their first meeting, and no efforts on his part to douse that desire had worked. And that one night, when he had held her naked body to his, feeling her arousal and watching her peak, had been a torturous one for him.

But this night . . .

They reached the stream and found a tent set up there. Roger stood before it, waiting for them. Brienne, fearless, brave Brienne, tucked in close to him, became suddenly shy.

"Roger," he greeted the man, and handed him the torch. They would have no need for it.

"Will." Roger held the tent open for him.

Inside was more comfortable than he could have expected. It would not be high enough for him to stand straight, but Brienne would fit nicely. Thick, lined blankets lay in one corner, with more piled on top. A skin of liquid, some food and bread, and an unlit candle sat on a small stool that served as a table. It would do nicely.

"See you both in the morn," Roger said, and with a bow and a wink at Brienne, he walked whistling back up the path. Only when the sound and light disappeared over the hill did Will let out the laugh that he held inside.

"Come. It will be warm inside." He felt the slight hesitation in her body. "Surely you are not nervous over this small thing," he said, kissing her on the mouth that beckoned him endlessly.

"Small thing?" she asked.

"Oh, aye, you have seen it." He was teasing her, hoping to ease her nervousness. "We will do only what feels pleasurable to you. You remember how it felt that first time?" Her body shuddered. She remembered. "Let me show you that pleasure again."

She nodded and went into the tent as he held the flap open for her. Once he closed it, the enclosure grew warmer just by having them in it. When he reached for the candle, she placed her hand on his arm to stop him.

"We do not need that," she said.

As he watched, she glowed, filling the tent with warmth and light. No need for candles at all. None at all when his wife could create fire, light, and heat with her thoughts alone. Remembering the hungry expression in her gaze when she'd found him naked in his bedchamber, he decided that was the best way to begin. Will reached up and loosened the ties of his tunic.

"Wait!" she said, her voice a bit breathless. "I should undress my husband."

"I want no 'should' between us, Brienne," he said, stroking her cheek with the back of his hand. "Only 'would' and 'want.'"

She leaned against his hand as he turned it to cup her face and stroke her cheek with his thumb. "I want to undress my husband," she said.

"Then do so, wife." He relaxed his arms and waited on her.

She reached up and untied the laces of his shirt. Then she took the hem of it and slid it up his body, pushing it over his head. Tossing it on the floor, Brienne turned her attention back to him, and he could feel her heated gaze touching his skin.

He watched as she moved closer, studying his chest and his stomach, before she reached out and touched the curly hair on it. She lightly grazed it, sending waves of sensation through his skin. He stood motionless as she traced the outline of his male nipples with her finger. But he lost his ability to breathe when he saw the tip of her tongue and realized her intention.

Imitating his own caress of her breasts, she stroked with her hands while her tongue licked the sensitive skin. Pleasure coursed through his blood then, and his body grew hard and ready for her. Her mouth moved over his chest, tasting and licking his skin, but her hands did not rest idly by. She embraced him, sliding her hands around to his back and then down until she held him as he'd held her.

"You have too many garments on, wife," he said. It came out sounding like a plea.

"Worry not, husband," she said. "I am not done undressing you yet." Meeting her gaze, he noticed that she was brighter, as though more light and fire raced through her blood. He worried then, not at her power but at the wicked glimmer in her gaze as she came closer to him.

She moved around him then, kissing and licking her way to his back. Her hands continued to touch and stroke him, and he let his head fall back, enjoying every touch, every caress. If it pleased her to pleasure him, he would, he decided, allow her. But he questioned the wisdom of that very thing when her hands slid around his waist and began working on the ties of his trews.

"Brienne, love," he whispered, placing his hands on hers to stop her. He learned the foolishness of his intention when she let the fire in her heat her skin, burning him long enough that he let go.

It took little effort for her to unlace him and allow his prick out, for it stood hard, long, and begging for her touch. She leaned her face on his back and slid her hands under the fabric, pushing it down away from his waist and over his hips. Brienne took hold of his flesh and sighed against his skin as it lengthened in her grasp.

He was going to spill his seed if she continued to touch him and make those noises that she probably did not even hear. But he did. They echoed through his body, increasing the need within him. "Brienne," he whispered harshly as she stroked his needy flesh. "Brienne."

She moved again, slowly releasing him and coming around to stand before him. She studied his erection much as she had that first night, and his hardness twitched under her gaze. But when she licked her lips and leaned over closer to it, he took her by the shoulders and pulled her up to his mouth.

And ravished her there. His tongue thrust deep until she suckled it the way he'd shown her. He undressed her without even lifting his mouth from hers, and when her naked skin was against his, she seemed to melt into him. William scooped her up and carried her to the blankets. She sighed as he laid her there and came down on top of her.

The warblood inside him urged to conquer, to take, to have, pushing power into his blood and pushing his body to change. But William tempered the warrior and contained him as he loved his mate, his love, his wife.

She felt him struggling to keep his warblood inside, much as she was barely holding on to the fire within her. Each touch, each caress, each kiss pushed her closer and closer to losing control and bursting into flames. But as he controlled himself, so did she. She held tightly to the boiling power as he unleashed a different kind of heat on her body and her heart.

Brienne had thought she knew what to expect, but when his goal was unlimited, unrelenting pleasure that would end with them as one, she lost the ability to think and almost forgot to breathe as he began his attack. And it was an attack—on her senses, on her skin, on every part of her—as he began using his mouth and tongue and teeth and hands as the weapons they were.

Her skin burned as he rubbed his face down her breasts and across her belly. She arched as her body

throbbed in anticipation of what was to come. Knowing the waves of pleasure that would result from his
hands, she urged him on.

"Impatient now that you've remembered, love?" He
laughed deeply in his throat as he raised his head and
looked at her.

His mouth now poised so close to the place between
her legs that she grew wet just seeing him there. When he
moved to kneel between her legs, her flesh between them
tingled with want. He stroked her legs, taking her ankles
and guiding them apart. Then he kissed and tasted his
way along each leg as she gasped and shook from the
sheer pleasure of each touch.

He reached the top and she waited, waited for what
he would do next, and when he did nothing, she rose
onto her elbows and looked at him. Wicked did not do
justice for the expression on his face now as he leaned
down and kissed the inside of her thigh. He glanced at
her once more and then licked the other side before
putting his mouth fully on the place that ached the
most.

She screamed then and fell back, part of her wanting
to pull away from such intensity and the other part
wanting to rock against his mouth. The other part won
out. She pressed against his hot mouth, and his tongue
darted along the swelling folds. Her body shuddered
with each caress, and he laughed against her—the
sound and feel of it going into her blood.

When he teased with his teeth, nipping to make it
ache more and licking to soothe it, she reached down
for him, sliding her fingers in his long hair. He did not
slow. Using his fingers to open her, he dipped into her
with his tongue, sucking in the moisture that flowed

from her body. She could not breathe then, only feel as he took control of her body and soul.

He slid his tongue along the folds up until he touched a spot with its tip that sent her reeling, shaking and keening out his name as he pushed her free of any control she had and into some mindless creature of his doing.

"Come for me, love. Let go. Let go," he urged.

And she did.

Flying free as her body came undone under his sensual assault, she could feel herself shattering and being remade from the pieces. Over and over, breaking and forming, breaking and forming, until she was empty and then refilled in the next instant.

She was panting in shallow breaths and still throbbing when he moved over her, spreading her legs wider and seating his body there. Brienne felt his hardness and knew that this was the moment that they would become one. She opened her eyes and met his.

She had no idea of how beautiful she was to him. It almost hurt to stare into her eyes when she was still shaking with pleasure, but seeing the love in her gaze captured him. Will slid a hand down between their bodies to spread the folds and find the place that would stoke her desire again. Her body reacted to his every touch.

She moaned, low and deep, and rocked against his hand as he stroked her heated flesh, readying her to accept him inside her. When her hips rose with each caress, he lifted his and placed his cock at her opening.

"Brienne," he whispered. "Open for me, love," he urged. Then, as she opened, relaxing her legs, he pressed into her. Not gently, but a constant movement, inch by inch, until he was buried deep.

Home.

He waited, gathering his crumbling control and waiting for her body to adjust to his invasion. When she rocked her hips and gasped, he knew she was ready for the rest of it. Easing out of her, he stroked back in, using his cock to rub against the walls of her channel. She gasped and then began to moan as her body became wild beneath his.

"Put your legs up here," he said, guiding them up to his hips. "Hold on to me, love. Hold on."

Will began slowly thrusting in and sliding out, alternating deeper and harder with slower and gentler, his own muscles hardening and urging him on. His bollocks tightened, and he knew he would spill his seed soon. Leaning down, he kissed her hard and deep.

When he opened his eyes, she whispered to him. "Bring on your warblood, husband," she urged in the husky voice of arousal. "Bring him now."

His vision had gone red and he had not realized it. He thrust harder then, aching to be part of her flesh, craving the feel of her tightening around his cock. Every part of him wanted her, wanted to conquer her, take, have, possess. He gave in to her begging sobs and took her, until she screamed out and fell apart under him.

He felt every wave of pleasure as it moved through her. Every muscle, every spasm as her body took his release until he was empty. He inhaled her; he exhaled her. Then they breathed as one. Their hearts beat as one, in time with the other until he could not tell which was his or hers. Their flesh, filled and filling, throbbed as their releases eased.

He could not move. He did not wish to. Ever.

The fireblood belonged to the warblood.

Mine. Mine. Only mine, the creature chanted.

She was his mate.

Brienne was his.

He drifted off a bit, undone by her reaction and the complete satisfaction he felt. He felt the laugh rather than heard it as she answered him deep in his mind.

As you are mine.

The night passed much too quickly for his liking. The only thing that comforted him was knowing she was and would be his for a long time. After the first time, he rolled to his side and pulled her into his arms, holding her and listening to her breathe in her sleep.

He would have been content, feeling lighter and more at ease than he had in years. He would have been fine if she had not shimmied herself closer to him and sighed. Thinking her asleep, he'd ignored the call of his flesh. Then she arched her bottom against it, and he gave up fighting it.

You will be sore.

I will be fine, he heard.

You have no idea what I want to do to you now that I have you. He let several things float in his thoughts, ways he wanted to take her, things he had not yet done with or to her.

Her body answered for her, pressing against him and rocking her hips until he lifted her to her knees and showed her one thing that he wanted to do. This time her release came quietly in a long series of gasps as her flesh gripped his and milked him dry.

When daybreak finally broke into their haven, William was not certain he would survive her *having* him if every night were like this one.

CHAPTER 27

Marcus and Roger watched as the couple walked back into the camp. They laughed at the bawdy comments thrown their way by his friends. The bride blushed at every one, more likely now to understand their meanings than before.

Warblood and fireblood joined, now in heart, mind, body, and soul. He watched as they did not need to say words to speak to each other. This was a blessing from the gods and would be helpful in the coming battles.

Marcus had no doubt that this would not end easily. Roger, the warblood's man, agreed. For, in spite of his resistance and in spite of Marcus's lack of battle skills or experience, Roger de Bardem and he had forged a truce.

Now they each had bad news to deliver to William.

They walked first to the fire, where they accepted a bowl of porridge and then they greeted him and Roger. Marcus invited them to sit, sending a few men down to pack the tent so they could leave soon.

"The others arrived late last night, Will," Roger reported. "None are happy that they missed the fight."

William's gaze narrowed for a moment while he listened to Roger's words.

"What are you not telling me, Roger?"

"How the hell do you do that, Will?"

"If you really want to know, I can smell it. Your smell changes as you try to hide something."

From Roger's expression, Marcus thought the man probably had not wanted to know. He wanted to laugh but held it back because he knew the rest of it. Before Roger spoke a word, William turned his head to face Brienne. She took his hand and held it tightly against her. Then she nodded. William stared at her for several minutes and then turned back to his friend.

He already knew the worst of it.

"The king is dead," Roger said softly. "He fell from his horse in the middle of a storm. They found him the next morning dead."

No one spoke then as they watched William struggle with the news. His father the king was dead. Enough of his men knew the truth that it took little time to comprehend it. Natural sons, and daughters, were common enough and nothing unusual among the nobles and royals. Alexander, he'd been told, never suffered an empty bed or a lack of offspring—except for the legitimate, living kind needed to inherit the throne.

"You knew, Brienne?" he asked.

"Aye. Lord Hugh told me that he was going to kill the king as part of his plan to unleash chaos even before the goddess does."

"And I knew he was in danger. I told his royal commander to be on watch for an attack. Where did this accident happen, Roger? Do you know?"

"They said he fell off the cliff at Kinghorn in Fife."

Marcus had not seen much of the country of Scotland yet so he did not understand the suspicious tone in Roger's voice. "Is that unusual?" he asked.

"There are no cliffs in Kinghorn, Marcus. Only straight, level roads and a beach."

William glanced over at Brienne. "A part of his plan that was successful."

"I am so sorry, William," she said, kissing his hand then.

William sat in silence for a few moments, and Marcus allowed him this short time to grieve. Another casualty in the evil one's war to bring chaos to the world. A dead king without a clear, viable heir would do that. There was a young granddaughter, offspring of a now-dead daughter, but she was not more than a bairn, and so many things could happen to wee ones.

"Marcus?" William broke his silence. "And your news?"

He could not help the smile this time. The warblood had some sharp abilities, including the ability to detect the truth by odors. It was but one that he would discover if the old legends and stories were true and accurate.

"The gods spoke to us last night while you . . . " He did not finish that. "Aislinn interpreted the signs and the words and knows where the next circle is located."

"North, based on the direction Hugh escaped in."

"Aye. In the Norse isles to the north. Orkney."

William nodded. "And the rest of it, if you please. I would know what we are up against."

"If we know, then so does he," Aislinn said from behind William. "He took one of our priests with him when he escaped. Devyn."

"Alive?" William asked.

"Aye. For now."

William began to pace around their small group. Marcus knew he was searching for a solution, but he did not know their ways.

"Can you break your connection with him?" he asked.

"No," Aislinn said.

"Aye," he replied. At Aislinn's startled glance, he nodded. "There is a way."

"Marcus, please," she begged as she walked to him. Lowering her voice, she whispered, "You know it will mean his death. Do not do this. I beg you."

"Aislinn," William began, taking her hand in his and making her look at him. "He will not be alone in his death. Some have gone ahead of him and others, many others who will follow us will follow him into it. But his death will be empty if he dies at Hugh's hands without purpose."

Marcus watched Aislinn's tears spill over, and Brienne went to her to comfort her. Whatever she whispered to Aislinn made the difference, for she nodded to her and then at Marcus.

"How do we accomplish this?" William asked again.

"We must break the ties we have among ourselves and weave another in its place."

"Another connection? Between . . . ?"

Marcus considered it for a moment and then glanced at those around him now. "I think we should try to form a link among us, though I suspect it will not work with Roger. No magic, you know." He could not help but tweak at the man.

"When can we do this? When can we try?" William

asked. Roger remained silent, a suspicious glint in his eyes.

"First I must prepare the others. I think we must do this to protect everyone. If Hugh thinks he can learn our plans in this way, he will continue to take and torture—" He stopped as the huge guard stepped forward. He was the one who'd tortured Corann.

"He will. He is," he said, confirming Marcus's fears. "He will."

"Then we must do this quickly. If he can learn nothing from Devyn, then he may . . . " The man shook his head, extinguishing any hope of rescuing the man he'd raised from a boy.

"I will summon them," Aislinn said, walking away. The man trailed not far behind her.

"It will take some time, Will," Marcus said. "We will call you when it is done."

"What do we need to do for this? Is there some way to prepare?" Roger asked.

"Nay. Nothing. Just be willing when we try, my friend."

Marcus went to where the priests would gather and explained the situation. Much discussion and disagreement followed, but Marcus wanted everyone to have their chance to speak when coming to a decision among their community. For most of them, it would be the first time without a connection to the others, and it made everyone uneasy.

The ritual took time, and Marcus was exhausted when they completed it. And alone. It was very strange not to feel the others with him. Not to feel Aislinn there. And from her pale face, she was experiencing the same thing.

And Devyn would suddenly be alone in the clutches

of the evil one's sycophant. Offering up prayers for a merciful death for a true follower, Marcus sought his sacrificial knife for the next ritual.

He called William, Brienne, Aislinn, and Roger together, and they sought out a private place in the forest to carry this out. Roger's face went gray and green when he noticed Marcus's blade, but he did not explain until they reached a place where he'd discovered several rowan trees growing. The tree, sacred to the gods, would add potent magic to his spell.

He sat on the ground and invited them each to sit in a particular place—priest, fireblood, human, priest, warblood—and then he prayed over the dagger. Then he held his hand out and asked for Roger's.

"What are you going to do with that?" William's man asked, not offering his arm.

"You carry no mark. I must make one before we can perform the ritual that will connect us to one another." Roger glared at him through narrowed eyes and then held out his arm.

Marcus leaned into the circle between them and took hold of Roger's hand. "Hold on to mine."

With practiced strokes, he cut into Roger's forearm, slicing deep into the skin, forming the same shape that he and the other priests, save Aislinn, bore—the stick figure of a man. His blood flowed onto the ground as Marcus chanted the words to sanctify the mark. Then he turned to Brienne.

"Burn it."

"What?" both Roger and Brienne said at the same time.

"It must be burned. It must be a brand, not cuts of a dagger that can heal. Purify it with your fire."

He watched as she struggled with the act of burning another human with her powers. He had no doubt she'd seen her father use his powers to hurt and maim, but it was not in her nature and never would be. He did not doubt that she would be called on to use it as a weapon in the days ahead of them.

"Go ahead," Roger said, grasping Marcus's arm tightly. "If it must be done, do it now."

He saw William nod at her, and then she looked to him. At his nod, the sliced flesh began to sizzle and burn. Each cut he'd made searing itself to the others until the skin branded and sealed. Roger hissed and clenched his jaws closed, but otherwise said nothing.

And then it was done and he released Roger's arm.

"I am sorry, Roger," Brienne said. Tears filled her eyes as she looked over at her husband.

"We all have our duties, Brienne. I've had much worse than this in skirmishes and practice," Roger said.

"Now we can do the rest." Marcus stood up. "We must connect our flesh in order to connect our minds. Like this." He showed them how to cover and clasp the person's mark with their opposite hand, creating a circle.

He and Aislinn began weaving the spell, teaching the others the words to chant as the connection between them wove threads between their thoughts even as their flesh touched. It took some time, more than it would have taken with priests, but he repeated it over and over until he could hear their voices in his thoughts.

Some time passed—he knew not how long—until suddenly he became aware again of the wind and the sun and the others around him. Glancing at each person, he spoke their names in his thoughts.

As they nodded in reply, Marcus offered a prayer of thanks to the gods for allowing this.

Aislinn? William spoke first. *Can you share the prophecies you've received with us now?* He glanced at Roger and Brienne.

Aislinn looked to Marcus for permission, for this was something else forbidden for anyone but priests.

Tell them, Marcus said.

"When the threat is revealed and the sleepers awaken, a Warrior seeks the truth while the Fire burns away the deception. Begin in the East, then North, then South, then West . . . Find the true gate among the rest."

He watched Brienne's eyes widen at the mention of the warrior and the fire. And now that they had the location of the first circle, north and south and west made sense. Scotland, Orkney, England, and Ireland. The path their journey would take to stop the evil one. The reverse journey of their Celtic ancestors in coming here and building these places.

And the next one?

"While those of the blood advance and the lost lose their way, Water and Storm protect the Hidden. The Hidden reveals its secrets only to those who struggle with their faith."

And Hugh will know that one? Devyn will tell him?

Aislinn and Marcus both nodded in reply. The young man would give up the words.

"Then we should begin now," William the warblood, their leader, said.

Within hours, they were on their way to the northern coast of Scotland and then on to the Norse lands of Orkney.

EPILOGUE

Eudes looked very, very worried. He had not the finer skills of Brisbois in prolonging life even while prolonging the anguish. How three brothers could be so different, Hugh did not understand, and it mattered not now.

"Is he dead, then?" he asked.

"Aye, my lord. Just now."

The burned and beaten body lay before him in the dirt. At least he'd given up the words that the powerful priest had received in prophecy before dying.

"And he said what else?"

"He just kept blabbering at the end, out of his mind, my lord."

"What. Did. He. Say?" he repeated slowly. "The exact words, Eudes. Now, before you take his place there." Hugh pointed at the tree where they'd chained the priest.

"He said—it is empty. It is empty. They are gone. Over and over. Makes no sense, my lord," Eudes said.

Hugh screamed out his frustration then, and all of

his men tried to be or look someplace else other than where they were. He understood it.

The damned priests had figured out a way to sever their connections with this one. Probably between all of them. They had to know it would mean this one's death. He shrugged, looking at the body. It was unexpected for them to be that ruthless. With a thought he finished the task begun earlier and burned the man to ashes.

Turning back to his commander, he gave new orders.

"Orkney. We head to Orkney."

"Very well, my lord." Eudes bowed and left him alone.

While those of the blood advance and the lost lose their way, Water and Storm protect the Hidden. The Hidden reveals its secrets only to those who struggle with their faith.

He would need to find the waterblood and the stormblood, and the wild, windblown isles to the north somehow seemed an appropriate place to find them.

Another chance to free his goddess and to destroy those who'd betrayed him. He would make them all pay for that.

Read on for a sneak peek at the next
Novel of the Stone Circles,
by Terri Brisbin

RAGING SEA

Coming in October 2015 from Signet Eclipse.

Spring, AD 1286
Kirkwall, Orkney

Soren Thorsson walked through the marketplace, greeting the merchants and nodding to the vendors selling their wares. Kirkwall was a blending place, filled with people from all parts of the north and beyond. The Norse, Scots, French, and English all used Kirkwall, as it was now called, and Orkney for replenishing supplies, and they stocked their ships there for travel while trading goods.

But something this day was different.

As he walked the streets that morning, Soren noticed a change in the air around him. In the colors of the fabrics offered in the weavers' tents. In the faces of the villagers. The brightness and hues had been leached from the world in which he lived.

The realization stopped him between paces.

He glanced around to see if something had thickened above him and had blocked the sun. The clear, cloudless blue skies answered him. What was happening?

And then she walked out from one of the alleys.

Ran Sveinsdottir.

The woman he'd loved.

The woman he'd betrayed.

Soren stepped back into the shadows and watched her. Tall and svelte, she moved with the same easy grace on land that she had on her father's ships. Her blond curls tamed into several small plaits framing her face and one larger unruly braid. 'Twas a hopeless attempt to control the uncontrollable, and the longer woven tresses lay down her back and swung in time with every step she took. His body recognized hers; his mouth remembered the taste of hers, and his hands itched to glide over those curves and touch every inch of her.

He shuddered and released the breath he did not know he'd been holding, continuing to watch her make her way through the crowded street. Without deciding the matter, he started to follow her, drinking in the sight of her, of her every smile and glance and movement. She bestowed her smile on many as she greeted the merchants and tradesmen along the street.

Ran was the one woman he'd loved and the one he could never have. It had been two years since he last saw her and yet—

His vision flickered then, and he realized that she was surrounded by color and light. They were missing in everyone else around them and were vibrant and almost alive in her. Turquoise—the color of the seas—surrounded her body, glowing and glimmering. He blinked several times, trying to clear his vision, for what he saw was simply not possible.

When that made no difference, Soren dragged the sleeve of his tunic across his eyes, but the sight did not change. Her blond hair was still bright and golden, her skin still glowed, and her eyes shimmered. He hissed in pain, unsure of what was happening, as his forearm began to burn.

Lifting his hand, he tugged his sleeve back and watched as the skin underneath grew red and an outline of a bolt of lightning became visible. It changed as he watched, growing brighter and clearer in shape. And it burned as it did. Covering it with his other hand, he glanced around to see if anyone else noticed his odd behavior.

Those seeking goods or food did not spare him a second glance. Those selling their wares did not either. Everyone else walked around him, ignorant or uncaring about this significant change in their world. As he looked around the area, Soren realized that Ran had the same bewildered expression on her face that his must have been wearing. She clutched at her arm, touching the same place on her forearm that yet burned on his.

He'd taken three steps out of the shadows and onto the street toward her when he finally pulled himself back and stopped. As much as he wanted to understand what was going on, he knew she would not welcome his approach. Or his questions.

Two years. Two years and much more than time separated them.

Since he knew her father would remain in Orkney while his ships and boats were preparing for the sailing months ahead, Soren knew she was not going anywhere. If this strangeness somehow involved her, he knew where he could find her.

He would always know where to find her. Now though, he turned and walked away.

*   *   *

Though he stood in the shadows between the merchants selling their wool and other fabrics, she would recognize him anywhere. Taller than her brother and her father, Soren towered over most men she knew. The years of working the fields and ships had built muscle and strength in his body, and she could not help but notice that he looked even larger now. Her traitorous body responded to the memories of their times together. The feel of his skin on hers. His strong hands moving over her and bringing her to pleasure. Relentlessly. As he did everything.

Could it be the mere sight of him that was causing this eerie feeling within her? The strange buzzing that filled her ears and dimmed her vision? Moments ago, all the colors of the world had disappeared and everyone looked like a pale, drab version of themselves.

Except Soren.

He had changed and not just by looking stronger and healthier. His skin gave off a silver-gray glow that outlined his body to her. As she watched this happening to him, her arm began to burn. Clapping her hand over it, she lifted her gaze and met his in that moment.

In that second, everything and everyone around them disappeared, leaving only the two of them. Time slowed, and she gazed at the man to whom she'd given her heart, body, and soul. Their life together had been laid ahead of them, shining like a jewel and holding the promise of happiness. That hope had crumbled in an instant, when he had betrayed her faith in him.

Now though, all that passed by in the blink of an eye, and she found herself staring at Soren as her arm burned fiercely. And, realizing that his action mirrored her own, she waited for his acknowledgment. Instead, he did again as he'd done before—he turned and walked away.

The bright, shimmering color of molten silver continued to swirl around him as he made his way along the street and away from her. Her heart, the one she'd sworn would never be hurt again, pounded in her chest, reminding her of the weakness of her will when it came to Soren Thorsson.

Her arm felt as though it was on fire, so she tugged her sleeve up to look at it. Her skin seemed to burn, reddened with heat and changing as she watched. A shape formed and smoothed away, only to form again. Two wavy lines etched into her then, undulating and moving as waves or currents did through water. For a moment, she believed them real. Then the burning began anew and the markings grew deeper and longer across her forearm.

What was going on? First the strange change to her vision and hearing. Then the alterations to the world's coloring—and Soren's. And last, this marking on her skin and, from his reaction, on his, too.

With more questions than answers, she wished there was someone she could ask. Someone who could counsel her and help her discover the truth of these events.

And she wished with all her heart that it was someone other than the man who had betrayed his every vow and his own words.

For two years had not been enough for her heart to heal. Ran had thought that distance and time would lessen the pain, but it had only taken one glimpse of Soren to show her how wrong she could be. How wrong she always seemed to be when it came to that man and her choices.

As Soren turned and walked off toward the edge of town, Ran knew one thing—she had lied to herself about her feelings for Soren. And the only way she would save her soul and her sanity was to keep away from him.

So that was what she would do.

Stay away from Soren Thorsson.

About the Author

In her previous lives, *USA Today* bestselling author **Terri Brisbin** has lived in ancient Egypt and medieval Scotland. In this one, she's stuck in the wilds of southern New Jersey with a hubby (a wonderful one!) and kids (three adorable and finally grown sons!). When not living the life of a glamorous romance author or suffering through deadline binges-o'-writing mania, she spends some of her time as a dental hygienist.

Terri's had more than thirty-four historical and paranormal romance novels, novellas, and short stories published in more than twenty-five languages in more than twenty countries! And there are a bunch more swirling around inside her brain just waiting to be written. You can find out more than you need to know about Terri or subscribe to her newsletter on her Web site, her Facebook profile, or her Facebook page.

CONNECT ONLINE

terribrisbin.com
facebook.com/terribrisbin
facebook.com/pages/terribrisbinauthor

LOVE
ROMANCE
NOVELS?

For news on all your favorite romance authors,
sneak peeks into the newest releases, book
giveaways, and much more—

"Like" Love Always on Facebook!
🅵 LoveAlwaysBooks

Penguin Group (USA) Online

What will you be reading tomorrow?

Tom Clancy, W.E.B. Griffin, Nora Roberts,
Catherine Coulter, Sylvia Day, Ken Follett,
Kathryn Stockett, John Green, Harlan Coben,
Elizabeth Gilbert, J. R. Ward, Nick Hornby,
Khaled Hosseini, Sue Monk Kidd, John Sandford,
Clive Cussler, Laurell K. Hamilton, Maya Banks,
Charlaine Harris, Christine Feehan, James McBride,
Sue Grafton, Liane Moriarty, Jojo Moyes, Jim Butcher...

You'll find them all at
penguin.com
facebook.com/PenguinGroupUSA
twitter.com/PenguinUSA

*Read excerpts and newsletters, find tour schedules
and reading group guides, and enter contests.*

Subscribe to Penguin newsletters and get an
exclusive inside look at exciting new titles and the
authors you love long before everyone else.

PENGUIN GROUP (USA)
penguin.com   s0151